If This Was a Movie

a film by

MORGAN ELIZABETH

To the hopeless romantics patiently waiting for their happily ever after.

PLAYLIST

Nonsense (Holiday Remix) - Sabrina Carpenter
Last Christmas - Wham
The 1 - Taylor Swift
The Prophecy - Taylor Swift
That's How You Know - Amy Adams
Tiny Dancer - Florence + the Machine
You Make it Feel Like Christmas - Gwen Stefani
Risk - Gracie Abrams
I Hate It Here -Taylor Swift
Invisible String - Taylor Swift
Santa Tell Me - Ariana Grande
The Very First Night - Taylor Swift
Juno - Sabrina Carpenter
The Alchemy - Taylor Swift

A NOTE FROM MORGAN

Dear Reader,

Thirteen years ago, I went to a party on Memorial Day at a house my friend was renting a room in. I'd broken up with my boyfriend (via an email, I know, I'm a horrible person, but I was also young and stupid) and was supposed to go on an internship in Florida in the fall. I told myself I was entering what the kids now call a *hot girl summer*, planning to have flings and kiss hot boys and live my life before I ran off.

At that party, I met my now husband. Over a game of flip cup and a night of watching some dumb movie where he very gentlemanly sat on the floor the whole time so I wouldn't feel uncomfortable, I decided I had met the man of my dreams. As a life long lover of romantic comedies, just like Jules, I had been looking for the *moment* since I was a kid. The moment when you see a guy and just *know* he's the one for you somewhere deep in your gut that you can't quite explain.

As a child of divorce, I also feared it would never happen, that it was all some kind of obscure fantasy people create in their head but doesn't exist in reality.

Spoiler: it was real.

We got married two years later and three years after the day we met, our oldest son was born on Memorial Day, another sign from the universe that we were meant to be if you ask me. But I never forgot that feeling, the one of both hope and excitement and a pinch of fear. Something so special and all consuming that lived up perfectly to all of the movies and books I've read and adored.

I say often all of my characters have a hint of me in them—I'm the only brain I know, so I can't really pull from anyone else—but Jules.... Jules is so very me. A hopeless romantic who wants to *believe*, waiting for some Prince Charming to come and sweep her away.

I hope you love her whirlwind romance and the chaos that ensues with our romcom obsessed bestie: I loved writing her for myself and for all of the other hopeless romantics out there waiting for the stars to align.

This book is a single dad/nanny holiday romcom and contains mentions of generalized anxiety, child abandonment, and parental divorce. As always, take care of yourself first and foremost. Reading is supposed to be our happy place.

Love you to the moon and to Saturn,
   -Morgan Elizabeth

ONE

JULES

"Miss Jules! I can't find my tutu!"

The shout makes me jump, forcing the tip of my mascara wand to poke me in the eye, and I'm reminded *once again* how badly I need to finish my office.

I sigh, blinking as my eye waters, a black smear of mascara ruining my nearly finished makeup. "Have you checked your bag?" I ask the adorable, if not incredibly forgetful, little girl who ran in.

There's silence before she says, "Not yet," running off to find what she was looking for, probably exactly where it's supposed to be.

I sigh, grabbing a makeup wipe while my assistant, Claire, laughs at me. I glare in her direction before she steps over, grabbing the makeup wipe from me, carefully cleaning the mess so I don't have to redo my entire face.

"I could have done this, you know," she says. "Filled in for Gina."

Standing in full ballet costume to understudy the Sugar Plum Fairy for our dress rehearsal of the Nutcracker, I groan. "Yes, except you're abandoning me tomorrow, and the point of today is to make sure the rest of the kids know how things will go for the performance.

If the twins aren't better by then, I'll be the one taking their place, unfortunately."

Claire, the godsend who fell into my lap just under a year ago, is leaving tomorrow to move across the country with her boyfriend. She showed up for an interview for a teacher and assistant and got the job on the spot, seeming to be everything I needed to keep my sanity. As excited as I am for her to have an adventure, I also have no idea how I'm going to function without her now that my business is booming.

"I'm not abandoning you, Jules! Stop making me feel bad," she says with a huff.

I smile and shake my head. "You know I'm just kidding. It's just a lot going on right now."

Two years ago, my best friend, Ava, joined a beauty pageant to help my and our friend Harper's businesses out, and it changed all of our lives for good. Then last year, I had my hopeless romantic heart broken once and for all, so I decided to fall into my work, to ignore any dreams of love and romance because it never, ever lives up to your dreams, and continued to build the dance studio of my dreams.

What started as one small dance studio and a waiting area is now two large studios, a lounge for parents, and a locker room with room to grow.

It's everything I dreamed of when I was a kid taking dance classes and daydreaming about the future. Even though I danced for as long as I could remember, I always knew I was never going to be some prima ballerina, performing on grand stages. I just love the feeling of losing myself, drifting to a secret place of content and safety in my mind where no one can touch.

No nagging mom, no men who always disappoint, no expectations, no reality.

Just me, myself, and the music.

"You just need to finish up the green room, Jules," she says, sitting on the edge of my desk as I finish the rest of my makeup. "And your office."

I groan aloud, knowing she's right.

Two years ago, when I bought the building and opened First Position, we were only two small studios, a lounge for parents, and a front desk on the first floor of the three-story building, my apartment on the top floor.

Slowly, I've been finishing each room to be the studio of my dreams, but I'm also only one person, and while the studio is doing well, I enjoy paying those who work with me a living wage. That being said, I'm still working to finish a formal office with a *working door*, another studio, and a dressing room for the dancers.

"I know, I know. I just need to save up a bit more, and then it's next on the list."

Claire shakes her head and rolls her eyes.

"You really should just let me call my brother. I know he would be more than willing to help out. I could even get you a family discount."

"And you know that I want to do this on my own. I don't need any help," I tell her, not for the first time.

"I think you've more than proved to your mom you can do it, Jules. You don't need to keep struggling just to prove a point."

She's never going to appreciate it anyway. Claire doesn't say it aloud, but the words hang in the air anyway.

When my grandmother passed, leaving me a small inheritance, my mother begged me to use it for something practical, like a nice house in a well-off neighborhood where I could go on hot girl walks and bump into some rich man and convince him to marry me.

Instead, I bought the building where First Position was born and have been barely scraping by, updating it room by room all by myself.

My mother doesn't get it, and Claire doesn't understand why I refuse to get help, but I do. It's mine. I'm proud of this place, knowing that every inch of this place has *my* blood, sweat, and tears.

Heavy on the tears, if I'm being honest.

I love walking into this place every day, knowing I helped to lay every plank of wood, that I picked out the fixtures and painted the walls. Knowing *I* built this wonderful, amazing thing all on my own when the people who were supposed to believe in me the most rolled their eyes and told me I'd fail.

"I'm just saying, if you had him help you six months ago when I first suggested it, you wouldn't have kids jump-scaring you every five seconds because the girls would have their own place to get ready and warm up." She is right, of course. "You could even have a man to get you out of your dry spell, since he's single and, objectively, because he's my brother and that's disgusting, pretty good-looking."

"I'm not looking for a man," I remind her.

"Oh, yes, yes, I forgot. You found your dream man a whole year ago, spent one night with him, decided he was the one, only to find out he was a piece of trash. Got it. That makes sense, you meet one piece of shit and rule out all romance for the rest of your life. Logic, you know?"

I glare at my friend. "It was two nights, thank you very much," I say.

Claire smiles and opens her mouth but is interrupted.

"Miss JULES!" another girl yells, entering my office.

A door.

First thing after the winter recital, I'm buying and installing a goddamn door. Who cares if I do things out of order if it means I get a *semblance* of peace?

"Martina says she's going to be the sugar plum fairy next year, but I said I am going to and—"

"How about we figure this out next year?" Claire says with a calm smile, ushering the arguing girls out of my office. "Part of those decisions are made based on how you do at this recital, so why don't you go warm-up with Miss Christine downstairs, yes?" There's more mumbling before Claire is back in my office, closing the door behind her with a sigh.

"You know, if this was a movie—" I start before she cuts me off.

"Let me guess, you'd have a group of hot men doing your hair and makeup rather than getting a cramp while doing it over a bookshelf in a messy office?"

I pause with the mascara wand once more near my lashes before turning to look at her.

"What kind of movies are you watching?" I ask.

"The good kind," she replies with a smile.

"Uh, I was going to say that this is where some rich billionaire would kick down the door and tell me I deserve the world and magically fix all of my issues."

She laughs out loud, grabbing a can of hairspray and dousing my tight bun before nodding like she approves of what she sees.

I wasn't supposed to get into a dancer's costume today, much less get completely dolled up, but it's dress rehearsal for our winter performance, and one of the dancers called in sick. I want to make sure the kids get the full experience, and considering I stupidly penciled myself in as Gina's understudy, I'm wearing a pink leotard and tutu while Claire finishes up my slicked-back bun.

It's just another moment in a series of shitty luck I've been experiencing as of late: a dancer calling in sick (which means I now have to stress for the next two weeks to see if it's the kind of sick that runs through the entire group or a one-off), the hot water in my apartment not working this morning, the kids reporting one of the sinks downstairs isn't turning on, my mom once again incessantly calling me to set me up on a date, the contractor who was supposed to help me this month finish up the final studio telling me he double booked himself and had to postpone, and, of course, Claire leaving.

This utterly horrid string of bad luck all started nearly a year ago, not that I'll let myself think about it that much. Instead, I force myself to think about the good: Ava meeting Jaime and getting engaged, Harper seemingly happy with Jeremy, even though he isn't my first choice in partners for her, First Position doing exceedingly well, and—

I don't have time to continue my list of things I'm grateful for when a noise breaks into my conscious thoughts, forcing my hand to shift and swipe the mascara well past my lashes to my eyelid. At least I didn't poke myself in the eye, right?

"Goddammit!" I groan, grabbing another makeup wipe and folding it to clean the spot precisely. When the blaring continues, I turn to Claire. "Can you please shut your phone up?"

She rolls her eyes and smiles. "Sorry, babe, that's your phone."

She's right, of course. I forgot Ava changed the song to "Barbie Girl" the other day, and it is, in fact, my phone obnoxiously blaring from my bag. With a sigh, I cap the mascara before reaching for my phone and seeing a number I don't know on the screen.

Don't be more bad news. Please, God, don't let it be more bad news.

Taking a deep breath, I hover over the answer button, but before I can, a fat drop of water falls on my head, trailing down my forehead to my nose, followed by another.

"What the—"

And then all hell breaks loose.

TWO

NATE

There are a million things I'd rather be doing right now than walking into the mall two days after Thanksgiving, but unfortunately, here I am fighting crowds and holding onto a small hand.

At least I dragged my sisters Sloane and Sutton with me, since it's Sloane's fault Sophie even got the idea to go see Santa on the worst weekend to visit a mall in the entire year.

"I hate you for this," Sloane grumbles.

"Back at you," I reply as Sophie stops at the back of a very long, winding line, dozens and dozens of sets of parents with over-excited kids in tow wearing puffy jackets and floppy hats the mothers shove into bags before their children sit on the big man's lap in perfectly coordinated outfits.

At least Soph is in a cute outfit, courtesy of Claire, who bought it for her months before. *It will be perfect for Christmas photos!* she shouted when she handed me the bright red dress with fluffy white edging way back in September.

I can't complain though, since two years ago when my ex and Sophie's mom told me she was done with the back and forth, didn't want to be a mother anymore and signed all rights over to me, my entire family jumped in to help. My three sisters and my mother created a schedule to babysit because, as a contractor, sometimes I work odd hours. My youngest sister, Claire, even moved into the small in-law cottage behind my house, becoming my full-time help with Sophie.

Now that my daughter's in kindergarten, I mostly only need help on the occasional night or weekend I have to work late, meaning when Claire's boyfriend asked her to follow him to California, she jumped at the prospect.

"Sophie, do you know what you want to ask Santa for?" my oldest sister, Sloane, asks my five-year-old daughter, using a hand to pull her into her side. She's getting big, but still barely hits Sloane's stomach.

Sophie's blonde curls I was barely able to calm this morning sway when she shakes her head. "Nope."

Sighing, I stare at the ceiling of the Evergreen Park Mall, praying for some kind of divine intervention. I've been begging Sophie for a Christmas list since November first, not wanting to brave the crowds, but each time, she comes up empty.

"You'd better figure it out soon, silly," my middle sister, Sutton, says, with a laugh. "Santa is right there!" She points to the old man in a bright red suit that matches Sophie's dress.

"Oh, I'm so excited!" Sophie says, jumping up and down swinging the Ashlyn doll she takes everywhere around so I have to dodge getting smacked in the knee with it.

Ashlyn, the doll I got on a whim when she broke her arm nearly a year ago. She's barely let it out of her sight since, changing her outfit daily and brushing her hair diligently to take care of her "best friend." My daughter doesn't know I have four dolls I rotate every few days, in case she loses one, so they'll all wear similarly, and two more in the box.

You can never be too prepared when it comes to a toy your child has determined is the reason for them to continue living.

We wait in line another fifteen minutes before a green-and-red-dressed elf takes Sophie's hand, leading her to Santa with an all-too-fake, much-too-high-pitched giggle.

"I hate this shit," I say to my sisters, watching my daughter climb onto some stranger's lap. "Who thought this was a good idea, letting small children be hugged by a total stranger and sit on him?"

"Probably capitalism," Sloane replies, and I can't argue that logic.

Instead, I move to the spot the employees guide parents to and listen intently to the interaction so I can finally know what to search online for. With my luck, it's going to be something she's completely made up in her mind, like a pink-and-purple unicorn she can ride around the house that shits glitter.

"What's your name?" Santa asks, and Sophie smiles wide, a recently lost tooth on the bottom leaving a gap before she answers.

"Sophie Donovan. I live on 6 Auburn Avenue, Evergreen Park, New Jersey," she says, and I run my hand over my face with a groan.

Santa makes a loud chuckle, cutting her off before she gives out my phone number and probably social security number for good measure. "Oh, don't you worry, I know exactly where you are, you don't have to tell me now!"

That's my Sophie, for you: not a care in the world, trusting everyone and anyone in her path, loud and self-assured, and friendly to a fault. It's a fine line I walk daily, trying to teach her to keep herself safe while not taking my favorite personality trait of hers away. If this was any other situation, I'd quietly remind her that we don't give total strangers explicit information about ourselves or where we live, but this is Santa Claus, and that would probably ruin the magic.

Again, who the fuck decided this entire schtick was a good idea?

Still, I put it on my mile-long mental list to remind her before bed that Santa is the exception, not the rule.

"So what do you want Santa to bring you this year?"

I'm hoping the answer will be something easy and attainable, not some Furby/Tickle Me Elmo/Eras Tour tickets level of impossible, even though, considering she is the center of my universe, I'd find a way to get it for Sophie if need be.

But I don't have to worry about dishing out five, ten, fifteen times the retail value on some junk she won't even want to play with in a month's time. No, because my sweet, loving, kind five-year-old daughter looks this man dead in the eye, lifts up her Ashlyn doll in the air, today in her little pink ballet costume and dark hair in a bun, and says, "I want my dad to marry the real-life Ashlyn and make her my mom."

You have got to be fucking kidding me.

"No, she did not," Sloane whispers under her breath, and Sutton barks out a laugh. But the wish we both have that we misheard her is swept away when, upon Santa's request for clarification, Sophie repeats herself with confidence.

"Where is she even coming up with this?" I say under my breath as Sophie fills in Santa on all the things she wants to do with "Ashlyn" when she's real. "I don't even date."

"Because you're too caught up on your mysterious dream girl," Sutton says with smugness in her voice.

Not for the first time, I regret getting drunk with my sister last February after Sophie fell asleep and telling her all about the woman I met on New Year's who ghosted me not long after we met. That's when I told her all about how I felt a connection I couldn't describe, despite the short amount of time I spent with her, how I was sure to my gut she was meant to be mine, and I had no idea where things went wrong.

"A dream girl?" Sloane asks, her interest peaked.

"Ignore her, she's insane," I say.

"He met a girl on New Year's and fell in love, but a week later after he canceled a date, she blocked him, and he hasn't heard from her since."

"Why did you cancel?" Sloane asks, always ready to tell me I'm the problem, as any good younger sister is wont to do.

"Soph broke her arm." I'm praying they leave it at that, really wanting this conversation to end, but I know better.

"Did you tell her that?"

I run a hand over my face before shifting my focus from Sophie to Sloane. Sutton is looking at me, now interested, probably realizing she didn't think to ask me that question.

"I told her I had a family emergency."

"But not that your daughter broke her arm."

Once more, I look at the ceiling, but unfortunately it still hasn't written the answers to life's mysteries there yet. "I didn't tell her I had a daughter."

Silence follows before my sisters explode.

"You fucking idiot!" Sutton shouts.

"You have to be kidding me, Nathan," Sloane says, using my full name. "Why didn't you tell her!?"

"Because I liked her, okay?" I say, getting frustrated, then lowering my voice. "I liked her a lot, and I wanted her to give me a chance without having to dump on her that I have a kid."

"God, Nathan, you really are so, so dumb. Have you ever considered that that's what happened? Evergreen Park is a tiny town. She probably asked around about you to a few people and they filled her in on you and all of your drama."

I actually...hadn't thought of that, if I'm being honest. I assumed she just got turned off by something I did or said and set a clear boundary, blocking my number so I couldn't contact her again.

"You think?" I ask, suddenly letting my mind see other possibilities. What if she learned about Sophie and thought the worst? What if she thought I was hiding even more things and decided to cut her losses before she got in too deep? Did I fuck up big time by letting things end where they did? "Things were good between us until right before my texts started marking as not delivered."

"God, and this society says men are the smart ones, the breadwinners, the rulers of the world, but then this is the kind of logic us women are dealing with. Yes, Nate. I would bet everything was fine and dandy and then she found out you omitted the vital fact that you had a child. She probably decided you were a liar, or even worse, thought you were cheating on Sophie's mother!"

Well, fuck. That *would* make sense, a potential new piece to the puzzle that's been plaguing me for months.

"You need to find her. At the very least explain so she doesn't go around thinking all of the Donovans are assholes."

There's a loud *Ho! Ho! Ho!* that breaks through our conversation, and I use it as an excuse to step away from my sisters and what I'm sure is going to be a long and painful beatdown.

I take Sophie's hand as the elf hands her back to me, ushering me to the kiosk where I can buy a shitty photo that costs fifty dollars and Sophie can get a candy cane before we start to walk toward the exit to get out of this madhouse. My mind is still reeling from my sisters' revelation, but now I have a more pressing issue in front of me as Sophie walks next to me with her wide, gap-filled smile, her doll in hand.

"Hey, bud..." I start, not sure where to go from here. Never once has my daughter implied she wanted a mother figure in her life, not even after she realized her mom wasn't coming back every other weekend like she was used to.

Never once has she mentioned my dating, much less getting married.

Where the fuck has this come from?

I settle on keeping it simple and straightforward. "Sophie, what did you ask Santa for for Christmas?" Maybe if I pretend I didn't hear, she'll give me something reasonable, something I can actually purchase with money. Maybe I misheard—I am getting old and—

"I told him I want you to marry the real-life Ashlyn and make her my new mom."

Jesus fucking Christ.

"Uh, sweetie, that's..." Sloane starts, turning a bit to avoid some asshole on his phone slamming into her. Sutton stayed behind to wait for the photos to be printed. "That's not exactly what Santa brings, you know. He brings toys, not people."

"Ashlyn *is* a toy. I just want him to use Christmas magic and make her real. Then Daddy can meet her and fall in love with her and she can be my new mom. I can be a flower girl at their wedding, and she can teach me how to dance."

I jump at that opening, thinking maybe I can make due.

"Do you want dance lessons for Christmas?" I ask, looking at her. Maybe that's what she really wants, and—

"No," she says simply with a small shake of her head. "I want Ashlyn."

"A new Ashlyn doll?" Another shake of her head. "The Ashlyn Dreamhouse?" I ask, mentioning the giant gift I thought she was going to request as a last resort. I have no desire to sit and spend three nights meticulously assembling that nightmare, but I'll do it if need be.

"No, silly. I want a *real* Ashlyn."

When we step out of the exit and into the cold November air outside the mall, I pull Sophie to the side and get to a knee in front of her, helping to zip up her jacket and getting on her eyes level. "Sophie, sweetie, I don't want you to be disappointed this year. Santa brings kids toys, not people," I say as I zip up her coat, trying to keep my tone even and kind.

"Yeah, but he's going to bring you a wife. He told me."

He very fucking well did not, because I saw the same panic on that man's face as the one I felt and heard him try and divert you.

"I think he told you that he only brings toys," I say.

"Aubrey asked for a puppy last year, and she got a puppy." Audrey is the brat in Sophie's class who gets everything and anything she's ever wanted. She even makes the occasional rude jab about Sophie not having a mother when she's at our house, and it takes everything in me not to snap at a five-year-old. She might have two parents, but her mom hits on me and not-so-subtly propositions me any chance she gets.

"Well, a person is not a puppy, Sophie," I say. She looks at me for a long beat, and for a moment I think I'm in the clear, that she understands and is going to accept my statement as fact.

But then she shrugs.

"I don't know, but it's going to happen. Trust me." I stand in defeat and reach my hand out for her, but she continues to stare at me, her little face suddenly fierce and stoic, like she really needs me to believe in what she's saying. "Trust me, Dad. Christmas is for miracles."

We are definitely going to need a miracle, I think to myself as we start to walk toward the diner I promised we'd go to after Santa. Unfortunately, when I look across the street, it looks like it might be closed. A bunch of police cars and a fire truck block the way, familiar faces gathering on the sidewalk in front of a building. For a moment, I wonder what's happening until a rush of water coming from the road catches my eye and I realize it must be some kind of water main burst.

"Soph, we might have to—" I start as we approach. I'm about to tell her we might not be able to go to the diner, which is one block further, and if it's still open, we'll have to detour our way there.

But before I can say anything else, my daughter shouts, "There!" pointing toward the chaos ahead, and bolts.

THREE

NEW YEAR'S EVE, LAST YEAR

JULES

If this was a movie, I'd be cozy on a couch with a glowing Christmas tree in my peripheral vision, a roaring fire warming me as I lay in the arms of the man of my dreams. Or maybe we'd be all dressed up at some chaotic, fancy party, getting drunk and preparing to ring in the new year in style.

But this isn't a movie, so instead I'm spending my New Year's Eve alone.

My life is anything but cinematic.

My two best friends are off living their best lives, Ava and her beau Jaime are hosting some crazy party on behalf of the Miss Americana pageant in California, while Harper is at some fancy work party with Jeremy. Both have someone to kiss at midnight, someone to start the new year in love with.

And I'm here.

Lonely and miserable but too proud to tell anyone, eating at a bar before I go home and take a melatonin so I can go to bed early. It's one thing to be alone on New Year's Eve, but it's a whole other to stay up until midnight and start another year alone.

"Hey, Donovan," the bartender says, lifting a hand toward the front of the bar as a cold gust of wind enters, dancing along my skin and leaving goosebumps in its wake.

"Hey, Tyler, how's it going?" a deep voice asks, getting closer with each word.

"Eh, you know, I'm working New Year's Eve, so it could be better."

The man laughs from behind me, getting closer before a tanned hand and gray sweater are stretched next to me, giving the bartender a manly handshake. I can't lie and say I didn't check the hand out, noticing a few small scars and calluses on his hands, implying he works with them and no ring on a certain important finger.

The bar is nearly empty, maybe half a dozen patrons in all taking up various seats, so I jump a bit when the stool next to mine is pulled, the legs scraping on the floor.

A tall man settles next to me, ordering a beer and bullshits a bit with the bartender, taking a look at the menu that is passed to him before turning to me.

"You come here often?" he asks. It's so bad, an overused and cliché line, but it makes me laugh out loud without thinking twice. "That bad, huh?"

"It wasn't great," I say as I take him in.

He's cute.

Really cute, with light brown, almost blond hair that screams he spent a lot of time in the sun before winter kicked in, pushed back with his fingers rather than some kind of product, a fitted dark gray sweater on, paired with a pair of worn jeans.

"Not really great at this whole thing," he admits, a light pink flush on his cheeks that I tell myself must be from the cold outside.

"This whole thing?"

"Talking to a pretty girl." He smiles, and that's good too.

"I think step one is telling her your name," I say, giving into the fun of flirting. My best friend, Ava, is the queen of flirting. She'll flirt with anyone if she's bored enough, and while I'm not on her level, I can't help but want to flirt with this stranger. This is how all of the best romance movies start after all: a lonely woman meets a man at a bar, and they begin their journey to forever.

My mother tells me at every chance she gets I'm too much of a hopeless romantic, that I need some realism before I get really and truly hurt. I know she's just projecting because when I was five, my dad left us to start a new family with someone half his age and never looked back. That was her reality check, and she tells me every chance she gets. Him starting over was the moment she realized she needs a man for stability, security, and status more than anything.

But I want nothing but true, all-consuming, movie-worthy love.

I know down to my bones, one day, it will find me.

"Nate," he says, putting a hand out for me to shake.

"Jules." I smile, taking his hand. It's rough and calloused, much bigger than my own, and after we shake, he holds in for a moment longer than necessary. "Are you from Evergreen Park?"

He nods. "Yeah, I was born and raised here, never left. I know nothing but this town."

"That must have been nice. I grew up a few towns over in Spring Hill, utter chaos at all times. Moving here was a nice change of pace."

"It's a great place to be," he agrees before we fall into a comfortable silence.

The bartender brings Nate over his beer and takes his dinner order. The entire time, I try to figure out how to comfortably and casually keep talking to this man. My belly is in knots, a slew of butterflies beating around my stomach, and it could be that I'm just single on one of the most romantic nights of the year, but I feel... something. Something I can't explain, a voice in my head that is screaming, *talk to him, get to know him.*

His fingers move over and over on something, and I look closer, eyeing it to notice a small matchbook. "Do you smoke?" I ask, because that's a deal-breaker for me, something I won't fuck with.

"What? No," he asks with a confused chuckle.

I tip my chin toward his hand where he's flipping a matchbook over and over in his hands, opening and closing it, fidgeting away.

"No, I'm just inexplicably nervous, and it's keeping my hands busy," he admits, a shy smile on his lips as he drops the matchbook.

I reach over and grab it, playing with it myself now. "Nervous?"

"Again, pretty girl, not something I do often...it might be a line, but I'm telling the truth. I feel very much out of my wheelhouse."

Something is refreshing about that, a man being nervous and embarrassed but not trying to play it off like some macho idiot. Because of it, I give him a wide smile, slipping the matches into my pocket.

"If it helps, I don't do this either. Sit next to a handsome man flirting with me, trying to flirt back."

His smile turns to a grin, taking over his entire face.

"It does. Okay, tell me about yourself," Nate says.

Relief that I won't have to find a way to break the ice myself floods me right before the panic of having to talk about myself kicks in.

"Tell you about myself?" I ask with a stutter. He nods. "Well, uh, what do you want to know?"

"Whatever you want to share," he says, but he must see the anxiety on my face because he chuckles before adding, "Okay, how about what do you do for fun?" he asks, and I contemplate how to answer.

I used to dance for fun, and I guess I still do, but it's a job now, as all good hobbies become. I used to do crafts, but I don't have the time or mental capacity anymore, so that feels disingenuous. Despite how often Ava recommends books, I never find the will, time, or energy to pick up one.

"I watch movies." The answer clearly takes him aback because he lets out a laugh, something deep and comforting that slides through me and settles in my bones like that's where he's meant to be, meant to stay. I smile back at him and shrug before he speaks.

"You watch movies? What kind, like the classics?"

"I mean, they're classics to me. I love romantic comedies."

"All right, so you watch romantic comedies for fun and you're sitting in a bar alone on New Year's Eve—am I safe to assume you're single?"

"Woooow," I say with a laugh. "God, that one hurt."

"Fuck, shit. I didn't mean it that way, I just—"

My laugh builds, and I touch his arm. The sleeve of his sweater is pushed up so my fingertips graze his arm, bare skin sending a bolt of recognition through me as I do.

"I'm just messing with you. Yeah, I'm single. Kind of obvious, unfortunately." I pause, trying to decide if I'm brave enough to ask, then do it anyway. "You?"

"Same," he says with a smile that goes wider. "Okay, now it's your turn."

"My turn?"

"That's how this game works, isn't it? You ask a question, I ask another. Get to know each other." I smile and nod in agreement, trying not to squeal as I remember Ava telling me she and Jaime did this when they were stuck in long car rides together before they were together. "So it's your turn," he says with a tip of his head and moving to take a sip of his beer.

I try and think of what to ask, what I need to know, before landing on the easiest one.

"What do you do for a living?"

"I own a contracting business. I renovate homes and businesses, do new builds, the whole nine." So he does work with his hands.

"That's interesting. Did you go to school for that?"

He shakes his head. "No, wasn't for me. I did a bunch of apprenticeships out of high school, and my dad's a carpenter. Learned about a lot, then started my own business."

"That's admirable," I say.

"And that was two questions," he says, and I blush.

"Oh, I didn't mean—" His hand reaches out, grabbing mine as he smiles at me.

"I'm just fucking with you, Jules. But I get two now. What do you do?"

"I own a dance studio downtown."

"Are you a dancer?"

I nod. "I danced as a kid and through college, but I always knew it wasn't going to be a forever thing. I danced because I loved it, not because I was phenomenal or I wanted to make it my life's career."

"I'm sure you're amazing," he says.

"I'm decent, but now I get to do what I love and I get to teach other people about it, give them the outlet that's always brought me so much joy. Best of both worlds, you know?"

"Kids? Adults?"

"Both. I have a few kid classes and adult fitness classes. But that was, what? Three questions?" Now it's his turn to smile and apologize before I ask what his favorite movie is. (*Top Gun*, a typical guy response.)

It goes like this for the next two hours, an entire meal, and countless light brushes of his hand on mine and shivers down my spine. I learn he has three younger sisters, that his parents have been happily married for forty years, he's thirty-five, and has never seen any of my favorite movies.

"You really love movies, don't you?" he asks after I tell him the entire plot of *You've Got Mail*.

"Only romance, really," I say.

"Why's that?" I shrug, but answer anyway.

"It's easier to relate to, and there's always a happily ever after. The world is chaos and full of disappointment and heartbreak. I like living in the fantasy of that, that two people could meet and go on some grand adventure and fall in love and ride off into the sunset." I shrug sheepishly, but continue anyway. "I picture everything as a movie. Romanticize it a bit, pretend that no matter what, everything is for the plot, that at the end, the happily ever after is impending."

He continues to stare at me for long moments, and I feel the self-consciousness sneak in, and instead of shutting my mouth, I keep speaking, trying to explain. "Plus, if you think of every bad moment as a plot twist, everything seems less...consequential. Then you can be excited, waiting to find out what happens next instead of stressing about it."

The silence swirls around us again, and I almost speak to change the subject, but then he gently shakes his head like he can't believe something before speaking.

"I've never met anyone like you, Jules." He says it in awe, and I panic.

"Is that...is that a good thing, or do you mean it in a you should seek professional help way?"

"In all the best ways," he whispers before he once more shakes his head before leaning in and smiling. "Okay, so if this was a movie, what would happen next?"

"Oh, we'd definitely leave together, go back to one of our places. You'd kiss me at midnight, and it would start to snow, probably. We'd be stuck inside and have to spend a few days together. You know, normal romance movie stuff," I say.

I don't know if the single drink I've had is going to my head or if I'm just drunk on the idea of Nate, but I'm not as embarrassed as I think I should be, saying that out loud.

"Sounds perfect," he says, his face serious despite the slight tip at the edge of his lips, like he really thinks that would be perfect.

"Last call, we're closing down early tonight," the bartender tells Nate with a tip of his chin, breaking the moment. "Holiday and all." I reach into my bag to grab my card to pay for my food and drink, but the bartender shakes his head. "It's covered." I turn to my dinner companion and smile.

"That wasn't necessary," I say.

"Happy New Year's, Jules. You being here made mine a hell of a lot better." Again, I smile, my cheeks starting to hurt as I do because it's pretty much all I've done since he sat next to me. But then he stands, his stool pushing back as he does, stepping down and away with a wave to the bartender. "Later, Tyler. Have a good one, yeah?" The bartender waves and wishes him a Happy New Year before Nate takes three steps away from the bar.

I watch him, unable to do anything else, my gut dropping to my feet as I watch what I kind of hoped was my own little rom-com in the making walk away. I shift a bit to grab my purse and leave, planning to go to the bathroom so we don't leave at the same exact time because it's embarrassing, before Nate's body shifts.

He looks over his shoulder at me, a wide smile on his lips and a bit of goofy confusion on his face before he speaks.

"You coming?" he asks.

"Huh?"

"Are you coming with me?"

Warmth rolls through me, slow and sweet like heated honey.

"What?"

He turns more fully toward me, then puts a hand out in my direction like he's expecting me to grab it and follow him.

"I'd love nothing more than to ring in the new year with you, Jules," he says, voice low, eyes filled with promise.

I should probably just give him my number at best and go home, take my melatonin, and go to bed, but instead, I stand. I slide my jacket on and loop my bag over my shoulder before stepping forward and taking his hand.

FOUR

JULES

"So, unfortunately, it looks like you won't be able to live here for at least a few days, probably longer," the fire chief says, looking genuinely reluctant to give me this news. "The pipe breaking means we can't turn on the water access until it's repaired. My guess is that it'll take a week since they can't do too much until this cold snap breaks. You'll need to do some repairs from this incident. Water can weaken structural integrity, and, again, with the cold, it can get into wood, expand, and cause instabilities. Not to mention, of course, mold."

The dripping on my face earlier was water from a burst pipe in my kitchen that flooded my apartment and then seeped down into my studio, making both unusable for the foreseeable future. I'm staring up at the all-brick corner building in downtown Evergreen Park I once thought was my dream come true.

"You know, when it's this cold for this long, you're supposed to drip your water lines so they don't freeze," he tells me, giving me a look I've seen many times before, most often when I'm at the hardware store and some idiot man comes over to ask if I need to be shown the paint section.

I try not to glare at him because, no, I did not know that, obviously. I mean, why would I? It's not like it's some kind of commonly taught knowledge. I need one person on this planet to explain to me why we don't have classes in high school to teach us about the important things in life, like how to do your taxes, assemble IKEA furniture, or, apparently, drip your water lines during a cold snap.

I'm a wiz with Google, but I have to actually know what shit to Google, first.

"Yeah, I'll remember that next time," I mutter under my breath before someone calls him over to ask a question and he gives me an *I'll be right back.*

"What's the verdict?" Claire asks, walking over after waving goodbye to the last kid whose parents we were waiting on.

"I can't stay here for at least a few days," I say, still in shock.

"A few days?" she asks, shocked.

I cringe and nod. "At best. He mentioned that the place will need some work that will probably make it longer." I sigh, watching the money I set aside for the final renovations drift away. "I'll probably have to find a hotel for the next few days then figure things out from there."

Claire shakes her head at me. "You can't stay in a hotel, Jules. With the town lighting coming up, the hotels are all overbooked or they will cost an arm and a leg." I groan, knowing that's the truth. "What about..." She pauses, cringing because she already knows how I'll feel about the idea. "How about your mom?"

"And have her spend the next month telling me she was right? Absolutely not. I won't tell her about any of this if I can get away with it." Evergreen Park is a small town, but she lives a few over in TK, so one can hope news won't travel too much.

"Ava?" I shake my head.

"She's in California with Jaime while they wait for their place to be done." They bought the most gorgeous old Victorian a few months back, and with Jaime being Jaime, he wants to make sure his fiancée has everything she could ever want, resulting in a near complete gut while they finish off the house."

"Harper?"

I give her a look.

"And stay on the couch while Jeremy grumbles about how her friends are all leeches, again?" I ask, then shake my head. "I love Harper, but I'd rather stay with my mom than with Jeremy."

"Honestly, that's so fair," she says, tapping her finger on her chin and trying to think. I see it before she says anything, some idea I don't think I'm going to like clicking into place. "You know..."

"I feel like I should preemptively say no," I say, and she shakes her head.

"No! No, seriously, it's actually a really good idea. You know I was staying in the in-law cottage behind my brother's house?"

"No, Claire."

"It's a good idea! It's going to be empty. You don't even have to talk to him if you don't want to!"

"I can't move in with a stranger. That's insane, and even you have to know that makes no sense." I shake my head.

"It's not even in his house," she assures me. "It's *behind* his house, fully detached. I usually nanny for him, but since I'm leaving, he's in a bit of a lurch. You could even help him out with his daughter, so you don't have to feel like you're taking advantage of him. I know he'd really appreciate it."

The downside of working so closely with Claire is she knows me really fucking well. She knows exactly what obstacles I'll use to argue and how to tug at my heartstrings. A single dad with no one helping to watch his daughter, who Claire is constantly going on and on about how sweet she is? Definitely a weakness.

"I don't know, I—"

She cuts me off, giving me a serious face, one she very rarely pulls out with her light and bubbly personality.

"What's your other option, Jules? You need somewhere safe to stay that won't cost you a million dollars. I'm leaving you with this mess, let me at least try and help." I can see it in her eyes—the urge for me to accept her help, so I sigh, not wanting to let her down. "Exactly," she says, that pout turning into a smile. "Let me go call him, see if it's even an option. If not, we'll figure something else out, okay? My mom knows, like, everyone in Evergreen Park."

Before I can further argue, she turns and begins walking to a quiet area, her phone already to her ear.

With a bone-deep sigh, I return to staring at the chaos that is going on in front of my place, trying to figure out some kind of makeshift plan that doesn't require spending all my savings on a hotel, staying with a stranger, or, worst of all, calling my mother. But I'm sidetracked when there's a tug at my tutu, and I look down to see a small girl with blonde curly hair.

"It's you!" she yells. "It's you! I told my dad it would be a Christmas miracle!" I stand frozen as she stares at me, wide blue eyes locked on me before her arms wrap around my legs and squeeze me tight. Then she looks at me again, determination on her little face now. "You need to come meet my dad," she demands.

"What? I'm sorry, honey, are you..." I look around to see if there's an adult around that she belongs to, but come up empty, everyone wandering around us completely ignorant of my panic. "Are you lost? Do you need help?"

The little girl shakes her head adamantly. "No, you're going to be my dad's new wife. It's my Christmas wish! Wow, Santa really does work fast."

My eyes go wide and my mouth drops open because, clearly, there's been some huge misunderstanding and somehow, some way, my night has just gotten worse. "I'm sorry, I—"

She tugs on my hand, trying to get me to move, determination in her tiny stance. "Come on! You've gotta meet my dad." She's quickly getting annoyed or fed up with my not doing what she's asking, and if I wasn't alarmed, I'd probably find it funny.

"Sweetie, I think we should stay here, we can—"

"Sophie!" a deep, loud voice calls from behind me, the voice far too familiar. A voice I do not want to hear on what might be the shittiest night of my life. Still, because I'm a glutton for punishment, I turn to where the frantic voice is coming from.

And then I see him.

Actually, then I see them, cementing the fact that someone up there really, truly hates me because my day just went from shit to absolutely horrific.

FIVE

NEW YEAR'S EVE, LAST YEAR

JULES

We walk out to the parking lot to find our cars are parked right next to each other, and once again, I can't help but think this is some kind of kismet situation. Like my time has finally come, and this is some kind of romance movie moment.

He takes me to the driver's side of my car, and we stand there for a moment.

"I'd really love you to come to my place tonight," he says, voice low and warm. "Or I could go to your place if you're more comfortable, or—" he starts, but I cut him off, knowing my place is an absolute disaster zone and I'd like to see where this man lives.

"Your place is fine."

"Does a friend have your location?" he asks. There's barely six inches between us, my mind reeling with all the possibilities this night could bring and not really listening to his question.

"What?"

"Does a friend have your location? Like on their phone?" He tips his chin to where my cellphone is in my hand.

"Oh, I mean..." I start, but the answer is yes, both Harper and

Ava have my location and I have theirs. He must see the answer because he nods.

"Okay, good. Tell them you're coming to my place, give them my address. 14 Oak Avenue."

Understanding what he means, I find myself smiling as I start to type out his name and info into our group chat before I look up with a faux glare. "You know, my best friend is engaged to a guy with a security firm. He could run a background check on you. Anything I should know?" I watch his face meticulously, trying to see if there's even the hint of some secret he wouldn't want exposed, but see nothing but an easy smile.

"Tell him to check away. I've got nothing to hide."

"Okay. Text sent," I say, my phone buzzing in my hand already with a response.

> AVA
>
> A MAN?
>
> HARPER
>
> Where did you meet him?
>
> AVA
>
> IS HE HOT?
>
> HARPER
>
> Are you safe?

I smile at their responses but look at Nate. "14 Oak?" He nods. "I'll follow you," I say, then look up at him smiling down at me. It wouldn't take much at all for him to dip his head, press his lips to mine, especially not with the way his eyes keep flickering to my lips. His hand moves up to cup my jaw, brushing a thumb along my cheek, and I think he's going to do it, he's going to kiss me, when he steps back.

"Follow me," he says, his voice lower now, almost gravelly.

Then he opens my car door like a true gentleman, watches me

slide in and start the car before slamming my door shut and jogging around to his truck. As he starts his car, I send a text to my friends, telling them I'm safe, that I met a hot guy at the bar, and I'm going home with him, promising to report back first thing in the morning.

A slew of squeal texts follow, including an *I love you, be safe* text from each of them before Nate's truck backs up and I'm driving to the other side of town.

It's barely a five-minute drive before I'm pulling into Nate's driveway next to his car. The house is cute and well maintained, something I wouldn't expect from a bachelor, unless he was both a contractor and had three sisters who are apparently as meddling as his mother.

He's already out of his truck and walking to my door, opening it and helping me out before helping me to the front door of his house.

"Talk to your friends?" he asks, digging in his pocket for a set of keys.

I nod. "They're a bit worried since I don't...do this," I say, waving at him and then at me. "But they know where I am."

"This?" he asks, letting go of my hand to pick the right key. He steps in front of me to open the storm door before working on the lock.

"You know, go home with a random guy from a bar—" I start to explain, but then, as seems to be my way, I make a fool of myself, tripping on the sidewalk and falling. I catch myself on my hands, my palms burning but mostly my own ego bruised.

"Fuck, Jules!" Nate says, stepping down the two steps, the storm door slamming behind him as he comes to me, kneeling before me.

"I'm fine, really. You'd think for a dancer I'd be a bit more graceful, but," I say as he grabs my hands, gently turning them over to inspect. Each has a small scratch, blood pebbling there, and he curses under his breath. "It's really no big deal at all, Nate. Seriously. I'm fine."

He looks at me then, genuine concern in his eyes.

"You're bleeding."

"I'm fine," I say, lower and quieter this time, but then I squeal as he grabs me, lifting me and carrying me up the two stairs and into his house. "Nate!" I say with a laugh. "Put me down! I'm fine!"

"You're a damsel in distress. Let me play Prince Charming." Then he sets my ass on the kitchen counter, turning my hands once more to inspect them. He brushes a few bits of dirt and a small piece of gravel that stuck to my palm before glaring at me. "Stay here," he says, then steps away, disappearing down the hall.

I take the opportunity to look around his place. It's clean, cute, and clearly decorated by a man with the minimal decorations, photos, and art. But it's cozy and comfortable.

There's two hallways, one he disappeared down and another to the left. The kitchen I'm in has an island I'm sitting on with stools as well as a dining table. Two giant glass doors face the backyard that butts up to the doors, and there's a small cottage or house on the property.

I'm tempted to hop down and inspect the rest of his home, but a door clicks and his footsteps become closer, his frame filling the hall in a few moments. In his hand is a white first aid kit.

"Glad to see you can follow directions," he says with a smile, setting the kit on the counter next to me, then rifling through it before setting two antiseptic wipes and two Band-Aids aside.

Next, he grabs me by the wrist, gently turning it over to inspect the damage. I watch with bated breath as he holds my wrist gently with one hand and tears the package open with his teeth before wiping the alcohol over the small cut. I hiss at the burn before he wipes on antibiotic ointments and puts a Band-Aid on.

"You really don't have to do this," I say with a small laugh as he moves to the next hand. "It's just a scratch. I've gotten worse."

"Not on my watch," he says distantly, attention diverted.

"What?"

"Not on my watch. When you're with me, if you get hurt, I take care of you," he says, eyes to my hand as he gently and almost reverently puts the last bandage on before staring at his handiwork.

Finally, he looks at me, a small smile on his lips as he stands between my spread legs. Like this, we're just about face-to-face. Suddenly, I feel brave, probably from the adrenaline of falling and the excitement of what I think is to come.

"You know, if this was a movie, this is where you'd kiss it better," I say with a smile.

"Is that the only time?" he asks, his voice low now, his eyes locked to my lips.

I shake my head, and when I speak, my words come out breathy. "No, you'd definitely kiss me a lot."

He gives me a boyish smile before lifting my hand to his face, pressing his lips to the bandage on my hand before repeating it on the other. Then his hand slides up my arm until it's on my neck, his thumb tipping my chin up as he leans down to press his lips to mine.

I wake up in a strange bed, but it doesn't feel strange at all: strong arms wrapped around my middle, a scruffy chin in my neck, and soft, warm breaths running along my skin.

It doesn't take long before it all comes back to me: meeting Nate at the bar, feeling a spark I couldn't deny, going home with him, falling and him bandaging me up, the multiple orgasms...

And now I'm wrapped in his arms in his bed, his breathing low and easy and comfortable.

I've slept with men, of course, and had long-term boyfriends and short flings where I'd spend the night, but I've never been able to sleep with someone touching me. I need space to sprawl, and I get way too hot, way too easily. I've always assumed when I finally found my dream man, we'd have one of those two-bed marriages in order to not go insane from lack of quality sleep.

Except I just woke up easy, feeling more rested than I ever have in my life, and there's a warm body wrapped around me. We're not just sleeping together, but sleeping intertwined.

The beating of my heart picks up just a bit, and for the first time in my life, I wonder if I've finally found it: my silver-screen worthy match, the person I was meant to be with.

Ever since I watched *My Big Fat Greek Wedding* at much too young an age, I saw a part of myself in Toula, in her bone-deep desire to find true love. It started my addiction to romance movies, and I watched every single one I could get my hands on.

I fell in love with the idea of love and told myself I'd only let myself fall when I met him—the one people wrote books and made movies about.

Over the years, I began to lose faith it would happen. How on earth could I find some kind of fictional soulmate naturally? Or even worse, on dating apps? Have you seen some of the men on dating apps? It's not even close to leading-man material.

But now...now things feel like they are clicking into place. Like maybe, finally, some goddess of love smiled down on me and decided I deserved even just the barest glimmer of hope, pushing me into that bar to...Nate, maybe?

As I lose myself in my thoughts, Nate shifts, quietly waking before pressing a kiss to the place where my neck meets my shoulder. "Morning," he whispers there, sleepiness in the word.

A chill runs through me, a bolt of excitement, and right there, I decide this is it. This is my chance to fall and fall hard, and I'm going to take it and trust in it.

"Good morning." I shift my body, turning until we're face-to-face, and then I see that it's not just his voice filled with sleep but his face. He still looks handsome, just a bit groggy, and his lips are tipped upwards with a smile. "Happy New Year."

"Can't think of a better way to start my year than this," he says. He moves up onto an elbow, looking behind me at a window facing the backyard, and then chuckles, the feel of it vibrating through me.

I hum in agreement, my hand lifting and drawing shapes on his chest, the fine dusting of hair there tickling my finger. God, he has a good fucking chest, doesn't he?

"Snowed in," he says, voice rough.

My head perks up, but his eyes are still on the window. "Hmm?"

"We're snowed in. At least a good foot dropped overnight." He looks down at me finally. "Maybe this really is a movie after all."

"No way?" His lips tip up at the corner with a smile. "There wasn't snow in the forecast, was there?" I'm absolutely terrible at keeping track, and I'm usually only up to speed about the weather when the parents of a class start calling and texting me to see if class is canceled.

"No, but there's definitely snow out there." He pauses before continuing. "I think it's still coming down, actually. Looks like you're stuck here for a bit longer."

Without warning, nerves and overthinking kick in because what if that's a bad thing? What if I'm just in a delusional bubble thinking he's some kind of miracle sent from the universe, and he was thinking this was just a one-night stand? What if he was hoping I'd leave first thing in the morning, and now he's stuck with me? What if—

My mind continues to fall down a rabbit hole, and I must show it on my face because Nate quickly speaks, changing directions.

"Unless you don't want to be here, then I've got a truck. I can get you home. It might take a bit since I'm not sure which roads are plowed. I didn't put the plow blade on my truck, but I could probably get to the garage to dig it out." His hand moves, pushing my hair back and over my shoulder before looking into my eyes, genuine concern on his face. "I don't want you to feel actually stuck here."

"I don't," I say quickly, then feel the need to explain. "But I also don't want you to be stuck with me."

"Not much I'd rather be doing than being stuck inside for a snow day with you."

"Oh," I say, warmth running through me.

"Yeah, oh." His head dips down, gently pressing his lips to mine, and even though I desperately want to continue that, to take it further, all my mind can think about is morning breath. He pulls back and smiles, and I wonder if he can read my thoughts somehow. "How about I roll out of here, leave you to wake up, and then when you're ready, you shuffle out to the kitchen for coffee? How do you like it?"

A bolt of heat runs through me because he definitely knows how I like it after last night.

"My coffee?" He nods, though there's a glimmer in his eye like he knows what I was thinking. "Milk and one pump of almond, one pump of vanilla." He laughs again, and I like how much he laughs, how he's so open with everything. He doesn't seem like the type to hide anything or try to act too cool to show emotion. "It's what I order at Evergreen Brew, which, in my opinion, has the best coffee in the world."

His smile goes wider, and he shakes his head. "Noted. Well, I can't say I have that on hand, but I do have vanilla coffee creamer or just milk and sugar.

"Creamer would be great."

He smiles wide before rolling over me, bracing his arms in the bed on either side of my face and doing a bit of a push-up until his lips press to mine. Once he's clear of the room, just a pair of low-slung sweatpants on, I can't help it: I take one of his fluffy pillows, put it over my face, and squeal into it, kicking my feet with glee and utter excitement.

"Do you have ingredients here, or is this a bachelor pad?" I ask ten minutes later, standing in his kitchen, a perfect cup of coffee in front of me.

After I had my moment, I hopped out of his bed, finger-brushed my teeth, and did some snooping in his bathroom, thankfully not finding anything but men's products. Next, I checked the closet and dresser, both clear of anything but men's clothing. Once I determined the coast was clear, I slipped into the kitchen wearing a giant sweat-shirt of his and my panties from the night before.

"What?" he asks, moving behind me and spinning me around to face him. His warm hand slides under the sweater to my waist, tugging me close. My chin tips up to look at him, a small smile playing on my lips that's reflected on his face.

"I know you're a single guy, but do you have ingredients to make food?" There's a quick moment, a glimmer of disappointment or something similar in his eyes that I think I see, but it's gone before I can identify it.

"Are you trying to cook for me?" I shrug. "It's a snow day. Snow days need snowman pancakes."

His smile goes wide, transforming into a grin. "Snowman pancakes?"

"Oh yeah. Snow days are for watching movies, pajamas, and snowman pancakes."

"You don't have any pajamas here," he says, his fingers playing with the hem of his sweater I'm wearing.

"Are you complaining?"

He shakes his head. "Not even a little. What do you need for these snowman pancakes?"

"Uh, you know. Pancake ingredients, then powdered sugar, chocolate chips...bacon for a hat would be great."

"A bacon hat?" he asks through a poorly disguised laugh.

"Or a scarf. Really depends on how you want to dress him up."

He smiles and leans a bit to press his lips to mine before stepping back and moving toward the fridge. "Not sure if I have powdered sugar, but I definitely have." There's a pause as he grabs something out then turns to show me a can of whipped cream. "Will this work? We've definitely got the chocolate chips and the bacon."

"I think we can make it work."

He comes back to me, pulling me back into his arms and using a hand in my hair to tip my head back. He's tall, maybe six foot to my five-five, and I like feeling small beside him. I don't have much time before his lips touch mine, opening so his tongue slides along mine, tasting of mint toothpaste and dark coffee.

We don't have pancakes for another hour, but when we do, they're the best snowman pancakes I've ever had in my life.

"Favorite Christmas movie?" I ask from the kitchen island I'm sitting on while I watch Nate do the dishes. I'm in his oversized shirt and a pair of his boxer briefs that don't quite fit. My hair is an absolute disaster, but something about the way he looks at me makes me feel hotter than I've ever felt in my skimpiest, sexiest outfit.

He smiles at me over his shoulder, a smile I feel in my lower half, but that also tells me whatever he's about to say is going to earn an eye roll.

"*Die Hard.*"

My jaw drops as I gape at him. "You have got to be kidding me. That's not a Christmas movie!"

"It so is," he says, a laugh in his words.

"Just because it takes place during Christmas does not make it a Christmas movie," I say with a laugh. His broad shoulders shrug as he rinses off a plate. I offered and even insisted on doing the dishes since he cooked, but he grabbed me by the hips, placed me on the counter, placed a kiss to my lips, and told me to just keep him company.

He seems to like having me up here.

Strangely enough, considering I like to always keep busy, I don't mind.

"Beg to differ. That's how they decide those kinds of things. It's got Christmas, it's a Christmas movie. It's got sappy love shit, it's a romance movie."

My eyes go wide with his wholly inaccurate statement. "So you're saying any movie with a romance subplot is a romance movie?"

"Hell yeah. *Top Gun* might as well be a chick flick."

I throw a chocolate chip at the back of his head. "That's...that's sacrilegious."

"I feel like that might be a small exaggeration."

Even though he can't see it, I shake my head, aghast. "Not at all. At this point, I find it necessary to warn you, I am an expert of all things romance movies."

"Oh yeah? What's your favorite?" He turns off the water as he sets the last dish into the drying rack, grabbing a dish towel to dry off his hands as he turns, leaning on the counter across from me and crossing his arms on his chest.

I think genuinely about his question for a moment before I answer.

"It depends on my mood, I guess. Do I want a Christmas movie? A contemporary? A romantic comedy? Or are we going by decade —'80s? '90's? 2000s? A Nora Ephron? A Nancy Meyers?"

His smile goes wider with each addition like he finds me wholly entertaining.

"Wow, I didn't know there were so many things to ponder."

"Oh, the list is endless."

"Okay, so, Christmas movies. What's your favorite?"

"*Love Actually*, obviously. *Serendipity* is second best. I love the whole invisible string theory, always pulled together despite not being together, you know?"

"Mm, yeah," he says. "So is that what you want? A romance that's movie-worthy, some invisible string kind of relationship?"

I shrug, not wanting to take this from fun and silly to something too much for having just met him. "Maybe. I don't know."

He takes me in for a moment before pushing off the counter and walking to me, standing between my legs and holding my gaze. "That's a lie," he says low. "Like a bald-faced lie, Jules. Something tells me you always know exactly what you want. You're just scared someone's going to belittle you when you tell them."

I think about telling my ex about First Position and my dreams for my little business and having him tell me it was a silly idea, a waste of time. *A fun hobby, Julianne, but not something to devote your life to.*

I think about telling my mother I wanted to find love, true love, instead of the security she always told me to settle for and her scoffing at the mere idea.

Might as well scare him off now.

"I want...I want to be loved madly. I want to live a movie-worthy life and wake up knowing every single day it's my reality. I want to find someone I wake up every morning excited to spend time with. I want someone who loves everything about me, even the parts I don't like. Some people in my life...they think I'm being crazy, that I'm being unrealistic, and that's fine. I know one day, I'll find it, even if it takes a lifetime. I refuse...I refuse to settle for less than I deserve." I stare at him, the way he's silently taking me in, and suddenly feel self-conscious, like I said much, much more than I should have.

"I'm sorry, that was...a lot for a first date," I say with a self-deprecating laugh and turn away, desperate for some kind of escape.

God, why am I this way?

But then his hand moves, grabbing my face and turning it so I have to look at him.

"I think we're well past the first date," he says with a smile.

"Yeah, I guess. But dumping all of that on you isn't exactly cool or coy or mysterious."

He keeps staring at me, his rough thumb brushing over my bottom lip gently, and I fight the urge to look away again.

"Do you feel it?" he asks in a whisper.

"What?"

"This...pull. There's something between us." My heart skips a beat. "It's crazy, Jules. I wasn't planning on going to the bar last night, but I walked past and couldn't stop it, like there was some thread tugging me right to you."

I swallow, trying to get words out.

"That's very romantic, Nate," I whisper.

"I've never been one."

"Never been what?"

"A romantic. I've never believed in any of the grand ideas of soulmates or love or invisible strings. My dad does; he says he saw my mom and knew that day she was meant to be his. They met at some party and talked all night, and then she disappeared." His lips crack into a smile, and it's contagious, spilling onto my own face. "A couple of years later, they met again, and he didn't let her run off the second time. A year later, they were married."

"A year!" I say with a laugh. "Kind of quick."

"Yeah, well, as my dad says, when you know, you know."

"Hmm," I say, running a hand through his hair.

"I think I understand what he means now."

SIX

JULES

Every prayer I send up to whoever will listen goes unanswered as the man nears, and it only gets worse when the girl at my side yells, "Daddy!"

I blink a few times, hoping my vision is just inexplicably fucking with me, but each time they open, he just gets closer.

Nate, the man I spent two magical nights with last year. The one I met in a bar and made me believe I'd found that once in a lifetime, love at first sight, what movies are made of kind of story, only to discover he had a wife and kid. His green eyes are locked on the girl now holding my hand as he moves toward us. When the gap between us is barely ten feet and quickly closing, he shouts, "Sophie, what were you thinking!?"

"I found her, Dad! I found her!" she replies, excitement in her voice as her hand squeezes hard on mine, keeping me grounded in reality. Something I greatly need when his eyes finally leave the girl and meet mine.

That's when his entire body goes still as he breathes out my name. "Jules." The single word makes me stumble, and I don't know if I do it physically or just internally when I see his face, the look of panic quickly melting into astonishment.

It's really him.

No wonder this girl looks familiar: she looks like him. Against my will and better judgment, I stare as he approaches, taking him in fully. Not much has changed since I saw him last: longish dark blond hair messily pushed back, a dark brown work jacket over an olive green sweater and jeans, and a pair of beat-up boots on his feet.

A tall blonde woman walks behind him, and I recognize the build and the hair as the woman I saw in the grocery store. She stops beside him, and my eyes lock on her, unable to look away.

"Daddy, I found Ashlyn!" the little girl shouts, tugging my hand.

"Uh," he says, looking from the girl to me, a flash of panic filling his face as he puts some kind of pieces together. "She does. What are you doing here?" he asks, his question directed at me.

I continue to glare at him.

"What are *you* doing here?" I ask.

The little girl tugs on my hand again and then shows me the doll in her free hand.

"We were seeing Santa! I made a wish that we would find the real-life Ashlyn, and it came TRUE!"

As if this night couldn't get any worse, this girl thinks I'm her Christmas wish come to life. I look down at my outfit, realizing with an ounce of horror I do kind of look like her Ashlyn doll dressed up like this.

"Jesus, Sophie, what was that all about?" the girl's mother asks as she makes it through the crowd, stopping right behind Nate.

"I found Ashlyn!" the girl, I'm assuming is named Sophie, shouts, and the woman gives me a head-to-toe before smiling.

"I guess you did, didn't you?" Nate sighs, running a hand over his face.

"Sloane, this is Jules. Jules, this is Sloane, my—"

Your wife, I think.

You know, this is so my kind of luck. The worst day of my life, standing in the cold in a ballerina costume while the entire city of Evergreen Park finds out I'm a moron who doesn't know to drip my water lines during a cold snap, and the man who fooled me and his wife get a full view of it.

"Sister."

His sister.

His sister.

His SISTER.

Oh god. This is definitely the same woman I saw in the grocery store, but if this is his sister...

"God, you guys are fast!" another woman says, and all eyes move to the new face, a girl in heeled boots and a sweater dress, whose face lights up when she sees me. "Jules! Hey!"

I recognize her as Claire's older sister who has come out with us to get drinks once or twice, and once more, my world tilts on its axis. Her eyes widen as she takes in the fire trucks and chaos.

"Oh my god, look at you! What happened? Is everything okay with the studio? Oh look, Claire is here!" she says, jumping from one topic to the next and looking over my shoulder.

When I turn, Claire is walking toward our little group with a wide smile.

"There you are! I was just trying to call you," she says to Nate.

No, no, no, I think, as things continue to click into place.

No.

My luck cannot be this bad, can it? But it gets worse when the little girl holding my hand tugs it and speaks. "Aunt Claire, look! It's her! It's Ashlyn!"

Claire looks from me to the doll in her niece's hand and smiles.

"Oh my god, she sure does!" Claire bends to grab and lift the little girl, placing her on her hip.

"I told Santa I wanted to meet the real-life Ashlyn for Christmas so she could fall in love with Dad, and now she's here!"

I think I'm starting to get lightheaded, and my friend's smile grows.

"You know Jules?" Nate asks, looking from me to Claire.

"Well, yeah, she owns the studio I work at." Her brow furrows and turns fully to who I understand is her brother, accusation filling her tone. "How do you know Jules?"

I open my mouth to give some explanation—literally any explanation for how I know this man other than I fucked him a few times before thinking he was a liar with a wife and kid—but Nate speaks first.

"I met her last New Year's," he says. It's not a lie, but thankfully, it doesn't reveal much. Or so I think, but Nate's sisters' eyes go wide before looking at me with wide smiles.

"Oh," Claire says. I have no idea what that *oh* means, but I somehow know it's not good.

"No way," the other sister says, Sloane just smiling wide.

"I, uh..." I start trying to find some way to get out of this hellscape so I can focus on more important issues. Right now, I need to get out of this costume, into my coziest clothes, and figure out how to get my things and where to sleep for the night before I have the world's biggest breakdown.

"So, wait, what's going on?" Sloane asks, tipping her chin to the fire engines with their lights on, the crew of men huddled around. They came to turn the water off in the building and are making sure it's cleared.

"I, uh...a water leak. Apparently, it's just too cold for these pipes, and my upstairs bathroom isn't insulated enough. Something must have cracked. I don't know; it flooded my place and the dance studio." I sigh before shivering from the cold, Nate's eyes narrowing on me.

"How long has it been, you out here in the cold like that?" There's an edge to his voice, like he's annoyed or mad, but I barely feel the cold at this point. I'm numb from it and the million other feelings running through me.

I try and ignore his glare as I look at my watch and shrug. "Not sure, maybe an hour?"

"An hour? Jesus. That's unacceptable."

He shifts then, shrugging off his thick tan jacket, draping it over my shoulders. In my peripheral vision, Claire elbows Sloane, and Sutton whispers something I probably don't want to hear.

"You don't have to give me this, I'm fine," I say, even though it's warm and smells like Nate and feels absolutely amazing.

Nate glares at me and opens his mouth, but his sister interrupts.

"You should go talk to Mark, see what's taking so long," Claire says with a smug smile.

"Yeah. Stay here; I'll try and move things along," Nate says with a nod.

"That's really not necessary—" I start, but he's already turning, moving to the fire chief, who greets him like an old friend with a handshake and a pat on the back.

"Let him do his thing," Claire says. "He knows everyone, can figure out what the next steps are, and when you can get some things to tide you over for a night or two."

I sigh, then slip my arms into the jacket. If it's already on me, might as well warm up. Or, at least that's what I'm telling myself. I definitely am *not* just trying to take in the smell and feel of Nate while I can. That would be crazy.

"Where are you staying tonight?" Sloane asks.

I shrug.

"I, uh." My mind moves over the money in my savings that I've been saving for a larger studio, groaning internally as I do, but using the money is much better than the alternative. "I think I'll have to go to a hotel—"

"Oh god, no!" Sloane shakes her head. "That's going to cost a million dollars, if they even have any openings," she remarks, using the same logic her sister did earlier.

They're not wrong. This weekend is the town lighting, one of the few times a year our tiny town is flooded with non-locals to see the wonder that is Evergreen Park at Christmastime. Because of this, hotels cost an arm and a leg and book up fast.

"It's really my only choice, you know? I don't want to bother my friends, and my mom isn't...the ideal place for me to stay. It's really all I've got right on such short notice."

"Are any even going to be open?" Sloane asks, grabbing her phone and scrolling. Looking at her properly, she looks so much like her sister but has a more professional, no-bullshit way about her that is completely the opposite of Claire.

"Probably not," Claire agrees. "I was calling you guys before because I told her she should just stay in Nate's guest house." A knowing smile pulls along her lips with the words, and I watch as her two other sisters smile and nod in agreement.

"I—" I start with a shake of my head, but Sloane cuts me off.

"Oh, that's genius!" she says.

"It's not even really attached to his house. I lived there for a bit when I moved back to Evergreen Park, too. It's really cute!" Sutton adds.

"I couldn't—"

Claire ignores my argument, turning to Sloane. "Has he found someone to watch Sophie when he's not around?"

"I don't need—" Sophie starts, but her aunt breaks in.

"You know, I don't think he has." There's a tip to her lips like she's catching on to whatever grand scheme Claire is hatching. "You know, Nate's a contractor. I bet he could help with the repairs." Sloane waves her arm at my building. "And you could help out with Sophie on the nights he works late."

I pull the edges of the jacket closer, needing the comfort of it now. "I really don't think—"

"It's perfect!" Claire says, then turns to me. "It's not often, the babysitting, just like, once a week and getting her off the bus if you're around."

"You're my new nanny?!" the little girl shrieks, and the panic continues to close in on me as her aunt puts her back down on the ground.

"No, no, I—"

"I mean, you're so great with kids, you teach all of those classes,

Jules! And you babysit, right?" Claire asks, knowing the answer. Sometimes parents of the kids I teach ask me to come sit for them on a date night, and I'm always more than willing to help if I'm free.

"Well, yeah, but—"

"It's settled then," Claire says, a self-assured smile on her lips. "God, if I had known you were her, I totally would have pushed for you to go on a date with my brother harder. I told you you would get along!" She did, months ago, and I turned her down, telling her I had a bad experience recently that put me off dating for a bit. Claire gives me a small smile. "You'll just stay in the cottage while this all gets sorted out and occasionally babysit."

I open my mouth to argue but don't even get a squeak out this time. It seems these women are hell on wheels when they get an idea in their heads.

"You can't trust me with your niece," I say, but she gives me a be-so-real look because even I know that's not true. We spend a lot of time together, nearly every day. "I could be dangerous, and you'd never know! I appreciate the offer, really, but I can't accept that. Plus, I doubt your brother would be okay with your friend moving in with him."

"Literally anyone on those nanny sites could also be dangerous, and we'd never know. I listen to true crime podcasts. Anyone could snap at any moment, becoming a total psycho. At least we know who you are," Sloane says, her sister nodding as if it's the utmost bit of logic.

"I actually don't know you," I say to Nate's other sisters.

"Oh, I'm Sloane. See? Now you know me. Perfect. So a place to live, got that. That's your dance studio?"

I nod, a bit frazzled. Everything right now is utter chaos, and it seems everything I'm saying is going right over these women's heads. This is so my kind of luck.

Let's see, first, I have nowhere to live and nowhere to work. Then, the man I thought was a piece of shit so I ghosted him, is actually my friend's brother, and his sisters are attempting to convince me to essentially move in with him.

Oh, and his daughter seems to think I'm her Ashlyn doll come to life to fulfill some kind of Christmas wish.

Claire, clearly either oblivious to my panic or not caring at all, turns to her sister. "Do you think Mom has any contacts at the community center? Jules could run her classes there in the meantime, it's usually pretty empty in December."

"Definitely," Sloane says, pulling out her phone and tapping on it. "I'll fill her in now, and she'll get working on it."

"Perfect!" Sutton says with a happy little clap of her hands. "It's set! Nothing to worry about anymore!"

"I'm sorry, I really appreciate all of this, but it's so very unnecessary. I—"

"Do you know if your clothes were damaged? We can try and see if we have anything that would fit you. You and Sutton look about the same size."

"I have way too many clothes! You can totally go shopping in my closet," Sutton says.

"If you need furniture, I'm sure our dad has—" Claire starts, but the anxiety bubbles over.

"Stop!" I shout as loud as I feel comfortable without drawing additional attention. Everyone around me goes silent, and I close my eyes, taking in a deep breath. "I'm sorry," I say, taking in a deep breath when all four women stare at me with wide eyes, including little Sophie. "That was rude. I appreciate the kindness, really. But I'm panicking enough, and I just need to make it through the night. I appreciate the offers, but I don't need you to go out of your way. I'll figure it all out myself."

All three of the sisters look at each other, not offended by my outburst or my declining their help, instead smiling at each other before Sloane puts an arm around my shoulder and sighs.

"So I hate to tell you this, but this is just the Donovan way,"

Sloane says. "You get used to it. We see someone in need, we chip in. Especially when we claim you as one of our own."

My eyes drift across the way to where Nate is talking to the fire chief, pointing my way and nodding. When he catches my eye, his lips tip up in a soft smile, and despite everything, butterflies in my belly flutter like they've never been gone.

I've completely lost it.

I sigh before turning to Sloane. "The only kind of help I need right now is a fucking lobotomy," I mumble under my breath.

SEVEN

NATE

"Are you terrorizing Jules?" I ask, walking over to where my sisters are nearly doubled over with laughter, Sophie smiling like she wants to get the joke but is only five, and Jules looking like she might try and run.

Claire stands and shakes her head, brushing a tear from her eyes as she catches her breath. "Only a little," she says. "We're Donovan-waying her, and it's sending her spiraling."

"Ah, yeah, that'll do it," I say, then look over my shoulder at where Mark, the fire chief, is making his way over to us. I turn back to Jules. "So I talked to Mark, and as you know, you can't stay here. So—"

"She's going to stay in the cottage!" Claire interrupts.

"And you're going to fix her place," Sloane says.

"She's also going to help babysit Sophie when you need her," Sutton adds.

"And Ashlyn is going to fall in love with you!" Sophie shouts, clearly excited by this grand plan.

"Shh! Soph, you're going to freak her out!" Claire says.

"Oh, sorry, Jules!" Sophie says with a giggle.

I look to Jules, who does, in fact, look slightly more freaked out than before, and sigh, turning to her completely.

My fucking sisters make everything so much more complicated than it needs to be.

"Ignore them, okay? First things first, you're going to go up with Mark and grab some things for a day or so. That's step one. Then we'll worry about step two when that's done." Slowly, the tiniest glimmer of relief flashes into her eyes, and I begin to understand just how overwhelmed she is. "I'll handle all of them, don't worry," I say, tipping my head to the four meddling Donovans, and Jules nods.

"Ready?" Mark asks, coming up beside our huddle. Jules nods, then tries to shrug out of my jacket.

"Keep it for now," I insist, my rarely used dad voice coming out.

She stares at me, ready to argue, but must see it's pointless. Without another word, she turns to follow him into her building.

"It's her, isn't it?" Sloane asks as soon as the door closes behind them, and I sigh, knowing my nosy sisters will never let this die. Even as it was happening, I knew I shouldn't have drank too much that night in February and let it spill to my youngest sister. "Your dream girl?"

"She's not my dream girl, Sloane," I say, running a hand through my hair. She was just a girl I thought was my dream girl before she ghosted me because I came on way too strong. And now it's like my fucking sisters are repeating history.

"If I remember when you were drinking that tequila, you told me you'd met your dream girl, hung out with her for two nights, and thought you were going to marry her just like Dad did with Mom. Then she disappeared," Claire recalls with a smug smile.

"Weren't you drinking too?" I ask, frustrated.

Her smile goes wider, and it looks exactly like the girl who used to make my life misery when we were kids, always finding out my secrets and using them as blackmail.

It seems that hasn't changed at all.

"No, my sweet Nathan," she starts, patting my cheek. "I saw it for what it was, a perfect opportunity to pull all of your deepest, darkest secrets out in your moment of weakness, and I pounced."

Sounds about right.

"You're the worst, you know that?"

"You love me. Now, about my friend being your dream girl. That's not a coincidence, and you know it."

My middle sister nods in agreement.

"Things like this, Nate...they don't happen for no reason. It's a sign, some kind of miracle, that you're finding her like this again," Sutton says. Of all of us, she's the most like Mom with her belief that everything is a sign.

"A Christmas miracle!" Sophie shouts, and I close my eyes to take a deep breath, trying to find the will not to lose it.

"You guys—"

"She has nowhere to stay. You know how the hotels here get during the holiday season," Claire adds. "Even before I knew all of this was happening"—she waves her hand toward me—"I was calling you to see if you'd be okay with a total stranger staying in the cottage while she figured things out. She's a friend, and I don't want her going three towns over and staying in a sketchy motel."

"But it turns out she's not a total stranger, so now there's no reason not to help out a damsel in distress," Sloane continues with a pointed look.

"Just like all of the movies! The prince saves the princess, and then they fall in love!" Sophie is nearly jumping with excitement now.

I stare up at the night sky, stars shining, and I wonder who up there is watching my life as their own personal reality show.

I hope it's entertaining, at least.

"Soph, we gotta play it cool," Sutton says to my daughter, pulling her into her side and lowering her voice. "If we freak your dad out with our super-secret Christmas plan, he's never going to agree." She winks at my daughter, and Sophie gives Sutton a sage, all-knowing nod.

"Got it," my daughter says to her aunt before giving her a thumbs-up. Claire and Sloane snort out a laugh.

"The reality is, Nate, if you say no, you're going to have the three of us, Sophie, and Mom, mad at you. You know this town: I give it three hours until word gets to Mom, and you know somehow she's going to know about everything."

Whether Sloane means Jules not having a place to stay or our history, or Claire's meddling, it doesn't matter, it's true either way. Sighing, I know there's no way to avoid this, so I nod. "Fine, I'll offer, but I'm not forcing her to stay with me."

"Of course! Of course!" Claire says, all three sisters nodding vehemently in a way I do not believe at all.

"And I don't want you to either. She stopped talking to me for a reason, and no matter what, we have to respect that. In fact, I think you should head out so we don't overwhelm her anymore. I'll figure the rest out."

To my shock and awe, there are nods of agreement, and Claire offers to drive Sutton and Sloane home. Never in my life have I seen my sisters leave anywhere so quickly, each giving Sophie a kiss and me a hug before walking off, whispering and giggling to each other.

Even though I want to be annoyed with their meddling, I can't.

Because whether she likes it or not, Jules is going to be sleeping on my property tonight, and I can't be mad about that.

⁂

"What are you still doing here?" Jules asks when she walks out of her building with Mark and walks our way. She changed while she was up there, now in a pair of leggings and a sweatshirt, my jacket pulled on over top with a large lavender-colored duffel bag over her shoulder.

The jacket looks much better on her than me, even if it's three sizes too big.

"Waiting for you," I say with a smile.

"Why?" she asks, clearly confused.

"Because," I start, taking her bag before she can argue and hefting it over my shoulder. "I feel like we have a lot to talk about."

She sighs, standing before me with her arms crossed on her chest, exhaustion clear in her eyes. "I've had a really, *really* long night, Nate," she starts. "I appreciate your con—"

"Where are you going tonight?" I ask, cutting her off.

"What?" She looks at me, brows furrowed in confusion like the words don't make any sense.

"Where are you going tonight? A friend's place? Family?"

"I'll probably book a hotel room for the night and figure something more long-term out after that. I can't move in until the town reapproves." She straightens her shoulders like she's preparing for an argument. "I'll get more info on timelines and whatnot tomorrow—"

"No, you won't," I say bluntly.

"What?"

"You won't get more information tomorrow. I work in this industry, and you're not going to get more info unless you already have a contractor on speed dial. And even then, it's Saturday. Chances of them being able to get the right info and rush things to get you answers tomorrow? Very slim." Her jaw goes tight, and I watch as she tries to rework whatever plan she's made in her mind, but I smile. "Luckily, I happen to be a contractor with all the right contacts."

"That's not—" she starts, but I interrupt her.

"When was the last time you ate?" I ask. It's almost seven, and I know by now that Sophie is starving, even if she won't admit it because of all the excitement.

"What?" Jules asks, confused by the change in subject.

"Last time you ate. I specifically remember you telling me you snack all day, eat every three hours, or you get cranky." Her head moves back like she's confused, unsure of why I remember that tiny fact she shared with me, but she doesn't know I remember everything about her.

"It's every two hours, but—"

"So let's go. Come to dinner with us," I say, tipping my head down the block and starting to move.

"Dinner?" she asks, moving to follow us reluctantly, though she doesn't have much of a choice, considering I have her bag. I wave at one of the firefighters wrapping things up, but I don't miss Sophie letting go of my hand and switching sides on the walkway to grab Jules's.

"Daddy said we'd go to the diner where they sing! Do you like grilled cheeses?" Sophie shouts, still not having figured out volume control yet.

Jules bites her lip, looking so fucking cute as she does, clearly trying to weigh her choices but not wanting to be rude to a five-year-old. Eventually, she nods. "Yes, I love them, especially from the diner. Have you ever had their milkshakes?"

Sophie squeals with excitement. "No! Can we get one, Dad? Please!"

I laugh, and Jules gives me a grimace.

"Sorry," she says under her breath.

I shake my head. "No worries. Yeah, Soph, but a small one and only if you eat real food, too."

Without looking, I know Sophie rolls her eyes at me, a habit she picked up from Claire. "Yes, Dad," she grumbles.

"Good thing your Aunt Claire is leaving, Soph, because you're getting much too sassy." My daughter just smiles at me.

"Where'd your sisters go?" Jules asks, belatedly looking around and realizing it's just us.

"Home, probably to call my mom and tell her all about this shit show." She gives me a small smile, and even though I'm pretty sure this, having an us, isn't an option anymore, it makes my heart skip a beat. "Come on, let's get you fed."

Then I'm opening the door to the diner, the noise tumbling out onto the street as we enter so I can get my girls fed.

EIGHT

NATE

"When you live with us, can we have a sleepover one night?" Sophie asks Jules after we place our orders and right before she takes a long gulp of her sugar-laden chocolate shake.

I groan out loud because, although I love my daughter more than anything on this planet, she cannot read a room to save her life.

Jules had just been starting to decompress, it seemed, relaxing a bit despite the strange circumstances. As we were deciding what to order, she even cracked a joke and told Sophie she could teach her a dance to do with her Ashlyn doll. But with Sophie's words, her shoulders return to their position at her ears.

"Sophie," I say with warning.

"What? When Aunt Claire has sleepovers with me, they're fun, but Jules is a real-life princess! Just like Ashlyn!"

"I, uh—" Jules starts, eyes wide.

"We don't even know if Jules wants to stay in the cottage, Sophie," I admonish, though I'm grateful she brought it up. Jules and I have a lot to talk about, but first we need to handle the situation of where she's going to be staying. I turn to Jules, my face trying to portray a casual offer even though it feels nothing of the sort. "Claire told me she mentioned the cottage to you. It's just sitting empty, and you're more than welcome to stay there. Actually, I kind of insist." I look at her pointedly before smiling. "I feel like we have a few things to talk about anyway."

Almost instantly, she averts her eyes, a blush blooming on her cheeks that match the color of the sweater she's wearing.

She's cute.

So fucking cute.

But, I have to remind myself, not mine.

"It's very kind, really, but I don't know if I'm comfortable with taking advantage—"

"Hotels are crazy," I add quickly. I have a few friends who work at the local hotels, and I can't stop myself from wondering if they'd be willing to tell a stranded woman they were booked so I could convince her to stay with me. It would be better than shelling out the money she could be using to fix her place on a hotel room.

Besides, she clearly is over me, over whatever there once was between us, since she let a whole year span without a word. Unfortunately for me, I haven't been able to think about anyone but her for a year. I wonder if it could give me the closure I need, some explanation as to where I went wrong with her all those months ago so I could finally move the fuck on.

Every night, my dreams are haunted by the promise of what I thought I had with Julianne, and despite it being only two nights, I can't seem to get over it, like some kind of lovesick middle schooler.

"Even if it's just for the night, you should stay in the cottage. Then, if you're not comfortable, I'm sure I can pull some strings tomorrow, reach out to some friends, and find you somewhere that won't cost you your entire savings. If I can't, my mom might as well be the mayor of Evergreen Park with the amount of people she knows. She'll figure out something."

"Nate—"

"I mean this in the most genuine way, you will be doing me a favor if you stay at the cottage tonight."

She gives me a disbelieving look before speaking. "I highly doubt that," she says with a roll of her eyes, but there's also a small smile on her lips.

Progress, I think.

She moves to say something else, but I interrupt her before she can.

"Look, Evergreen Park is small, and my family is nosy. Word travels fast in this town and faster when my sisters are involved. If it gets out I didn't do my best to give you a safe place to stay for the night, I'd never hear the end of it from my mother."

"You're thirty-five, Nate. I don't think your mom has that much sway on you." She looks me over, and that smile spreads. "Unless you're a total momma's boy, which is a red flag by the way."

I laugh out loud and shake my head.

"Not a full-blown momma's boy, though I'm close with my whole family. It's just that my mom raised me to always help someone in need, and I know Sloane is probably going to call her tonight and fill her in. We're tight like that, and my sisters love to meddle. If my mom finds out I wasn't a proper gentleman, I'm toast." I nudge Sophie under the table with my foot, but she doesn't need the hint to help me out.

"Yup, he is! Grandma will yell at him," Sophie says, and I look at my daughter with a smile. "And probably take him off her Christmas list, and she gets really good presents."

Never in my life did I think I'd use a five-year-old as a wingman, but here we are.

"See? Don't get me in trouble with my mom. And then we can talk about the rest." I shift my eyes to Sophie. "Later. Only if you want, of course. But even if you just want to spend one night in the cottage and never see me again, that's fine, too. I think I fucked up big time a year ago, and if I can only make it up in this small way, so be it."

Her brows furrow, a quick jolt of guilt flashing over her face as she bites her lip. What I wouldn't give to get into her head for just a moment.

"I don't know…" she says, hesitating, but I can also see her resistance is less now like she's coming around to the idea, so I try another angle, trying to knock out any and all arguments.

"Your friend's dating some security wiz, right?" She nods, and I reach for my wallet, slide out my license, and hand it to her. "Go. Call him, give him my info. Run me by him, look up my record so you know I'm not a psycho."

"I don't think all psychos have it written on their record, you know," she says.

I smile at her, and she returns it, even if she doesn't want to. I stare at her for a few more moments, waiting to see what she does. Eventually, she sighs and nods. I lift the license to her once more, and reluctantly, she takes it, sliding out of the booth and heading toward the bathrooms.

And even though I think she's going to take me up on my offer, I send a few texts to friends, telling them if a young woman named Julianne calls, I'll owe them a favor if they tell her their hotel is completely booked up for the night.

NINE

JULES

Once I'm in the bathroom, I pull my phone out and dial a familiar phone number from heart, not even bothering to find the contact as I pace.

"Hey—" Ava starts, but I cut her off quickly.

"Put your man on."

"What?"

"Put your man on. I know he's glued to your side every waking moment; so put him on," I tell her, no time to stress about niceties or explanations.

"Uh, excuse me?" she asks, her sassy nature coming out. "What am I, nobody? You just call me up to talk to my hot—"

"I'm in a crisis, Ava, and I need to talk to Jaime. Please, for the love of fuck, put him on the phone."

A beat of silence before she speaks. "A crisis? Are you okay? Are you safe? Did—"

I groan to the ceiling before speaking, taking a deep breath before I do. "I'm fine. I'm safe. There's an issue with my place, and I need to ask Jaime to check someone out before I take him up on an offer. I promise I will call you first thing tomorrow morning to explain, but in the meantime, can you please put Jaime on the phone so I can have him do a quick little search and make sure this person is not a murderer?"

Another pause before she speaks again, and I can hear the smile in her words now.

"Well, is he hot? Because I could maybe forgive a murder—" There's a scuffle before the phone switches, and Jaime's deep voice fills the line.

"What's going on, Jules?" Jaime asks.

"I was talking to her!" Ava shouts from the background, followed by a huff. I picture him standing there, Ava jumping and trying to grab the phone from his hand but failing miserably, and it makes me smile.

"And now I am. What's up? You got an issue?"

I sigh, knowing Jaime is not going to like this at all. "Yes? No? I don't know."

"I don't like how this sounds," he says with a grunt.

"A water line broke in my building, flooded my place and the dance studio," I say, deciding to get right to it is the best point of action.

"Fuck," the man of few words says, somehow encapsulating everything I'm feeling in one simple word.

"Yeah. And, as I'm sure Ava has told you, Evergreen Park gets crazy during Christmas. So considering how much I'm going to have to shell out to fix my place, I don't want to spend a ton on a hotel for an indefinite stay. Luckily, a, uh...friend of a friend offered me a place to stay in an in-law suite behind his house. I just want you to look him up to make sure he's not going to murder me or something."

"No," Jaime replies instantly.

"No, you won't look him up?" I ask, confused.

"No, you can't stay with him. Jesus, I thought that was common sense—not sleeping in someone's house right after you meet them."

"Technically, I've slept there before," I say without thinking.

"What? What did she just say? You've got that face!" Ava shouts in the background and instantly regrets it.

"How have you slept there before?" he asks.

"She what?"

"Look, I'm not really interested in—" I start.

"Is it the New Year's guy?" Ava yells.

Why do I tell my friends anything at all? I ask myself.

"What?" Jaime asks his fiancée.

"That guy she slept with on New Year's that has a family! Is it him?"

"Ava wants to know if—"

"I heard. Tell her yes, and it wasn't his wife; it was his sister."

"You are not staying somewhere where a man was caught sleeping with his sister," Jaime says.

I look at the ceiling of the bathroom and pray for patience as I hear Ava scream in the background.

"He didn't sleep with his sister," I say with as much patience as I can put in my words. "I saw him with a kid and a woman at the store, and I came to the apparently incorrect assumption that he had a family and he was a cheater. It turns out the woman at the store was his sister."

"And the kid?" I sigh, knowing the answer is going to require an explanation that I don't want to give, mostly because I can't give that answer. I have no idea why Nate didn't tell me he had a kid, but if I'm being completely honest, I can see why a single guy might not be willing to info dump that kind of thing right off the bat.

"It was his kid. Can you background check him or not?" I ask, letting some of my irritation seep into my words.

"Whose kid was it!?" Ava asks.

"His. I'm gonna do a background check, and I'll have more information then," Jaime says to my best friend before directing the rest to me. "Yeah, I'll do it. Can you get me his full name and address?"

"I can send you a photo of his license," I say.

"His license?"

"He knows who you are and told me to call you and give you his information. The background check was his idea." There's a beat of silence before Jaime speaks, and I can almost hear the approving nod I know he's making.

"Got it. Yeah, send it to me. I'll do a preliminary one now, which should let us know the basics tonight, and start a deeper one after. I'll probably have the full results in the morning. Though, I'm gonna guess he's probably fine if he's got a kid and gave you his license to run him."

"Thanks, Jaime."

"No—" he starts, then there's a scuffle before Ava's voice is coming through the line clearly again.

"You listen to me, Julianne Everett. You text me as soon as you get settled. You call me first thing in the morning, no questions asked. I don't care if you wake up at four a.m., you call me."

"Ava, you're in California. That would be one a.m. your time."

"Do I sound like I care?" she asks, and I can almost see her foot tapping.

"Your fiancé would."

"Jaime won't care, trust me." There's a grumble in the background of disapproval, and Ava whispers something that's probably much too spicy for my ears but makes the grumbling disappear. "I'm serious. I'm not going to hound you now because Jaime's going to make sure you're safe, but my god, Jules, if I don't find out everything ASAP, I'm going to snap. You hear me?"

On account that my best friend runs a business teaching women self-defense and once incapacitated a man on a live using little more than hair tools, I'm forced to agree.

"Yes, Ava, I'll call you as soon as possible tomorrow morning." I expect her to argue, to tell me she means to do so first thing when my eyes crack open, but she doesn't.

"Love you, Jules. Remember that sometimes things happen for a reason. If this was a movie—" she starts, a smile in her words, saying my signature words, but I'm not in the mood for it, so I cut her off.

"Goodbye. I love you." And then I hang up, giving myself a few more moments of peace and quiet before I head back out to face whatever the next wave of drama is bound to be.

TEN

LAST YEAR

JULES

"He's it," I say as I drive to the grocery store, my friends on the Bluetooth of my car.

"It?" one of my two best friends, Harper, says in disbelief.

"I know it's crazy, but he's my dream man. My love at first sight, knew it from the very first moment I saw him, absolute perfection. He's my rom-com," I explain, feeling a bit silly but unable to really care.

I spent two nights at Nate's house before I had to reluctantly leave to live my real life, but we've been talking non-stop since then, and somewhere in my heart, I know this is special.

"Jules—" she starts with a sigh because she's seen some variation of this a few times.

Of the three of us, Harper is the most practical. Ava is the fun, impulsive one, always ready for some grand adventure. Harper is the one who keeps our feet on the ground...and out of prison. While I'm the romantic, living in my head where I'm safe from reality and waiting for my love story.

My entire life, I've seen signs and meanings at every turn, making it easy for me to twist the most basic nicety into something more. I meet a man, and before the first date is even over, I can envision white dresses and the two-point-five kids, even when the dresses are really just red flags waving.

This isn't the first time I've come home from a date and said that I was wildly into a man, only to have my heart destroyed a week later.

But this time is different. I can't explain it other than something in my gut knows this is different. Even though I know it sounds crazy, I can't deny it.

"I'm serious! I know it sounds crazy, but I know it to my bones."

"I get it," Ava says in my defense as I park and transfer the call to my phone before heading into the store. "I saw Jaime in that bar, and I think part of me knew; we were just way too stubborn to even consider admitting it. I think that's the way you know someone is your person. All of the books and movies have a moment where they meet, and they know to their bones, you know? Sometimes, it just takes a bit for them to get to that point. Jules is just skipping all of the bullshit."

"Exactly!" I say, glad someone understands and confirming that I'm not completely insane.

Just a week ago, Nate and I spent almost two days holed up together before the roads were cleared and he had to take me home. Every moment since the time he kissed me on his kitchen island has felt almost magical.

Like I'm walking on clouds and it's finally my turn to live the fairy-tale love story.

"I mean, didn't you have that with Jeremy?" Ava asks, and I know she doesn't mean it in a mean way, thinking Harper would agree without hesitation. Instead, I watch on the FaceTime call as her nose scrunches up and she shakes her head.

"It's not a need, Harper, to have that feeling from the start," I say, jumping in to save her feelings. "You're much more practical than Ava and me." Ava catches on, nodding with wide eyes.

"Oh, for sure. So much more logical. Jules and I just jump in headfirst and hope we don't break our necks."

Harper's lips purse, and she sighs.

"I'm just saying that you should be careful, Jules. We don't want you to get hurt. You are the most amazing, loving, trusting person I know, and I love that. One day, though, you're going to get hurt. You know, sometimes when you jump in without looking, the water is deep, and sometimes it's too shallow, and you get hurt."

I sigh. I knew Harper would be the one to worry because that's just her nature.

"And I'm just saying, I know it's deep, Harper. I feel it in my gut." My phone is balanced between my shoulder and my ear as I grab a cart.

"I'm just worried about you. You love so hard and so completely, but not everyone deserves that, you know? I think—" she starts, but my mind stops processing her words when I hear a newly familiar voice speak from one aisle over.

"Come on, honey, let's go," a man's voice says.

"Daddy!" a small, squeaky voice responds.

"Sloane, can you grab those crackers Sophie likes?" the man asks.

Nate. It's Nate speaking, and a small voice calling him daddy, I think. I step closer to the end of the aisle then peer around, seeing his tall build and broad shoulders, a little girl with a curly blonde mop of hair on his hip, a pink cast on her arm, and a ballerina Ashlyn doll dangling in her hand.

My breathing stops.

Vaguely, I hear Ava and Harper in my ear, but I can't process them or hear any words they're saying. Not when a gorgeous blonde turns to smile at him. "Yeah, no problem. You want princess ones, sweetie?"

The girl on Nate's hip nods, squealing something and smacking Nate in the head with the doll in her excitement. The whole precious little family laughs at the mishap, and I fight getting sick right there in the cereal aisle.

My mind starts reeling as it becomes clear: He has a family.

I was some kind of fling, an affair on New Year's Eve.

I'm a homewrecker.

The flashbacks come pouring in: my mom crying late into the night after she thought I was long asleep, the yelling and throwing of plates at my father when she accused him of what she already knew to be true.

The visits to see my dad and his new family twice, maybe three times a year. The way I felt so completely and totally out of place no matter how wide of a kind smile I put on my face, or the way I always felt like a burden, an unsavory reminder of what my father was always trying to forget: his past.

The way my mother changed that year and decided there was no such thing as love; instead, searching for security. I had to watch countless shitty men come in and out of her life until she finally settled for Stanford and a loveless, but wealthy, marriage.

And here he is: the man I was sure was my dream man come true, someone who stepped out of the scenes of one of my favorite movies and came to life, standing with a gorgeous young daughter on his hip and laughing with an even more gorgeous woman.

Her mother, from the looks of it.

A perfect little family. I can't have been much older than that girl when everything fell apart for my family. If I continued this thing with Nate like I was living in some kind of fairy tale, would this have been a case of history repeating itself? If I wasn't at the store at this exact moment, would I one day be the source of some deep-rooted daddy issues in that pretty little girl?

Was it his place he took me to, or was it some crash pad? Does his perfect little family live there too? Where were they? Did he really have an affair with some stranger in a bar on New Year's Eve?

But most of all, how could I have been so stupid?

I was so lost in my delusion and seeing the best in things; being a hopeless romantic at heart, I missed all of the signs.

Oh god.

Oh *god*.

This is why men are only good when they're fictional. Because in the real world, they're always a fucking disappointment.

As I process this, he starts to turn in my direction, the little girl locking eyes with me, and suddenly, my body can move again, my legs forcing me to turn as fast as humanly possible toward the exit before Nate—and his perfect little family—can see me.

When I make it to my car, I take a deep breath, trying to steady myself before I open my phone, realizing he must have texted me between my leaving my place and making it to the store.

NATE

Can't wait to see you tomorrow. I miss you already. Is that crazy to say?

If I had seen this text five, ten minutes ago, I would have squealed at my luck, at the joy of this man and the excitement I was feeling for the future. Instead, it makes me sick to my stomach and makes my eyes burn at the cruelty of fate and reality.

Shaking my head, I remind myself there's a reason I live in my head, why I choose to watch movies instead of chase romance, that everything always works out in the fictional world, but out here, in the real world, no happily ever after is ever guaranteed.

The real world brings nothing but blow after blow. It's time to accept that soulmates and happily ever afters are myths so you don't lose hope. Sure, there are the one-in-a-million situations, like Ava and Jaime, but overall, it's all bullshit.

Just one big lie meant to keep the world spinning.

I make my decision then, tapping on his contact and staring at it. I take a moment to mourn what could have been—the silly thoughts and dreams I'd dreamed up after only a day and a half before I sigh, hit the block button, and start the car.

My mind is blank as I make the familiar drive to my best friend's apartment on the outskirts of Evergreen Park. Anytime my thoughts start to drift, to unpack what just happened, I shake my head fiercely, check the time and how far I am, and count down.

Just five minutes until I can lose it.

Only four minutes.

I only have to keep it together for three more minutes.

Two more, almost there.

I'm shaking by the time I pull into the parking lot for Ava and Jaime's place. When I step out, I slam the door without bothering to grab my bag, lock it, or do anything like that.

I just move, muscle memory carrying me to the front door, where one shaky finger reaches for the doorbell.

"Hey, babe," Ava says as she opens the door, distracted. "Are you —" And then she stops, taking in me, my tear-stained cheeks. "Oh no," she whispers, opening the door fully and pulling me inside where I can let go.

Because even if I'll never have a dream man to spend forever with, the universe did give me the blessing of really good fucking friends.

And that is the moment I swear off men. I swear off love. I swear off hope, feeling the gate slam shut over my heart.

It's not worth it: the pain, the disappointment, the heartache.

It's not worth it, surely not for a momentary shot at some far-off moment of bliss. No.

I'm not going to reach for that ever again, not when I've seen the destruction that small glimmer of hope can wreak.

Never again.

ELEVEN

JULES

Walking into Nate's house, a sense of déjà vu takes over. Not much has changed, though there is a pink blanket on the couch and a few toys scattered on the floor. It looks almost as if Sophie shuffled out of her room that morning, wrapped in her blanket, and left it there, which is the mere proof that a child lives here.

I've beaten myself up a bunch over the last year, wondering how I didn't see the signs of him having a family. A single man living in a decently sized home without a wife and kids should have been the first red flag, especially considering it was barely even decorated, but as I look around now, I at least have the comfort of knowing I didn't completely ignore some giant waving red flag. Aside from the blanket and the toys, Nate's home is still genuinely not very decorated and screams bachelor with no one relying on him.

"Soph, go get in your pajamas. It's way past your bedtime, and I have to show Aunt Claire's old place to Jules," Nate says as he puts a set of keys on a hook. I continue to jingle mine in my hand, staring around. I followed him here, taking note of everything as I drove, since I didn't pay much attention the last time I came here. I definitely wasn't taking in details like street names or neighborhoods; I was just excited to be alone with him.

"Will she put me to bed?" she asks, glaring at her dad, hands on her hips.

"Sophie," he starts, but his daughter's eyes go wide, and considering it's well past 8 p.m. and she's had what I can assume was a long day, the fight starts to build.

"I want her to put me to bed! She's my Christmas wish!"

Nate sighs before getting on his little girl's level.

"Honey, you know that's not how that works: we don't tell people what to do. You heard me tell Jules she could stay here, no pressure. You also heard me tell her that she wouldn't have to spend time over here if she wasn't comfortable. We're helping her out because her house is all messed up, not because we want her to be here." Despite his calm, reasonable words, she's still a five-year-old, and she pouts at her dad, eyes welling.

"But I do want her to be here," she says, low and sad, and something in me breaks. Nate's helping me out; I need to do the same.

"It's fine, really; I don't mind," I say to Nate. Sophie looks at me, her eyes going wide and filled with hope. "Go get your pajamas on and brush your teeth and whatever else you normally do for bed. When you're done, I'll come in and say good night."

"And you'll read me a book?" I can't help but laugh at the sudden look of determination on her little face and the way her hands go to her hips like she's in a board meeting and trying to secure a deal. Something tells me she's going to be an absolute powerhouse one day.

"Sophie," Nate warns, but I'm fine with bartering.

"One," I say.

"Three," she demands, and I raise an eyebrow.

"One." Her lips purse, and she looks at her dad and then at me.

I look to her dad, who is clearly fighting a smile but lifts his hands as if to say, *this is your fight.* "One," I repeat, knowing from my past babysitting experiences that if you win the first battle, the rest are much easier to triumph over. If I do end up helping out and babysitting in exchange for a place to stay, I'll need to start on the right foot.

Don't ask me why I'm even contemplating staying as an option when it so very clearly is not.

She glares at me, trying to read me and determine if I'll break before sighing.

"Fine. One," she says with a pout, then turns on a foot toward the hall where I assume her room is, more sass than I thought could be possible for one small body.

I laugh silently as I watch her retreat before looking at Nate, who is leaning against the kitchen counter, arms crossed on his chest, and taking me in.

"You did good," he says. "Showed her who's boss. She can smell weakness, I swear."

I smile and chuckle at him before shrugging.

"Like Claire said, I've babysat a bunch, and I teach a group of girls how to dance. Plus, my best friend is the sassiest person I've ever met, so I'm well trained. It's almost second nature at this point."

"You fit right in here," he says, staring at me with a contemplative gaze. He opens his mouth as if he wants to say something else but closes it when a light down the hall turns on, and Sophie calls his name. Then, without a word, he heads to help his daughter.

As I watch him walk down the hall, standing in his kitchen and not feeling a bit out of place, I think to myself, that is exactly what I'm afraid of.

"So this would be your place," Nate says as he walks me into the small cottage behind his house. It has everything one needs to survive in a cute studio apartment style. There's a tiny kitchenette and bedroom sharing a space, a cozy-looking loveseat in a corner, and a small enclosed bathroom with a standing shower, sink, and toilet. It's bigger and comfier than I could ever afford for any stretch of time and much nicer than I anticipated. "Will it work?"

I laugh at his nerves.

"It's...it's perfect," I say, shifting curtains to see an arched window facing the woods that butt up against the back of his property before turning to look at him. As much as this feels like fate at a time when I really, *really* need just a hint of good luck or a right place, right time moment, my mind still can't accept this as a reality. "I can't thank you enough, really."

"Well, it's the least I could do, all things considered. I have a feeling I did something to make you want to block me."

I close my eyes and sigh, feeling the blush burn at my cheeks but knowing I have to get this over with once and for all.

"I thought you were married," I blurt out. "And that I was some side fling."

He stares at me for long moments, and my heart pounds nearly audibly.

"You thought I was married?" he asks with a disbelieving smile, leaning against the doorway of the cottage, his arms crossed over his chest.

I wonder if this is some kind of signature move or if he uses it to get anything he wants because I can definitely see how that would work. It's probably why I find myself rambling my excuse without trying to avoid it.

"I went to the grocery store, and I saw you there, Sophie on your hip with Sloane. I..." I sigh once more and roll my eyes. "Okay, I jumped to conclusions and didn't give you any chance to explain, but in my defense—"

"It was a perfectly reasonable thing to assume, and I hope when Soph gets older, if she sees a situation like that, she will do the same." He pauses before he tips his head. "Maybe add in slashing his tires."

I smile in return.

"It wasn't very grown up of me, but...I have some previous baggage that kind of bit me in the ass when I saw that. My dad left my mom and started a new family when I was young. I saw history repeating itself, and I didn't want to deal with it. I didn't know you had a daughter, so seeing her with you and me—" I start, but he cuts me off.

"I should have told you about Sophie," he says, a sigh of his own.

"Probably," I say with a shrug. "I get why you didn't, though."

He looks up, shifting his gaze from his feet to my eyes, clear shock on his face.

"Yeah?" he asks.

"I'm sure dating is hard. I'm assuming you're the only one raising her?"

He nods. "Her mom signed her rights away two years ago."

I sigh, irritation brewing under my skin because I've barely spent more than a single meal with that girl and can't imagine wanting to give her up, much less being her mother and feeling that way.

"So I can imagine being her father becomes a part of your identity. You had a chance to introduce yourself as Nate, not Nate and Sophie. I get it." I shrug before laughing to myself. "It probably would have saved me a lot of heartache and tears if you hadn't, though," I add to break the ice, but regret it almost instantly when his smile tips down with my words. "Nate, really, it's not a big deal. I was kidding."

"I hate that I spent an entire year not knowing what went wrong, knowing somewhere deep down I fucked it up but no idea how to fix it. I should have...I should have found you. Reached out," he says, words drifting off. "I regret it. Especially now, seeing you again. It's all coming back." My heart skips a beat, and he shakes his head, eyes directed at his boots before he looks at me again. "I won't stand here and lie and tell you I have no interest in seeing where this could go." He stares at me, waiting for me to fill in whatever blanks I can.

"I..." I start, and for the smallest moment, I contemplate telling him it's a clean slate, that we could pick up where we left. But that girl, the hopeless romantic who believes love can find you at any turn, is gone. She's been put in a cage and boarded up to keep her soft heart safe. I'm coming to terms with the fact that what I saw was a miscommunication, but the pain I felt was real, and I don't want to feel that again. I'm more guarded than I was a year ago, regardless of if what caused it wasn't what I thought it was.

"I, uh, I'm not dating. I'm focusing on my business and my friends and...other things," I say, suddenly realizing my life truly isn't much more than those two things. "And considering what just happened with my place, that's something I need to do even more. So while I appreciate your words and, even more, I appreciate the closure and knowing I wasn't a total idiot homewrecker, it would be best if things stayed...platonic," I say, and I hate how the lie feels on my tongue, even if it is the safest option for me.

He waits a long beat, reading me before he nods. "All right. Got it." The disappointment he's clearly fighting back covers his face before he gives me a wide, if not a bit forced, smile. "Got it. But I still want you to stay here until your place is fixed up, Jules," he says, suddenly looking serious, and I shift at the abrupt change in topic.

"What?"

"Stay here until your place is fixed. Let me make it up to you. I fucked up by not telling you from the start, and that clearly impacted you. Let me give you a safe place to stay, no strings attached. Plus, with Claire gone, this place is going to sit empty, and it's ridiculous to spend money on a hotel your insurance probably won't cover."

"I don't know. One night is kind enough. I can't—"

"You can. You don't have anywhere to stay, and your home needs work before the township allows you back in." I groan at the reminder I wish he hadn't given me. "And if you won't accept my doing it as an apology for hurting you last New Year, do it as a favor for a friend. Sophie is fully convinced you're her wish come true, and I don't know how to handle that without breaking her heart."

The words remind me no one has told me what this Christmas wish is.

"What does that mean exactly?"

Nate steps further into the tiny cottage before flopping back on the bed, running a hand over his face as he does.

"We were at the mall today to see Santa. She told him she wanted me to fall in love with the real-life version of her Ashlyn doll. I was gearing up some kind of way to rationalize with her, to break the truth to her easily, but when we walked out..." It becomes clear the sticky situation he's in.

"I was there."

"You were there, and she sees it as some kind of sign or holiday magic. She's stubborn as all hell, so she's not going to back down from it. She thinks you're her Christmas wish come true."

"Does she ask about things like that frequently? You getting a wife or whatever?"

"No, so I don't know where it came from. I can only assume it's that she's a little girl who has friends with two-parent households, sees my parents who have been happily married for decades, sees my sister falling in love and moving away, and hears my mom and sisters jab at me for being single and never dating. But if that's all she wants, it's the one thing I can't just give to her. I know it's cliché, but she's been let down a lot, so I try to make sure she can have whatever she wants. She doesn't ask for things much, so it hasn't been much of an issue until...now."

I think about how when I was her age, I wished and wished my mom would find a new husband who would make her happy, someone who would make us feel like a family again. That was all I wanted, though I never verbalized it. Something in me breaks a bit for this little girl—a shared longing I wouldn't ever wish upon her.

"I don't know what to do, but I believe in signs, and I believe in things happening for a reason. The world did not put you on that sidewalk just minutes after she made that wish because I wasn't supposed to help you out, mend that fence. You can stay here, and I'll do everything I can to help speed up the work at your place if you help me give her this, if only for a month. We'll sell Sophie on this little romance and convince her that her Christmas wish is coming true. In the meantime, you'll stay here while I fix up your place until you can move back home."

I shake my head. "It seems a little one-sided to me," I say with a half-assed laugh. "I don't know how I feel about that."

"You can help me with babysitting when you can. Claire usually helps get Sophie on the bus and watches her occasionally when I have to work late." I think about how, with the recital next week and classes mostly shelved for December, for once, I don't have much on my plate. It's almost like my calendar is open just for this reason.

"Let me..." I say with a sigh. "Let me just double-check my calendar, make sure I can help out before I offer." I move to grab my bag, reach in to grab my old-school calendar, and flip through to find the dates I'm busy and when my next classes are.

"It's really not necessary," he says. "If you can't watch her or get her off the bus one day, I can find something that works."

"I'd be much more comfortable with this arrangement if it was actually mutually beneficial," I say under my breath, flipping pages to find December. In my peripheral, Nate stands and walks closer, bending to grab something.

"If you're agreeing to help me with the mess I've gotten into with Sophie, we're more than even, trust me," he says, the words trailing off.

"Well, it turns out I think I can—" I start, lifting my head to look at Nate, who has gone quiet and is staring at something in his hands. "What's that?" I ask, but panic fills me because I know what he's holding. It's worn and weathered, but it's been in my bag for almost a year, despite changing bags relatively often.

"You kept this?" he asks. "This was from that night."

I bite my lip and lie. "How do you know I didn't go back and get a new one? I could be a smoker." He gives me a look, and I shut my mouth.

"Why?" he asks, voice quiet.

"Why am I a smoker?" Once again, he glares at me and I sigh. "I don't know," I say. "It was a reminder of sorts, maybe. It made me... happy. Reminded me of something special."

"I thought I was a bad reminder. Put you off dating, didn't I?"

"I mean, yeah. But for a moment..." I let it hang there, not wanting to finish my sentence. I'm tired, and the adrenaline from my long, long day is wearing off, meaning nothing good can come from the rest of the day.

"For a moment, it felt magical," he says, stepping closer. I watch his hand slip into his pocket, taking the matchbook, and I fight the all-consuming urge to ask for it back.

That would give away way too much.

"What happens after?" I ask.

"After?"

"After the holidays, after the new year, after my place is all done, and I can move back." A small smile tips his lips, and I realize I just admitted that I was thinking about taking his offer. "I mean, if I stay here and we pretend, what will happen then? What will you tell Sophie? She's expecting some Christmas miracle, but while I appreciate the offer to help me out, I'm not marrying you just to make some Christmas magic for your kid."

He smiles wider and then shrugs, that calculating smile filling his eyes now.

"Eh, I'm sure she'll have already forgotten about her wish by then; it's fine. Kids are resilient." I give him a disbelieving look, but he continues. "And at Christmas, she'll get spoiled to death by eighteen million toys and new clothes and who knows what else. She's the only grandchild and has three aunts to spoil her. When you eventually head home, she won't even notice."

When I get a pang of sadness at how quickly it seems I'll be brushed out of their lives once more, I realize I should say no.

I should say I can't do this, spend one night here, and find new plans tomorrow. Call a million contractors all over the state and pay hand over fist to get my place done as soon as possible.

But now that I know Nate wasn't actually a piece of shit all along, a part of me is desperate to get to know him again, to see if my gut was right or if I was delusional. And despite myself, I really, really want to give Sophie a spark of Christmas magic so one day, when she looks back, she can remember that her father did absolutely anything and everything to get her her every single wish.

A little girl deserves that, to believe in magic and true love and wishes coming true.

"Fine," I say despite my best interests. "I'm in. But only until my place is done and only if I can pay you for the work and materials." He makes a face, but I keep speaking. "I'm serious. I'm proud of First Position, and I've done it all by myself. I don't need some random guy coming in and taking that away."

He takes another moment, clearly contemplating if that's my breaking point, but when he sees I'm not bending, he nods.

"And this? Us? It stays platonic. I'm not in the market for a real relationship," I say.

"Deal," he says almost too quickly, putting a hand out. I stare at that hand as his smile widens. "Gotta shake on it, dollface," he says, and I glare. "You gotta admit, you look just like her." His smile widens, and I shake my head, unable to fight the small smile. "Come on. Let's make a deal, Jules."

I spend a moment contemplating all of the ways this could go wrong before I sigh and put my hand in his. "Deal," I whisper as his hand closes around mine.

He uses the leverage to pull me in close, forcing my heart to pound.

"Deal." He holds me there for what feels like a lifetime, neither of us moving before he speaks. "And Jules? There hasn't been a single day in three hundred and thirty-two days when I haven't thought of you. What you look like, how you made me feel, how you taste. I won't fuck this up this time." He says it with such conviction and determination that I can't breathe, despite his breaths grazing against my lips.

Finally, he steps back, leaving me unsteady on my feet.

"See you tomorrow, Jules," he says, walking away.

I watch him from the doorway of the cottage, watch him close the back door, and shut off the lights inside, leaving the back porch light on low.

It's not until I take a shower and get in bed and see a text from Jaime telling me Nate is completely spotless that I let myself pull up a calendar and discover the last time I saw Nathan Donovan was three hundred and thirty-two days ago.

TWELVE

JULES

I wake in an unfamiliar bed, and for a split second, I panic.

Where am I?

How did I get here?

And most importantly, as my hand slides across the sheets carefully, am I alone?

When I realize that the answer is, thankfully, yes, it all comes back to me.

The pipe in my place breaking.

The little girl telling me I was her Christmas wish.

Seeing Nate again.

Learning I completely misunderstood everything a year ago.

His sisters meddling, telling me to live with him.

Nate and me making a bargain.

I'm staying in a cottage behind Nate's house, and we're...what? Pretending to be together for her sake? For my sake?

I have no idea what I'm doing.

What made me think this was a good idea? What made me accept his offer?

Clearly, insanity.

Clearly, I've lost my damn mind.

Staring at the ceiling, I decide I need coffee, an emergency Face-Time with my friends, and a lobotomy.

Not necessarily in that order, either.

I stand up, use the bathroom, then move across the tiny cottage to get my phone before I see a piece of pink construction paper that seems to have been slid under the door. The words "coffee in the house" were scribbled on it in messy boy writing with a red marker.

While a lobotomy isn't something I'll find in Nate's kitchen (probably, the jury is still out on whether or not he's an insane mass murderer), it seems I can probably count on coffee, and once it's a reasonable hour, I can call up Ava and Harper to beg them to knock some sense into me.

With a sigh, I roll off the bed, slide a bra on under my sleep shirt (I refuse to walk around his house free boobing it), and shuffle to the bathroom, where I brush my hair and teeth before slicking on a bit of tinted lip balm on my lips. It's a bit too early for lipstick, but I refuse to be caught completely off guard yet again with this man.

Slipping an oversized sweatshirt on and a pair of sneakers, I close the cottage door behind me and shuffle to the back door of their house, finding it unlocked. Quietly, I make my way down the completely silent hall, jumping when I see Nate sitting at the island in the kitchen, with a cup of coffee in front of him and an iPad in hand. Instantly, his head lifts, and he smiles wide at me when he sees me walk in, completely ignoring my panic.

"Hey," he says low. It's not a whisper, but it's quiet in a way that makes it obvious he's trying not to wake Sophie. My eyes flit to the over and catch the time, blinking at 6:41.

"Why are you up?" I ask in lieu of a greeting. "How long have you been up?" If you ask Ava, who would enjoy sleeping until ten every single morning, I am a morning person. But after the night I had, it feels much too early to be awake.

"About an hour. I always wake up before Soph, get some coffee, and have some alone time." I cringe at his words before biting my lip. He wakes up early for alone time. Should I leave or—

Before I can even find an excuse to back away, he sets his iPad down and shakes his head, standing from the kitchen island barstool and moving toward the counter behind him.

"No, stay," he says, his eyes locked on me. "Please." Something about him saying please—both the word and the way he says it—has me nodding before moving to the stool furthest from him and sitting quietly. "Coffee?"

"What?" I ask, distracted.

"Do you want some coffee?"

"Oh, yeah, I can—" I start before trying to move again, and he glares at me, making me shut my mouth.

"I got it," he says with a smile.

"I feel bad having you do things for me. You were relaxing before I came in."

"I was getting the courage to go wake up Sophie in a bit," he says, moving to the coffee machine, putting in a capsule, then pressing the button to brew me a cup. It brings back memories I've long tried to forget, only carefully letting myself pull them out when I'm at my loneliest, to remember the precious, tainted moments before putting them back away.

"The courage?" I ask.

"Oh yeah," he says with a smile. "She can be a bit of a terror first thing in the morning."

"Not a morning person?"

He shakes his head, and I smile. We're silent as he moves around the kitchen, and I make every effort not to watch. He's dressed for the day, it seems, in a pair of jeans and a long-sleeved shirt with Donovan Contracting on the back. It's clear he owns the business, but I wonder how much of the work he actually does or if he hires it all out, doing clerical work most of the time.

I'm still lost in my head when he slides a cup in front of me, a light brown, the exact shade I prefer, a familiar vanilla-scented steam wafting up before I look at him, a bit confused. Then, on the counter, I see it.

Two bottles: one with vanilla syrup, the other with almond.

"One pump vanilla, one almond," he says, and I shift my eyes to look at him. "That still how you take it?" I'd told him the morning I spent here that was how I liked my coffee and that I'd been taking it that way for as long as I could remember.

"I bought the syrup the day you left my place. Never had a reason to use it, though." I continue to stare, unsure of how to respond before he fumbles on his words, shaking his head as if my scrutiny means something it doesn't. "A few months ago, I replaced them. They're not expired or anything." Somehow, this shocks me even more.

"You replaced them?"

"I, uh..." He puts a hand on the back of his neck, holding it there and looking at the mug with a small pink handprint on it in front of me. "I figured I'd make sure they were fresh. Just in case."

He doesn't finish his statement, but he doesn't have to.

Just in case.

Just in case I came back one day. Just in case we met again.

He's kept the syrups I like for my coffee in his house for a year just in case I made my way back into his home.

A year of remembering how I like my coffee after barely two nights together.

What the fuck does that mean?

Instead of thinking about it, I lift the mug to my lips, taking a small sip before closing my eyes and sighing. It's perfect, exactly how I like it. A small smile plays on my lips when I slowly open my eyes again, only to see Nate's gaze locked on me.

So hot and intense that it sends a bolt of heat through me that has nothing to do with the warm mug in my hands or the sip I took.

Thankfully, before I can say or do anything truly idiotic, a noise in the hall, a singsong little voice, trickles toward us and breaks the moment. "That's Soph," he says with a smile.

"Yeah," is all I can reply.

"I'm gonna go get her, feed her breakfast, and whatnot. If you want some peace and quiet while you wake up, I suggest taking your mug to the cottage. She's a bit of a tornado in the morning." A moment passes where I think that's his dismissal. "Though, you're more than welcome to stay in the kitchen. Just wanted you to know you have the freedom to do...whatever. If you need time alone, you can have it."

From the hall, I hear her singing again.

"I'll drop Soph off at my mom's on my way to work, and when I get to the office, I'll call Mark. See if I can get a time when he'll let us in so I can assess the damage, and you can grab more of your stuff to bring here. I'll call you later and let you know what he says."

I nod, and he stands, moving around the island toward the hall. Sophie is now singing to herself, clearly keeping herself occupied but very wide awake.

"I appreciate it. Do you, uh, think it would be okay if I stay here and say good morning to her?"

He smiles wider than I think I've ever seen.

"I know she'd love that," he says before disappearing down the hall to Sophie's room. There are murmured good mornings and a low laugh before I hear Sophie's little voice yell, "Jules!" before feet pad down the hall.

"You're here!" Sophie shouts. She's in the light purple nightgown she put on last night, her hair a complete mess, her eyes a bit sleepy, but her gap-filled grin is contagious all the same.

"I told you I would be," I say with a smile. "Princesses never tell a lie." I probably shouldn't lean into the whole *I'm a magical Ashlyn doll come to life,* but when I see the look of joy and excitement cross her face, there's no room for regret, not even as she runs full speed into my legs, hugging them tight.

"Are you staying for breakfast?" she asks, leaning back.

"If your dad says it's okay," I say, looking at Nate, who shrugs.

"Oh, he doesn't mind. He's in love with you. He told me! Do you like cereal?" she says like she didn't just drop a bomb on me.

When I look back at Nate, he's moving around in the fridge, completely ignoring me.

"I...yeah. I love cereal," I say, deciding it's best to just go with the flow at this point.

We spend the early morning together, Sophie somehow convincing me to help pick out her clothes and braid her hair. *"Daddy can only do little braids, not French braids!"* she explained. She then started packing her backpack, Nate handing her the lunchbox I watched him pack and add in a little note to while we ate.

"When are you guys going to go on a date? Christmas is in less than a month, and you still need to fall in love," Sophie asks incredibly bluntly as her dad helps to put on her jacket.

I roll my lips into my mouth, biting on them to fight the laugh when his face goes to one of complete and total exasperation.

"Why don't we give Jules some time to settle, Sophie? We don't want to overwhelm her."

Sophie looks at her dad, and some kind of silent conversation transpires before she smiles wide. "You're right," she agrees happily.

"All right, time to get your behind out the door," he says, clearly trying to get her to leave before she drops some other bomb that sends me into a tailspin. "I'll call you once I know more. Does around noon work?" he asks me.

I nod, thinking that gives me plenty of time to have a mental breakdown and make a dozen calls, both to vent and to figure out the next steps for the studio. I'm hopeful I can move my lessons this month to the community center where our actual recital is held, but I need to double check.

They're almost gone, closing the door to lock me in when Nate turns to look at me, a smile on his lips. Somehow, I know he's been holding in whatever he's about to say for a while.

"Oh, and Jules?" He looks at me, and I don't respond, but he still knows I'm listening somehow. "Unblock me, okay?"

THIRTEEN

JULES

"Hey, babe," Harper starts when she answers my FaceTime call, "Wait, where—"

"Please hold, I'm only having this meltdown once," I say, watching the icon where Ava's face is.

"What—"

Ava pops on, and I breathe deep. "Oh, thank God," I say, collapsing onto the loveseat in the cottage.

"Jules? What's wrong? Wait, where are you?" Harper asks, looking past me at the unfamiliar location.

"Nate Donovan's house."

"Nate? Why is that name familiar?" Harper asks.

"Because it's the NEW YEAR'S DUDE! Also, Jaime did a deeper dive, and it's like this guy is from some magical world of perfect men. Comes from the most precious family I've ever read about, pays all of his bills on time, has never married, donates to an animal charity, sends his kid to a public preschool where his mom is a teacher, and, get this—he's even a class parent."

I blink a few times, staring at her. "How did he find that out?"

"My man is good," she says, a smile on her lips. "Also found out two years ago, his ex-girlfriend, who he had his daughter with, decided she didn't want to deal with the whole being a mom thing. Signed over full rights to Nate, ran off to bumfuck Montana where she's a bartender."

Huh. Well, that's good to know, I suppose.

"Wait, wait, wait. Can we reverse things? Who are we talking about, and why does Ava know this and I don't?" Harper whines.

"Technically, I don't know anything except for the fact that Jules called me last night to talk to Jaime."

"To talk to Jaime?"

"She needed him to run a background check, make sure the guy she's moving in with isn't a serial killer. You know, normal things."

"Moving in with?"

"Oh, yeah, according to Jaime—"

"God, that man gossips like an old lady," I mumble under my breath.

"To be fair, I can be very convincing if I want," Ava says with a wicked smile before continuing. "Anyway, as I was trying to say before I was rudely interrupted, according to Jaime, there was a water main break at her building, and the fire department closed it down. Word on the street was that they called the whole department there, though this guy is a contractor, so I'm not totally sure—"

"Can I tell my own story?"

"Oh. I mean, yeah, I guess," Ava says.

I roll my eyes before stepping in.

"My apartment flooded, and it leaked into the studio, so all of the police and firefighters showed up, shut down the entire road, and turned off the water main. I was standing outside in the winter recital costume because I was subbing in for Gina because she was sick, waiting for them to let me know when I could go in and get a few things. "

"You were standing outside in the middle of November in your leotard and tutu?" Ava asks.

"Pretty much," I say with a laugh. "I had a sweatshirt, too, but it was also pink, so it matched."

"What shoes were you wearing?" Harper asks like that's a pressing statement.

"What?"

"Were you in your dance shoes or—?"

"Uggs. I hadn't changed into my pointe shoes yet, thank God."

"Huh," Harper says, probably picturing the complete fashion faux pas in her mind.

"And then you're standing there and...?"

"A little girl comes running up to me. She grabs my hand and tells me I need to meet her dad because I'm her Christmas wish." Eyes go wide, and I think they're starting to put the pieces of my chaotic night together. "Yeah. Then I see a man walking up, clearly worried his daughter is gone, only to realize it's Nate."

"The guy with a whole-ass family you thought was the love of your life after a one-night stand?" Harper, who's always to the point, asks. I glare at her. "Sorry! I'm just getting my facts straight."

"It turns out the woman I saw him with that day was one of his sisters."

"His sister? Oh, babe, that's the oldest—" Ava starts, her face falling like she knows she's about to break my heart all over. Though my heart is much more guarded than it was the last time I met Nate, she doesn't have to worry this time around.

"She introduced herself to me as his sister," I say, knowing exactly what she's going to say. Before Jaime, Ava had just as much luck with men as I have had. "And Claire, you remember her, right? My assistant, we've gotten drinks with her before?"

Nods before Ava says, "Gorgeous blonde, and a great sense of humor?"

"Yeah, she's his other sister. He has three."

"No way! Wasn't she trying to hook you up with her brother the last time we were out together?" I nod. "God, it's almost poetic, you know? Like a romance book."

"I don't know about that," I say with a laugh. "More like a sick and twisted thriller."

"I'm sorry, I just don't get how we went from him running into you to you now sleeping at his place," Harper says.

"Did you sleep with him?" Ava shouts.

"Why didn't you call me?" Harper asks. "You could have stayed at my place. Jeremy wouldn't have minded."

"The fuck he wouldn't," Ava says under her breath because it's no secret Jeremy is not our biggest fan, and the feeling is so very mutual. I decided ignoring them both would be better.

"There's an unattached cottage behind Nate's house that Claire used to live in as his nanny, but she's moving, so it's empty."

"Oh, I see where this is going," Ava says.

"Long story short, we've come to a bit of a...pact. I'm staying in the guest house, babysitting occasionally when he needs it, and helping to convince his daughter that Christmas miracles do happen. In exchange, he's giving me a place to stay and helping me fix my place."

Neither of them say anything, which is both a relief and a bit of a surprise. While Ava loves to jump into chaos and, pre-Jaime, would absolutely have done something like this, Harper is logical. At the very least, I expected her to have a few more questions.

"So what now?" Ava says.

"Well..." I start. "Well, I guess I have to unblock him first."

"You're living in his house, and he's blocked?" Harper asks, and Ava just laughs.

"God, so typical," Ava adds through her laughter.

"Jules, you need to unblock him," Harper insists.

"Yeah, yeah, yeah. I know."

"Like, now." Harper's mom voice comes into play, and I groan before tapping at the screen of my phone and scrolling to where the contact Nate with a pink heart is.

I don't know why I didn't delete the contact or why I simply blocked him and left it that way, but I never looked at that too closely.

Now, I guess I can be grateful for that small oversight. I tap on the screen a few times until I see unblock and hesitate.

"Did you do it?" Ava asks. I shake my head. "Why not?"

"I'm...nervous?

"You're living in his house and agreed to watch his kid, Jules. I think we're a bit past being nervous to unblock him," Ava says.

Taking a deep breath, I press the unblock button, then stare at my phone, waiting as if something magical is going to happen instantly.

"Did you do it?"

"Yeah," I say, and a moment later, a new message pops up.

NATE

Did you unblock me yet?

Finally.

I smile at the screen, and Ava laughs. Harper shouts, asking what happened. "He texted me," I say, panicking a bit.

"What did he say?" Ava asks.

"And why are you smiling like that?" Harper asks.

"He asked if I unblocked him yet."

"That was quick," Harper says with a smile directed at Ava.

That was quick.

Again, he replies almost instantly.

"Oh my god, he already answered me."

Both of my best friends squeal with excitement.

"What did he say?!"

I've been texting you every twenty minutes to see if you'd unblocked me yet.

I read it out loud, and Ava cackles. "Every twenty minutes! Oh, girl, he's down bad!"

Only once every twenty minutes? Not very diligent.

"You know, if this was a movie..." Ava starts, and I roll my eyes.

"Stop it, this is not a movie. It's just a shitty string of events leading to a very strange circumstance," I say, justifying.

"Isn't that how all rom-coms start?" Harper asks.

"Oh, definitely. I mean, look at me. I literally joined a pageant for shits and giggles and ended up with Jaime." That *did* happen.

"You're in a once-in-a-lifetime situation, Ava," I inform her.

"And you're not?"

I shake my head. "I've sworn off men," I remind them.

"Does Nate know that?" Harper asks.

"What does it matter?"

"Because from what I can tell, he likes you. You like him, but you're being too stubborn to do anything about it. I just want to make sure you're both on the same page."

"You know, I think you should just go for it," Ava says with a giggle.

"What?"

"Go for it! *Lean* into it. It could be fun."

"Go for what?" I ask.

"Nate. The magic of finding him again. Lean into the whole Christmas miracle thing for his kid, but do it for you too, Jules."

I sigh and shake my head, knowing that just isn't an option. Not if I want to stay sane.

"I've sworn off love, Ava," I repeat, hoping this time it sticks. For us both.

"Again, because you thought a guy fucked you over. Now we know differently, and the world has dropped the movie-worthy chaotic adventure in your lap. Just do it! If not for love, do it for the story of it." I pause, taking in her words and wondering what that would be like, leaning into it. Playing house with Nate for the month. "What's the worst that could happen?"

"Well, for one, she could get hurt," Harper says. "I think you're forgetting what a mess she was after everything in January."

Ava rolls her eyes and groans. "Isn't that exactly why we should be encouraging her to go for it? You don't get that upset over some random hookup."

"And after?" Harper asks.

"After?"

"What happens after Christmas when her place is fixed, and he doesn't need her to play this game with him?" she says, speaking my nerves aloud. I know how torn apart I felt the first time when we'd barely spent two days together. What happens if I have time to become attached, not only to Nate but his daughter, and it goes bad? "Then what?"

"I don't know, but we won't find out if she doesn't try."

"Jesus, Ava—" Harper starts, but I hear it then, Ava stepping onto her soapbox.

"Who says it has to end in January? You told us last year you'd felt it—that instant, once-in-a-lifetime feeling. Now we know he wasn't a douchebag. Why not give it a shot?"

"I'm scared," I whisper my confession.

"Well, duh. It wouldn't be worth it if you weren't scared. That's the fun part, Jules. Grab hold of that man's hand and jump in." She smiles at her words, as if they bring back a happy memory, and I love that for her.

I want that for me, but I don't know if I'm brave enough.

"You're the brave one," I say. Her smile goes wider.

"Anyone can be brave if they want it bad enough, Jules. You know what I say: Shoulders back, tits out, bitch. You were born for big things."

And then we all dissolve into giggles.

FOURTEEN

NATE

"Daddy, are you going to fall in love with Jules?"

"What?" I ask, pretending I didn't hear what my daughter asked as I turn left onto Main Street. It's not the normal way I drive to my parents' house that's on the other side of our two-square-mile town, but I want to pass by First Position and make sure everything looks okay.

"You and Jules. Are you going to fall in love with her?"

"I, uh," I start, unsure of how to answer. We pass the studio that, despite a sign on the front door from the township stating it's closed for renovations, looks pretty much the same as last night. Crazy to think I've driven past that place a hundred times since I last saw Jules in January and never once bumped into her in town.

"I just think that you should, you know? Because I asked Santa to make you a real-life Ashlyn, and then we saw her, and that seems like a miracle." It sure as fuck does, doesn't it? "So you should marry her," she declares, and I snort out a laugh, shaking my head and turning onto my parents' street.

"Not really how that works, kiddo," I say. Especially not when the girl you've got your sights set on clearly has a lot to unpack, including the shit you put her through a year ago, unintentionally or not.

"Then how does it work?"

"Well, you meet someone, you talk a lot, and you become good friends, then best friends, then you get married," I explain as simply as humanly possible

"Hmm," she says. "So what step are we on?" The way she says *"we"* makes me laugh, but it stops abruptly when I approach my childhood home and see two extra cars parked on the street.

Sutton and Sloane.

Fuck.

"I, uh..." I start, parking and sighing, knowing this is about to be a fucking ambush. "I don't know."

"Well, we talked yesterday. So maybe good friends?"

As I park, I think about how when I originally offered Jules a place to stay, insisting she spend at least last night in the cottage, I thought it would end there. She was making it very clear that she wasn't looking to date and that whatever was once between us was no longer something she was interested in. I got the impression that after she got over the hurt of my not telling her about Sophie, she also got over the idea of us.

And then I found that matchbook she'd been carrying in her purse. It was a different purse than the one she had that night at the bar—I know because I took note of every tiny detail of Jules that night, replaying it over and over again over the last year—so that means she moved that matchbook from one bag to the next instead of throwing out the reminder of us.

And when that nervous blush crept over her cheeks and down her chest, I knew she kept it because it meant something to her.

That was when I decided that one way or another, I was going to convince Jules to give me another shot. I just needed to figure out how. Maybe it isn't so bad that my sisters are here today, because I could use all the help I can get.

"Grandma!" Sophie shouts as she bounds into my childhood

home. My mom is standing in the living room and scooping her up when she reaches her. It's a well-practiced routine at this point, and every time, it makes me smile wide. "Grandma! Daddy met the real-life Ashlyn, and she's living in Aunt Claire's house, and they're going to fall in love!"

The smile melts off my face as I look to the ceiling and groan aloud.

My mom's head jerks back in surprise, a smile on her lips before she looks at me. "Are they now?"

"Yup! It was my Christmas wish."

"Well, it sounds like we have a little cupid on our hands, don't we?"

"No, just a really good wisher," my daughter says matter-of-factly as my mom shifts her onto her hip.

"Yeah, Nate's in love with Ashlyn," Sutton says as she walks into the living room, making kissy noises. She's twenty-five and barely acts older than my daughter. I glare at her. "We need to figure out how to make her fall in love with him. That's going to be the harder part since he's...well...Nate."

"Well, hold on because last night, Nate said he wanted us to ease off him," Sloane, my oldest sister and the most level-headed, says as she enters the fray. "He didn't want to force her into anything."

"Thank you, Sloa—" I start, but she cuts me off.

"Even though he's clearly head over heels in love with her."

"Jesus," I grumble.

"He told me falling in love is the step right before getting married!" Sophie says, clapping her hands excitedly.

"Sophie," I start, ready to warn her not to get her hopes up too high, but my mom saves my ass as she tends to do.

"Hey, Sophie, baby, can you go find Grandpa? He wants to show you something in his workshop," she says, setting Sophie on the floor.

Eagerly, knowing that in the workshop there's a bowl of candy my dad thinks I forgot exists, she runs off.

"So, tell me everything," my mom says, sitting down on the couch and smoothing out the skirt of her apron. For a split second, I contemplate lying or avoiding the subject altogether, but I know three things as facts in this world.

One, my mom can always tell when I'm lying.

Two, my sisters have big fucking mouths.

And three, nothing stays a secret long in Evergreen Park, especially when a Donovan is involved.

So with a sigh, I sit on the loveseat across from her and spill, telling my mom and sisters the whole story. How I met Jules in a bar, how I took her home (leaving out all of the gory details, of course), and we got snowed in. I tell them about how I felt that feeling Dad always talked about—that gut knowledge that I found my person—only to have her disappear from my life completely. Finally, I filled my mom in on last night about meeting Jules again and finding out the true reason she stopped talking to me and how it was all just a messy, stupid string of events.

"I wasn't going to push any kind of romance on her, I swear," I say finally, getting to the end of my story. "I just wanted to give her somewhere safe to stay, and with my workload being light this month, I have the time to fix her place without having to charge an arm and a leg. You know how Pete down in approvals can be a dick about recertifying the occupancy." My mom nods, knowing all too well about peers. "But then I found out she'd been keeping this matchbook in her bag." I pull it out of my pocket and show them.

"Why?" Sloane asks, looking at me like I'm insane, which is valid since it's a fucking matchbook.

"Is she a smoker?" Sutton asks through a grimace.

I laugh and shake my head. "No, I was fidgeting the night we met and—"

"Always were a fidgeter when you got nervous," my mom says with a smile.

I roll my eyes and continue my story.

"And I was playing with it. She asked me about it, and I told her I fidget when I'm nervous, like when I'm talking to a pretty girl." My sisters let out a small aww. "She kept it all this time. If she was done with me, if there was nothing between us, I think she would have gotten rid of it, right?"

My mom nods before giving me a knowing glance, and I know why. The night my dad met my mom, he bought her a soda. She ran off with her friends before he could get her number, but she kept the bottle cap from it. When they met again later, she still had that bottle cap, and he knew they were something special. It's in a frame now, hanging over the sofa she's sitting at, a part of a gallery wall containing memories and photos of their life together.

I can't help but wonder what this matchbook would look like framed in my living room as I flip it mindlessly between my fingers.

"So you're going to go for it," Sloane says with a smile, now understanding.

"I'm going to go for it," I say with a nod. "But she's scared, and I'm afraid if I go too hard, I'll scare her off. So for now, I've convinced her to pretend we're a thing as a favor to me, to help with Sophie's wish."

"Ooh, good call. She says no, she's ruining Christmas magic," Sutton says, nodding.

"So what's your plan?" Sloane asks.

"What?"

"Your plan of attack. How are you going to convince her to stay forever?"

"I don't think I should be—"

"She swore off men because of you, you know," Sutton says, instantly quieting my protests.

"What?"

"I got drinks with her and Claire a while ago. She told me this whole story about this guy she met, thought he was it. Her romantic comedy come to life." My gut drops knowing where this is going now that I've got the full picture. "Then she saw him out and about with his wife and kid."

"It was Sloane! I don't have a wife!"

"I know that, dumbass. I'm just saying, that was…it was her final straw, according to her. She's had some shit luck with men, and I think there's some daddy issues there, too. She decided it's not worth her time. Dating. Men. The whole nine."

There's silence as I take that in before my mother cheerfully says, "So now it's your job to fix it."

"I'm sorry?"

"You messed it up, now it's your job to fix it. Show her she wasn't wrong to believe in whatever is so very clearly sparking between you two." I open my mouth, and she says, "No, not that I want to know about any of that, Nathan Donovan."

"So again, I ask what you're going to do to convince her to stay forever?" Sloane asks, bored with the subject.

"Well, for one, I'm not going to try and get her to stay forever," I say with a shake of my head. I just want her to give me a chance to make things right. Maybe if we got past that first hurdle, we could take things further, but step one is getting her to trust me and trust in me again.

"Why not?" Sutton asks, aghast.

"Uh, because she's an adult with her own thoughts and feelings."

"Shmoughts and shmeelings, Nate. She's your dream girl, and she's Sophie's Christmas wish! It's meant to be," my mom says with a wave of her hand.

"Mom—"

"No, listen to me. You're telling me your daughter makes some obscure Christmas wish out of the blue when she has never once told any of us that's something she wants and you walk out to find exactly that and it's not some miracle?"

I sigh, reluctant to agree, even though that same thought kept me up half the night. I just know if I do, my mom and my sisters will never stop pushing.

"I want to keep things easy. Yes, I like her, yes, she's the girl I thought I'd lost, but she's also incredibly hesitant, and it's not just my emotions at play here. If I bring her into the fold, it's her emotions and Sophie's."

"Okay, so what's your plan?" Sloane says impatiently, and I groan. Maybe this was a terrible idea. I should have known better than to think my family would be levelheaded in any sense of the word. "Look, I get it and I agree—we should play things safe. But you need a plan."

"You can't fuck this up, Donovan," Sutton says. "Or you're going to have all of us on your ass. Even Sophie."

"She's right, Nate. I'm going to be very disappointed if you fumble this," my mom says.

"Why can't I have been born into a normal fucking family?"

"If you were, you wouldn't have Jules sleeping under your roof right now, would you? You can thank Claire for that."

She has a point, though I don't want to give it to her. Long moments pass before finally, I let out a sigh in resignation. "Fine. What do I do?"

"God, I've been waiting all my life for this moment," Sloane says, a near evil smile on her face. "Mom, do you have a pen and paper?"

"Fuck."

FIFTEEN

JULES

Nate offers to pick me up from his house and bring me to the studio to come to get whatever stuff I need and check my place out, but being trapped in his car with him seems like an absolute recipe for disaster, so I take a cab to the coffee shop around the corner and wait for him to tell me he's here.

The only way I'll survive the next few weeks while Nate fixes my place is to maintain whatever distance I can. I need it for my sanity, because just one morning with him and I'm suddenly rethinking my assertion that we wouldn't work.

But I wrote off dating for a reason, and I need to stick to it.

When we walk into my place, I realize that in the light of day, it's even more of a gut punch than it was last night. There are wet towels piled up in the sink and spread around on floors, though the bulk of the water seems to have dried, thanks to half a dozen industrial fans and dehumidifiers placed all around. My rugs are rolled up and in the hall to be thrown out, and anything on the floor that wasn't damaged has been raised.

"Who did all of this?" I ask, looking around. Last night, there was still a thin layer of water over the entire floor, my feet squishing in it as I went.

"I got the go-ahead from Mark as soon as I dropped off Sophie. I wanted to come in before I brought you over to do what I could to make it less scary."

"You didn't have to do that," I say, my words soft and filled with appreciation even to my ears.

"I know," he says, looking at me. We're both quiet for a moment, and a million different things are silently transmitted before he clears his throat. "It needs work, but honestly, Jules, I've seen worse. We mostly need to fix the cracked pipe and insulate it wherever we need it so this doesn't happen.

"Some of the floors need to be pulled up and replaced, but not a ton. You have tile in most of the rooms, which makes things easier than if you had wood floors that absorbed all of that water. Downstairs got water, but not nearly as much as up here, so it's looking like it's just a few places where the walls and the ceilings got wet.

"I'll double-check the structural beams, but I'm optimistic they won't need replacing. Once it's relatively dry, I can check to see what drywall we'll need to replace. I think the kitchen cabinets might need replacing, but...overall, it shouldn't be too bad. You should be back in here in a couple of weeks."

I try not to panic at the long list of what needs fixing and instead focus on the positive. It sounds like I'll be back in my home in a few weeks and able to start the studio back up as normal with the new year.

"Come on, let me show you the second floor, I have a few questions," he says, stepping toward the front door of my condo. "Then we can come back up and pack what you'll need for the next few weeks."

We make our way down the stairs to the second floor of my building, where, thankfully, there isn't much that was finished, so even if it flooded completely, it wouldn't have been the end of the world.

"What's this room?" Nate asks, poking his head into one of the studios I'd been working on. I tore down the walls and the floor, and in the corner, there's a case of mirrors and hardwood stacked, ready to be installed.

"Another studio. Next to that is an unfinished dressing room-slash-greenroom."

"Who's working on it?" He steps out to look at the other room.

"I am." He turns to look at me with shock in his eyes—shock I'm very used to seeing at this point. My ex-boyfriend, Jared, never understood my need to do everything by myself. He told me over and over that my little hobby would be much easier if I just let him handle all of the man's work and hire it out.

Let's just say we didn't last long for a reason.

"You don't have a professional doing it?"

I shrug. "I had someone come in to do the wiring and make sure it was safe and got the plans approved by the township. When I was doing the initial renovations to open, I had a team come in to do one of the two studios downstairs. I asked them to teach me the basics, and I finished the second studio. This is the third."

"You finished the studio downstairs yourself?" he asks, clearly impressed.

A warmth of pride runs through me, and I nod.

"My friends help occasionally." I give him a smile. "Actually, your sister helped demo this room."

He rolls his eyes. "I'm sure she loved that."

"She did. Maybe a bit too much," I say, remembering how scary it was watching Claire with a sledgehammer.

"Why not have someone else do it? It would be quicker."

I shrug even though I know the answer.

"It's much more economical to take my time and do it myself," I say, giving the easy answer.

"I could finish it, you know. A couple of men, a couple of hours... it wouldn't take much or cost much, and we'll already—"

"No," I say, cutting him off loud and firm, the word echoing around the empty room. His head snaps to me, confusion written across his face. I shake my head. "I'm sorry, that was rude. But I've got it. I like doing it myself, and you're already helping me a lot."

"It really wouldn't—"

"I can do it, Nate. I like knowing I built this place all by myself. No one will ever believe in me the way I do, and this place is a testament to that in a way. I just need help getting the rest of the place back to whatever standard Evergreen Park needs for me to move back in here in a reasonable time frame."

He looks at me, reading every muscle, every shift of my eyes before he nods.

"All right. Got it. Let's get you upstairs to start packing while I make some more notes."

With a sigh of relief that he won't push the subject, I nod and then follow him back upstairs.

An hour later, I've finished packing up my clothes and putting anything I don't need to bring to Nate's into the big plastic bins he brought so we can keep everything clean during construction. He's carrying what I packed so far down to the truck while I stare at my movie shelf, trying to decide which I absolutely need to bring when he walks up behind me.

"Anything else ready?"

I topple over from my crouch, holding a hand to my chest as my heart pounds. "Jesus, you scared me!"

He lets out a chuckle as he offers me a hand to get back up. When I stand, we're face-to-face, barely a few inches between us, and I hold my breath at the closeness. It wouldn't take much to move up to my toes or for him to dip his head down just a bit, graze his lips over mine, press my body to his, and pretend like there isn't a year standing between us.

He stares at me, and somehow I know he's thinking the same exact thing, his hand still holding mine, his thumb shifting the tiniest bit to graze against my skin, calluses catching in a way that makes me remember what his hands felt like everywhere.

"What are those?" Nate asks, tipping his head to the small bookshelf in the corner of my bedroom and breaking me from my daydream.

I step back quickly, looking at where my DVDs are stacked up.

"You're not that old," I say, knowing he's barely six years older than me. "I'm sure you've seen a DVD before."

"I just didn't know anyone had them anymore." He walks up to the shelf, reading the titles. "I've only heard of a third of these," he says.

"They're all romantic comedies."

"I remember you saying you liked romance movies. I'm glad that hasn't changed. Is *Love Actually* still your favorite?" he says, and I shrug, secretly wondering what else he remembers about me. My favorite coffee, my favorite movies...

"Christmas wise, yeah. But romance movies are the best. Predictable and funny, they always end happily. My favorite kind of stories."

"Why DVDs?" he asks, sifting through them.

Suddenly, I feel self-conscious, like he was finding something about me I wasn't ready to show.

"I, uh," I start, stacking up the DVDs I'm bringing. "I find them secondhand. Most of them are on streaming services, but it's across like a million of them. I would have to pay a couple hundred dollars a month just to watch whatever I wanted, whenever I wanted."

"So you watch these often?"

"Every night."

"Maybe you'll have to come over one night; make me watch some of your favorites," he says, voice low, eyes locked on the movies before him.

I don't open my mouth, for fear I might tell him just how much I'd like that.

SIXTEEN

NATE

I'm sitting at the kitchen island when there's a jingle of keys at the front door. The locks click before it opens, Jules slipping in nearly silently before locking it behind her.

After we packed up all of Jules's things, I helped her bring them back to the cottage before she headed out to teach a couple of classes at the community center.

I texted her two hours ago, telling her that I forgot to give her the key to the cottage and that she could come into the house tonight to grab it from the kitchen island. It was Sloane's idea, one that was confirmed by Claire, Sutton, and my mom to be a good one. An easy way to convince her to come into the house and see me after her classes.

"Hey," I say, trying to keep my voice low so as not to scare her. Clearly, I fail at that when she jumps, putting a hand to her chest and gaping at me.

"My god! You scared the shit out of me," she says before walking further into the kitchen. She's wearing a puffy winter jacket and a pair of tight pants that leave nothing to the imagination, not that it would stop me. She could be wearing baggy sweats and an old tee, and what lies beneath it would still be burned into my mind.

"What are you doing?"

"Waiting for you," I say simply, and she stops moving, the duffel bag on her shoulder slipping down onto the floor.

"What?"

"I was waiting for you. I wanted to make sure you got home okay." I love how that sounds. Home, as if this is Jules's home instead of some temporary solution to a problem she has. "You've never driven here yourself."

"You...you waited up for me?" she says, seemingly in shock.

"Well, yeah."

Softness moves through her eyes as she tips her head at me. "You didn't have to do that, Nate."

"It's not like it's midnight, Jules. It's barely past nine." Something flits over her face, but her mask goes back in place before I can grasp it. That softness of hers, the one she let out that first night, trusting me with her vulnerability, is now hidden behind armor.

"I appreciate it, but it's not necessary. I'm already intruding on your life here."

"You're *helping* me," I argue.

"I have yet to see that happen. All you've done is be incredibly kind and generous with your time and your home, and I feel like I'm causing more trouble than I'm worth."

"Well, tomorrow, if you'll be around, it would be great if you could help Sophie off the bus and keep her busy until I get home. Though if you have—"

She nods, cutting me off. "Yeah, absolutely. I don't have a class tomorrow." I look at her with a smile because the way she jumped on the smallest opportunity to help with Sophie is cute. "I'm just feeling like this deal is very much unbalanced. You don't need me at all, Nathan Donovan."

I need you more than you could ever know, Julianne, is what I want to say, but I don't.

"Well, helping with Sophie will be a huge help with Claire gone."

"I'm excited to hang out with her. I like her a lot from the little time I've spent with her."

"She's the best," I say, then turn to the oven, opening the door and pulling out a plastic wrapped plate. "Dinner if you haven't eaten." I place it on the island between us, the plate still warm, and we both stare at it.

"You cooked for me?" she asks, shocked but stepping closer to me.

"It's nothing fancy, just pasta and meatballs. But I figured you may not have eaten and..." The words trail off as I suddenly feel silly, like a kid trying to get the popular girl to give him the time of day. What if she had already eaten? What if this makes her uncomfortable, if it's too much too fast? What if she developed some kind of gluten allergy in—

"No, it's great. I didn't eat," she says with a small smile. "So this is really kind." Finally, she sits on one of the barstools at the island, pulling the plate toward her and undoing the plastic. I move, grabbing a fork and sliding it her way.

"I'll...uh," I start, once again self-conscious as I stand here, watching her eat. "I'll leave you alone. You—"

"You..." she starts, then bites her lip. "You can stay. Keep me company." I take her in, trying to read her face and determine if she's saying that because she feels like she has to or if she really wants that. "Unless you—"

"No, no. I'd love to," I say, pulling out a chair. "How were your classes?"

A smile lights up her face as she starts to tell me about the classes she taught today, the upcoming recital, and the parents of the kids she teaches while she eats, and I realize I would give just about anything to do this every night: have dinner waiting for her, sit with her after Sophie has gone to bed, and hear all about her day.

I just want to spend *time* with her in any way I can.

Ten minutes later, she's standing, rinsing off the plate, putting it in the dishwasher, and turning to face me, worrying her lip between her teeth.

"I, uh, I guess I should probably let you get to bed or whatever. I feel like I've taken up more than enough of your time today," she says.

"Would you want to..." I start, then stop, suddenly feeling dumb. When did I turn into a fifteen-year-old who was nervous about talking to a pretty girl?

Since Julianne Everett fell back into your life.

"Would I want to what?" she asks, brows furrowed, and she looks so damn cute; I can't even focus on nerves, just on the all-consuming urge to convince her to spend more time with me.

"I have some work to do on my computer; I usually do it on the couch. Would you want to watch a movie with me? Keep me company?" I ask.

"A...a movie?"

There's no going back now, I think as I run a hand through my hair and nod.

"Yeah. I got...I got a bunch of the streaming services, so I should have just about any movie you want to watch."

"You *got* them?" she asks, and I feel it then—something that only seems to happen around her: a blush burning on my cheeks.

"Yeah, I mean, I had one or two for Sophie since all she watches are the Ashlyn movies and princesses, but—"

"When did you do this?"

"What?"

"Did you always have them? All the streaming services?"

I look at her in the eyes and see it there, the tiniest flicker of hope. It's like she *wants* me to tell her I went out of my way this afternoon to find *every* streaming service I could, make fifteen different accounts, and then hook them up to the television in hopes I could maybe possibly convince her to spend a few hours with me, even if we're on opposite sides of the couch and neither of us makes a sound.

Which is *exactly* what I did, of course.

It was tedious and might all have been for nothing, but if it gives me even the *chance* that she'll hang in here with me, it would be worth it. While we were at her place, I realized I just wanted to *spend time* with Jules. It's like now my body knows where she is, knows she's close, and knows she wasn't just some figment of my imagination. I'm aching to be in her proximity at all times.

"No," I confess. "I got them while you were at work."

A long beat passes as she takes me in before she asks, "Why?"

I shrug. "I don't know. I saw you trying to pick your DVDs like you were choosing which child to spare and wanted to make at least one thing easier on you. If you're not comfortable hanging in here, though, I can give you the log-ons; you can set them up in the cottage," I start. "I don't want you to feel obligated—"

"No," she says quickly, then bites her lip. "No, I'd like that. I'd like...the company."

My own lips tip up at her words, and for the first time since that night on New Year's, I feel it.

Hope.

SEVENTEEN

JULES

I yawn as the credits for *Sweet Home Alabama* begin to scroll on the screen. I stand up from the couch and turn to Nate. He's been on his computer the entire time, typing away and barely even paying attention to the television. For a bit, I forgot he was even there.

Until, of course, I looked over to see a tissue box pointed my way, Nate holding it out to me when I cried as Reese Witherspoon found out her ex-husband created an entire business inspired by her.

I mean, really. How could you not sob at that?

"I should get to bed," I say, low.

Nate's head pops up, a wide smile pulling at his lips as he shuts his laptop and sets it aside, standing as well.

"I'll walk you home," he says.

I shake my head. "That's really not necessary, Nate."

"Well, it's going to happen anyway, so get over it," he says.

I roll my eyes before silently grabbing my things and slipping my shoes on at the back door. Maybe that's the key to successfully handling the next month or so while maintaining my sanity: just giving in and letting Nate do whatever he wants but keeping my walls way up high, keeping myself safe.

It's worth a try, I suppose.

"So, this is me," I say, standing outside the small cottage, my new key in hand, even though I didn't lock it before leaving.

He smiles, stepping closer to me. "Yeah, I know," he says.

"Thanks for...everything. Dinner. The movies."

"Thanks for keeping me company," he says. He gets closer to me, and I realize too late that it's me shifting closer to him, not the other way around. "You should come tomorrow, watch another one. Continue my romance movie education."

I bite my lip to fight a smile, and his eyes watch, tracing the way my teeth dig into my lip there.

"We should talk, Jules," he says, voice husky.

"About what?" I ask stupidly, even though I know the answer, of course.

"Us."

"There isn't an us to talk about," I whisper.

His hand lifts, then pushes my hair back over my shoulder. I can tell myself it's the winter chill that has a slight shiver running through me, but I know it's the barely there graze of the tips of his fingers on the skin of my neck. His lips tip up like he saw it and knows my truth as well.

"You're a shit liar, Jules."

Irritation flares through me, and I step back, snapping at him

"You should know I've sworn off men."

"What?" he asks with a smile as if he finds my irritation adorable.

"I swore off men. And love. And romance." I purse my lips and put my hands on my hips. Maybe if I make myself seem bitchy and standoffish, he'll be uninterested. "So nothing is going to happen. We had one night, and that was it."

"It was two."

"What?"

"Two nights that changed everything for me, and I know they did for you too. Or else you wouldn't have kept that matchbook."

My jaw goes tight, and I try to seem unaffected. I should have just tossed out that matchbook when I found it, but instead, I kept moving it from bag to bag. I don't like what it reveals about me, not when I'm trying to play it off to protect myself.

"I didn't even realize that matchbook was in there. It doesn't mean anything," I lie, and he smiles. He *smiles*, the arrogant asshole.

"What about bumping into each other? You can't tell me that wasn't some kind of sign. What did you call it then? Some invisible string kind of story, the world pulling two people together?"

My jaw tightens, but my heart skips knowing he remembers that too, a tiny thing I mentioned a year ago.

"That's just silly movie things. Not something that happens in real life."

His head tips to the side, assessing me, and I hate it—hate how I can feel him reading me.

"What happened?" he asks.

"I don't know what you mean."

"What happened to the Jules who was searching high and low for her movie-worthy romance? Looking for signs and messages every-where she looked?"

I roll my lips into my mouth and bite, trying to fight the gasp. How much about me does he actually remember? And why?

And what does it mean when my heart skips a beat each time he does?

"She got a reality check," I say finally.

"Me? Was I the reality check?"

I blink and sigh. I should avoid the question to the best of my abil-ity, but for whatever reason, I don't.

"Yes. No? I don't know. It was eye-opening to see how deep I was in my delusion, reading into things and finding signs everywhere. It was a wake-up call that I really needed. I was living with my head in the clouds, and I hurt myself doing it. Now, I'm only focused on myself, my friends, and my business. I...I don't have time for anything else." I mostly lie because my business is closing up for the rest of the year, and my friends are all off with their significant others.

The truth of the matter is the last year has been the loneliest I've ever felt.

"And me and Sophie," he adds.

"What?"

"You're focused on me and Sophie, too. Watching Sophie and helping me out with her Christmas wish." My jaw goes tight because he's got me there, of course. Diversion seems to be the only way to go, so I take a page from Ava's book and turn my sass on.

"Well, you know, I wouldn't want to hurt your ego, but I'm really only in this because your daughter is super cool. You're just...a boy who happens to be there."

He lets out a small laugh and shakes his head before stepping closer to me, closing the gap. We aren't touching, but with each breath, the bulky material of my jacket brushes his sweatshirt, and I feel it as if it were his skin on mine.

"Are you going to make a single moment of this easy on me?" The words should sound annoyed, but there's a smile on his lips.

I shake my head. "Probably not. It's not my specialty." He stares at me for long moments, and I try to decode whatever he's thinking before his smile widens further.

"Good."

"Good?"

He nods, then takes a step back. "Wouldn't want to win you so easily."

"Excuse me?" I ask, appalled but also trying to ignore the butterflies in my belly. Stupid, idiotic, gullible butterflies.

"It'll be much sweeter, winning you over my way."

"You are so not going to win me over, Nathan Donovan."

"Keep telling yourself that, dollface." I open my mouth to argue, to yell something to tell him what a pompous, presumptuous ass he is before he steps back and tips his head to the cottage. "Go inside, Jules. It's cold out here."

I stare at him and his smug smile and decide at that moment I will not let him win. No way in hell. Even if he gave me the best orgasms of my life, and I haven't been able to think about much else other than the way he kissed me for an entire year.

I repeat that to myself over and over as he opens the cottage door, and I glare at him as I walk past him into the house.

But as soon as that door is closed and locked behind me, I can't help but do a silly little excited dance because even if he could totally break my heart if I let him in, Nate Donovan *so* likes me.

EIGHTEEN

JULES

The next morning, I wake up to a text from Nate asking me over for coffee, and I know I can't do it. I can't be with him early in the morning before I'm awake enough to put my defenses up, not when he's apparently adamant about trying to break through the wall I'm desperately trying to keep up between us.

I shouldn't have stayed to watch a movie with him last night, even if he was sweet, saved me a plate for dinner, and subscribed to every streaming service under the sun because he knew I couldn't bring all of my movies. I need to keep things professional and friendly and, most importantly, keep my heart out of it.

> Sorry, I can't, I've got so much to iron out at the community center today. I'll be back before 2 to get Sophie off the bus, though.

He gives me a thumbs-up in reply, and my mind has to remind me eighteen thousand times he is a man, so a thumbs-up isn't a weirdly passive-aggressive move, and even if it was, it doesn't matter.

Nate isn't mine.

So instead of sitting in his kitchen and drinking coffee with him while he gets ready for his day, I chug an energy drink on the drive to the community center, teach an adult dance fitness class, and spend the rest of the morning making sure everything is ironed out for the final rehearsals before our winter recital on Tuesday.

I get back to Nate's with plenty of time to get Sophie off the bus, give her a snack, and play Ashlyn dolls with her for two hours, but as soon as Nate gets home, I head out, telling Sophie I'll see her tomorrow and barely giving Nate a wave. It works so well that I decide this is going to be my routine, because the easiest, if not the most childish, way to keep things completely professional with Nate is to simply avoid him.

But the next day, when he walks in an hour early and Sophie is still eating her snack, I'm foiled by a meddling five-year-old with a wickedly effective pouty face.

"Can you stay for dinner, Jules?" Sophie asks as I start to close my laptop. I was doing administrative work, which I usually put off until the last minute.

"Oh, I don't think your dad—" I start, but Nate cuts in quickly.

"If you stayed, it would actually be a huge help," he says, and I glare at him as Sophie smiles next to me. He has to know that my wanting to help is going to make me cave, since no matter what he says, getting Sophie off the bus occasionally is not equivalent to fixing up my place and giving me somewhere to stay.

"Pleassseeee, Jules?!" She begs, pouting at me.

"I..."

"I have to fix this sink," Nate says, tipping his head to the kitchen sink that definitely works just fine. "And I don't want Sophie to get all the parts mixed up."

"And we're having pizza for dinner! We each make our own pizza, and we put on the toppings ourselves. It's so much fun! I use extra extra cheese because that's the best part."

"Well, I'm sure your dad doesn't have enough—"

"I have more than enough. Do you have a class tonight?" he asks, and before I can lie, Sophie speaks.

"She doesn't! I asked her when I got off the bus!"

The way Sophie is looking at me with big, blue puppy dog eyes, I can't find it in me to say no, so I sigh and nod. "Yeah, I guess I can stay if it's cool with you guys."

"It is!" Sophie shouts. And it sounds crazy, but the way Nate and Sophie look at each other when I agree, it's like this was, in fact, planned like some orchestrated exchange to...what? Get me to stay for dinner?

You're out of your mind, Jules. Be realistic, I tell myself, sighing as I settle back to open my laptop and respond to another email.

"What are you doing?" I ask a few minutes later when Nate sets a worn tool bag and a box on the kitchen island. "I didn't realize the sink was broken."

His forearms flex, the sleeves of his long-sleeve tee pushed up to the elbows as he opens the box, pulling out instructions.

No one should have forearms that good-looking. Add in a fading tan and the perfect light sprinkling of hair—it's actually criminal.

"Jules?" he asks, snapping me out of the forearm porno running through my mind, my head snapping up to look at him. His lips are tipped up like he knows what I was thinking about, and a blush burns over my cheeks.

"Yeah?" I ask, fighting the urge to shake my head out, to dislodge my thoughts from the incredibly inappropriate place they had wandered.

"You zoned out."

"Sorry, I, uh..." *Think, Jules! Think!* "I saw the tools, and my mind went straight to how much work my place probably needs. What did you say you're doing with the sink?"

He looks at me, eyes dancing with humor, and I know he knows I'm full of shit, but what else can I do?

"Replacing this sink faucet. It drips, and I've meant to swap it for months." I remember this: him telling me the sink drove him crazy back in January, and once again, in the way Nate always seems to be able to do so, I think he reads my mind, knowing what I remember because his lips tip in an embarrassed smile before he shrugs. "Never got around to it."

"Huh," I say, then watch as he starts to take parts out of the box, the instructions spread on the counter. "I'm surprised you use those."

"What?"

"Instructions. I would have thought a real manly man like yourself would just jump right in, figure it out as he goes."

Unexpectedly, his lips tip up, a full grin taking over his face.

"You know, a real man isn't afraid of a little instruction. In fact, he might find a step-by-step tutorial is quite...enlightening." The glimmer in his eye has my face burning with a blush as I recall the first time I was in this kitchen, spread on this very counter, and showing him how I liked to be touched before he took over.

I clear my throat.

"Yes, well, I'm also quite the do-it-yourselfer these days. I just find it more...satisfying, you know?" I flutter my lashes at him, attempting to ignore the absolute need to hide away. Backing down means Nate wins, and I hate losing.

He looks at me, his tongue tracing his teeth in a way I tell myself I would not like to feel before he speaks. "I think I'd like to see you do it yourself sometime, dollface."

I stare at him slack-jawed, unable to think of a witty or a biting remark, instead once again flashing back to almost a year ago on this counter. "Show me," he had said, and I'd be lying if I didn't occasionally bring that memory out of storage to use on particularly lonely nights.

"Do you like my picture?" Sophie asks, pushing a coloring book into my arm and breaking the moment. I don't know how I had forgotten the little girl who sat next to me, but when I look down, there's a princess colored in wildly, the lines of the page mere suggestions, but it looks perfect all the same.

I clear my throat before answering. "Oh my goodness, it's beautiful!" I say with a big gasp. "You're an amazing artist!"

"Thanks, I know," she says with a confident little shrug and a smile. I let a small laugh out and wish I had a third of her confidence. "Do you want it?"

"Me?" I ask, and she nods.

"To decorate Aunt Claire's cottage."

"Oh my goodness, yes! I'd love it. That's a great idea, thank you so much." I watch as she carefully tears out the photo, a look of fierce concentration on her face. "I can't wait to hang it up," I say, meaning it.

She smiles and then gives me a big hug before returning to her coloring.

"Now I need to make one to send to Aunt Claire. She probably misses me, like, a lot."

I nod my head and go back to attempting to reply to emails and ignore the man working at the sink.

My plan is ruined just few minutes later when I watch as he reaches behind himself with both arms, grabbing the back of his sweatshirt and tugging it over his head, leaving just a tight fitted white T-shirt underneath before opening the cabinets beneath the sink and looking in there, fiddling with pipes or whatever it is he's doing.

I wouldn't know, I'm too busy watching the muscles of his back shift beneath that tight T-shirt.

It's incredibly distracting. So much so that less than an hour later, I get exactly zero of the emails I needed to send and reply to done. Instead, every moment was spent trying to sneak coy looks at Nate's arms and back. A few times, he even reached up to grab something, his shirt shifting up and revealing a line of smooth skin, a hint of light hair leading to a happy trail on a toned stomach, and I think I swallowed the moan that almost left my lips.

I hope.

Either way, I am so totally fucked.

And when Nate turns the tap on, looking satisfied with his work, then turns to me, arms crossed on his chest with that same self-satisfied look on his lips, I know I'm fucked.

"So, tomorrow," he starts, looking at me, "What's your schedule look like?"

My brows furrow trying to remember what day of the week tomorrow even is since my mind is still muddled, watching his arms pull at the sleeves of his white tee. Shaking my head, I click a few things on my laptop and open my calendar.

"I..." I start reading the day's schedule. "Just a rehearsal at five. We have to redo the dress rehearsal at the community center before the recital."

"Oh, I forgot about your recital. When's that again?"

"Tuesday, so I won't be able to help much with Sophie early next week." He shakes his head and waves at me in a don't worry about it gesture. "And then, for the most part, the season will be done until January. Hopefully, everything will be...done by then," I say, biting my lip.

I try to close up the kids' practices after the winter recital and start back up mid-January once the chaos of the holidays and winter break end. Each year I think about doing a one-week intensive camp to help with the parents who have to work while the kids are off because I miss them, but I'm glad I didn't do it this year.

"Hmm," he says, looking at his daughter then back to me. "Well, tomorrow, in the morning, would you want to go tree shopping with us?"

"What?"

"Oh, Jules, you have to come! Daddy and I go to the farm and we pick the perfect tree and Daddy chops it down and then we go into the shop and get hot cocoa! With MARSHMALLOWS! And lots of whipped cream."

"Well, you can't have cocoa without marshmallows," I say with a smile.

"Exactly!" she exclaims, hands tossed in the air. "And then we go to get new ornaments and bring the tree home and put up our decorations. You have to come!"

"It kind of sounds like something you and your dad do to bond, sweetie. It should be just you two, I wouldn't want to intrude."

She groans aloud. "No way! How are you ever going to fall in love with my dad if you keep avoiding him?"

Nate's head pops up and he looks at his daughter, and I expect him to argue or to tell her that's not cool, but he doesn't.

Instead, he smiles.

"Yeah, Jules. How are you ever going to make a Christmas miracle happen if you keep avoiding me?"

My mouth drops open at his open taunt.

"I...I..." I start, looking from Nate to his daughter. "I'm not avoiding you!"

"Then prove it. Come with us tomorrow," he says.

I glare at him, knowing I am so screwed.

He smiles wider, and then, because I have seemingly no choice, I nod tersely. "Yes. I would love to come get a tree with you two tomorrow."

NINETEEN

JULES

The next day, when I walk over to the main house bright and early, Sophie is already awake, bouncing off the walls with excitement and telling me I need to dress extra warm for our outing to the tree farm. We're in the car before nine and get there as soon as it opens.

Once we park, I watch Sophie and Nate argue about whether or not she has to wear a scarf and a hat and gloves. Nate wins, only for Sophie to tell her dad five minutes later thank you for making sure she was warm.

It's interesting to watch them interact. Nate, who clearly wants Sophie to have the world—everything she ever wants or could want, yet having to weigh that against what's best for her. Meanwhile, there's Sophie, who thinks her father hung the moon, even if his rules suck sometimes.

I don't have many early memories of my dad before the divorce, and the ones after are tainted with an air of not belonging or being a burden. Watching Nate interact with his daughter with a wide smile and a tap to her red nose, her resounding giggle at almost anything he does, heals something inside of me I thought I had long bandaged over.

After entering the farm, we wander for what feels like forever, and it takes us much too long to pick out a Christmas tree, with Sophie and I nitpicking at each and every option then shushing Nate anytime he has input. Eventually, we find the perfect tree that even Nate approves of, and I hold Sophie back while he cuts it down and hauls it back to the registers before we sit in a small cozy café for the required cocoa.

"Can we please pick out an ornament in the shop now? Please, please, please?" Sophie begs her dad, a chocolate mustache over her lips. I sit back and watch them, Nate sighing and grabbing a napkin before wiping his daughter's face.

"We have a million at home," he says, and Sophie rolls her eyes at him like she's fifteen instead of five.

"So? We get one every year! It's a tradition." She stares at her dad, and eventually he smiles and nods. "Yay!" she shouts, standing and then reaching for my hand. "Come on, let's go pick some out!"

"One," Nate yells from behind us as she tugs me out of the café to the ornament shop next door.

"I need to get an Ashlyn ornament," Sophie says, looking through the racks and racks of ornaments along the back wall of the store. It's a mess of reds and greens and pinks and blues and whites, each meant to symbolize different milestones and interests in someone's life. There's a new baby one, an engaged and married one, ornaments for pets and sports and hobbies.

"You don't have one already?" I ask with shock.

In the few days I've known her, I've come to realize Sophie's biggest interest and obsession is Ashlyn. Most of her clothes are licensed for the magical doll, her entire room is decorated with it, and I don't think I've ever seen her without the doll in hand.

"Nope, last year I didn't even know about Ashlyn," she says, as if to say, a year ago she was such a baby, she didn't even know about the world's coolest toy.

"Really?" I ask, still a bit shocked, considering her level of devotion. I suppose kids do fall in and out of interests rather quickly, though. Hell, I think in the span of one year I told my mom I wanted to be a horse trainer, a ballerina, and an astronaut. It's actually a miracle dance ever stuck.

"Yup! Daddy got me her when I broke my arm last year. He said she was magical and she'd make me feel better, and she looked like a pretty ballerina he knew. That's why I knew that Santa could make Ashlyn come to life and marry Daddy." A rush of heat rolls over me with understanding. "She already existed! He just had to find her again."

A ballerina he knew.

"When did you break your arm again?" I ask, trying to be casual.

"Uh, I don't know. The beginning of the year. I was with Grandma and Grandpa at their mountain house, and I slipped on ice. I wasn't too sad because even though it was right after Christmas, I got so many presents."

"Yeah, that sounds pretty cool," I say, but my gaze is scanning the store, looking for her father. When I find his tall frame, though, his eyes are already on mine, taking me in and watching us like he's afraid if he blinks we'll disappear.

I understand that feeling.

A week ago, Nate Donovan was a sour memory that hurt when I touched it. Now, it's holding this tiny spark of hope I keep trying to put out, but I can't seem to make myself do it. I've sworn off love and men, but maybe I was too hasty? What if this really could be something special, some once in a lifetime, movie-worthy romance, and I'm just too scared to give it a shot?

A few hours later, we're back at the house, watching Sophie put on the final ornaments. We stopped for lunch on our way home before we came back, Nate and I putting up the tree, stringing the lights, and hanging all of the delicate bulbs out of her reach.

I move to stand beside Nate, who's watching Sophie show each ornament to her doll with a small smile on his lips.

"Found out the Ashlyn obsession is pretty new," I say, trying to break the ice.

"Did you now?" he asks, eyes not moving toward me like he's afraid to hear what I'm about to say, what Sophie may have revealed.

"Oh yes," I say. "Your daughter told me you got her because she looks like a pretty ballerina you know."

A light blush crosses over his cheeks. "She told you that?" he asks.

I smile and shrug. "Something tells me she isn't very good at keeping secrets."

Nate shakes his head with a small laugh. "The worst, actually. But you can't deny you look just like the doll."

"So you bought it..." I start to say, watching the doll dangling in Sophie's hand.

"After we met."

"Before or after I blocked you?"

"Before. I remember thinking about texting you, taking a photo, and sending the doll to you, but you didn't know about Sophie and..." His words trail off, and suddenly I feel the urge to know, to ask once and for all.

"Why didn't you tell me about her?" I ask.

He lets out a bone-deep sigh before running his hand over his head.

"You know, I've asked myself over and over since I saw you again. Probably would have saved us a lot of heartache. At least a dozen times when you were here, I almost mentioned her, but there was never a good time to bring it up, you know? We were...brand new. I didn't want to fuck it up. Turns out, not mentioning it was our downfall."

"I get it," I say, because I do. "I get protecting her until you knew for sure there was something there you felt comfortable exposing her to." I think of all the men my mom dated before she met Stanford, the way she'd parade them as some new dad. The way they'd buy my affection with toys only for them to leave, my mom in tears and me just confused.

A heavy silence hangs over us, and I hate it, feeling like I steered us in a shitty direction, so I try and move forward.

"So you bought your daughter a doll you thought looked like some chick you hooked up with?"

He looks at me, gives a light shake to his head before taking two steps and cutting the distance between us in half. His hand moves up then pauses, like he wants to touch my face, before it falls again.

"You were never *just* some chick I hooked up with, Jules, and you know that. You were always more. So much more, I didn't understand it at the time. But then my daughter ran to you on a crowded street, as if she knew too, like she could feel the pull of you to us."

My heart skips a beat or two before it kicks back into action doing double-time.

I open my mouth to say something—to remind him that I'm not here for that, to remind him and maybe myself that I've sworn off love and men and it's all for the best, really, it is—but before I can, an alarm goes off on my phone, reminding me to leave for my class that's in thirty minutes.

"I gotta go," I say in a whisper. "Practice at the center."

"Yeah." This time, when his hand lifts, he lets it rest there on my cheek, the warmth of his palm radiating through my skin in a way I really, really like. "Yeah, you do."

"Will you come see our decorations when you're done?" Sophie asks, her voice high and squeaky and hopeful and breaking the moment. I step back from Nate and slowly, like he's still categorizing what it was like, lowers his hand. "We're not done, but it's going to be magical!" She closes her eyes as if she's visualizing their future masterpiece, and I smile. "I just know it."

"I don't want to interrupt—" I say, but she cuts me off, moving closer and holding her hands together like she's pleading.

"Please?" Her eyes go wide, and I wonder how anyone is ever able to resist her, or if she genuinely always gets her way.

I'm leaning toward the latter as I find myself speaking without the approval of my logical mind. "Okay, fine," I say. "I should be back around six."

"Perfect. I'll make dinner, if you're okay with eating with us," Nate says.

Once again, I answer without thinking.

"Yeah, that works." My voice is breathy as I speak, his eyes still locked on mine as they go warmer, as my belly flips over and over in ways it should not. Finally, he breaks the look, and I turn away like I'm meaning to escape.

But even when I'm across town at my studio, I feel that tether in my chest, just like Nate mentioned and I denied, pulling me back to the place where a little girl and her dad are decorating their home, waiting for me to return.

I think about what Nate said the entire drive to the community center and then throughout the entire rehearsal. Thankfully, Gina was feeling better and able to dance tonight, so I didn't need to dress up, but unfortunately, that means I had time to think.

Think about the mess I had gotten myself into.

Think about Sophie and her sweet smiles and her all-consuming belief in Christmas magic.

Think about how I swore off love and romance and how my commitment to that is wavering in just a few days in the presence of Nathan Donovan.

What would happen if I risked it?

What would happen if I fell into the fantasy of it for the next month and let myself believe this was real, that this wasn't dangerous for my sanity?

This is what's running through my mind as I park in the drive at Nate's house and walk in the front door with a gasp, Sophie running my way in excitement.

"Do you like it?" she yells.

"Wow, you guys did an amazing job," I say with an impressed laugh, toeing off my boots in the entryway. Nate walks over to me, grabbing my coat and hanging it as I step into a Christmas wonderland.

The tree we decorated together stands in the corner, glowing bright and covered in multicolored ornaments, a red and white tree skirt at the bottom, an angel that looks suspiciously like Sophie at the top.

The mantel over the fireplace has faux green garland and snow, and on every surface there's something Christmassy, from holiday art Sophie has done over the years pinned to the walls to a tiny Christmas village taking up the dining room table.

"My mom and sisters have given me very specific decorating notes over the years," Nate says, explaining.

"It wasn't like this when I came," I say, still looking around, then going red as I realize what I just revealed.

He comes over to me, standing next to me in the doorway to the living room and smiling.

"The clutter gets to me. I can deal with it for only so long, so by the day after Christmas, I'm itching to take it all down. When Sophie leaves to be with my parents in the Poconos, I always use it as an opportunity to pack everything away and clean."

"Ah, makes sense," I say.

"I wish it could be like this forever," Sophie says with a wistful sigh, and I smile at her, but then her eyes go wide and a giddy, excited smile spreads over her lips. "Look!" She points over my head.

"Wha—" I start confused, but when Nate and I both look up and see a bundle of white and green tied with a red ribbon over the doorway we're standing in...

"Mistletoe! That means you have to kiss!"

"Oh, I—"

"It's a Christmas tradition!" she shouts, then claps her hands. Glancing at Nate for some kind of out, some explanation to his daughter as to why that's not how that works, all I see is a small tip of his lips.

"Sophie must have hung them up when I wasn't paying attention." There's a chair a few feet away, and when I look up, the sprig is taped to the frame haphazardly. It's not like it wouldn't be very on brand from what I'm learning of her. Meddling seems to be in her nature, just like her aunts. "It is the rules, though," he says in almost a whisper, lips spreading in a bigger smile. "We wouldn't want to let the girl down."

"What?"

His body shifts then, his hand moving to my hip in a way that burns through my thin leggings. It's gentle and hesitant, and the look in his eyes—the mix of nervous and excited—has my body shifting unconsciously to face him.

"If this was a movie, I think this is when I'd kiss you," he whispers under his breath, mine catching with his words.

"Yeah, probably," I say back, and he smiles again, pulling me in a bit closer. Again, without the permission of my logical side that has seemed to have gone dormant, I move to my tiptoes, shifting my body as his head dips down.

Somewhere in the back of my mind, I hear a tiny gasp from Sophie, but it only takes a moment before I'm lost in the feel of Nate's lips on mine.

It's gentle and PG-rated at best, just a soft brush of his lips to mine, but it has my heart racing all the same, even more when his hand moves to my jaw, pulling me a bit closer, deepening the contact of our lips.

My hands move up, winding around his neck and holding him there, and all I can think is I am so totally fucked.

TWENTY

NATE

I lied, I hung up the mistletoe.
  And it was so fucking worth it.

TWENTY-ONE

NATE

Jules eats dinner with us and, just like Sophie and I schemed together while she was at practice, my daughter begs her to stay, read a book, and get her ready for bed—a request Jules doesn't even bother trying to decline.

As we go through the routine of the night together, I find myself wondering what this would be like if it were our real life: Jules helping to brush the tangled knots out of Sophie's curly hair, making her giggle instead of whine like she does with me, picking out her book and reading it to her while I clean up the kitchen and close the house up for the night.

Like a team.

Someone on my side. Someone on Sophie's side.

I've never had that. Her mom was someone I barely was with before things ended, and I've never felt comfortable enough with a woman to introduce her into Sophie's life this way.

Until Jules.

When she slips outside of Sophie's room, clicking the door quietly behind her and tiptoeing toward the kitchen where I'm standing, watching her, there's a small smile on her lips.

"A success?"

"She's out like a light," she says.

"Yeah, she gets like that after a busy day." I continue to take her in and watch Jules's demeanor go from comfortable to unsure, her eyes moving back and forth from the back door that leads to the cottage and the couch in the living room.

Hesitation, like she wants to sit with me there but isn't sure where we stand.

"I guess I should…" she starts, letting her words trail off, and even if this isn't her intention, I take the open door she offers me.

"Stay," I say, tipping my head over to the couch.

"Stay?"

"Yeah. Watch a movie, keep me company. Like the other night."

"I don't—" she starts to argue, but I don't let her.

"Do you have something else to do tonight?"

"What?"

"Do you have something else to do when you get to the cottage?"

Slowly, she shakes her head and bites her lip.

"Come on. Pick a movie, keep me company. I'll just be answering emails and whatnot."

She hesitates, once again biting her lip and glancing from me to the couch and back again before finally, she nods. "Okay."

A couple of hours later, Jules is dabbing at her eyes, watching some actress stand in the foyer of her home, her husband's best friend proclaiming his love for her via fucking flash cards, and I can't fight the laugh back anymore.

"Are you crying?" I ask.

She turns to me and gives me the world's fakest glare before slapping my arm that's around her shoulders. I kind of lied when I said I had something to do. I kept my laptop open for maybe thirty minutes, clicked around before putting it down, and moved one cushion over so I was sitting beside her.

It felt like high school, sitting stick straight beside a girl and trying to spot the hint that it was okay for me to put my arm around her. But it came ten minutes or so later when her body shifted just a bit, her arm brushing against mine. I kept my eyes on the television as she quickly looked at me to check my reaction—a reaction I didn't give her for fear I'd scare her off.

Ten minutes after that, I got tired of playing games, wrapping an arm around her shoulder and tugging her close. I didn't care if it was the most uncomfortable, juvenile position to sit with a woman on the couch. It felt fucking great, touching her, holding her.

It was even better when a few minutes later, her body relaxed, her head resting on my shoulder as we watched the rest of the movie together.

I'm learning that with Jules, I need to give her time, ease her into things. If I do that, the overthinking slows, and she doesn't panic about her fears, instead letting me disassemble her wall brick by brick.

Now she's looking up at me with glassy eyes, glaring. "Stop, don't make fun of me," she says, trying to lean back but wearing a smile all the same.

"I'm not," I say with a laugh, my arm tightening to pull her in close once more. "I'm laughing at the writers, thinking this is romantic enough to put in a movie."

"It is romantic! It's an iconic moment. He's telling her she's perfect to him, that he's in love with her and knows she'll never be his, but that's okay, knowing her is enough." That's Jules's problem: she's willing to settle for someone who thinks knowing her is enough.

Simply knowing Jules will never be enough for me. I know that now.

"No, that's not romantic. Romantic is a man who will move heaven and earth until she's his."

She gives me a small, nervous smile.

"I don't know, this is a pretty popular movie. It's a famous scene," she says, tipping her head toward the TV.

A beat passes before I lift a hand and brush a dark lock of her hair back, smiling.

"What's more romantic, this movie or meeting a girl in a bar on New Year's Eve and knowing she's the one for you?"

Her mouth drops open a bit, and her eyes go wide in a way that is too fucking cute for her own good. "Nate..." she says low, and I smile.

"I'm just saying. Pretty romantic, that happening. Even more romantic walking out of a store and bumping into her a year later. Like it was meant to be or something."

"Nate," she whispers.

I smile then settle back again, her tight against my side.

"Watch the end of your movie, dollface." Her body is tight for just a second before she sighs and settles back into me.

"I should probably head to the cottage," she says as the movie's credits run, though she doesn't move when she says it.

"Mmm, I guess," I say, even though I'd be happy to sit here all night. Even if she fell asleep, I'd stay awake, documenting every single moment of her body touching mine, trying to convince myself this is real and not some figment of my imagination.

"I have an early class tomorrow," she explains as if I asked. All I can think of is how I can try and steal some time with her after, since it seems I won't be able to convince her to stop by for a cup of coffee before she leaves in the morning. "And it's a crazy day, preparing for the recital."

"Yeah," I say simply.

"I gotta get up really early," she says in a near whisper now, but snuggling deeper into my shoulder.

"Mm-hmm," I agree.

"So I should really get up and head to bed."

I smile wide, listening to her try and convince herself to get up when she clearly doesn't want to. Her guard might be up still, and she may tell herself she's sworn off relationships in order to protect herself, but brick by brick, I'm working past that wall.

I know once I get there, it's going to be fucking beautiful.

"All right, beautiful," I say, forcing myself not to let her fall asleep here, since she really should get a good night's sleep in an actual bed, and I don't think I'm far enough past her walls to be able to convince her to sleep in my bed with me, even if it's just for sleep. With a sigh, I shift her and force myself to stand before putting a hand out for her to take. "Let's get you to the cottage."

For a second, so quick I almost miss it, she pouts, and it takes everything in me not to smile.

"Let's?" she asks, an eyebrow raised.

"It's a dark and treacherous walk to the cottage. Wouldn't be a gentleman if I didn't go with you."

"I don't need a chaperone."

"I know that, but if there's anything I've learned from these movies, it's that you always walk a lady to her door after a date."

She tips her head, giving me a glare.

"This isn't a date," she says as I shake the hand I put out to her, ignoring her. She stares at it before finally grabbing it, and I help her up, not letting go when she's standing just inches before me, our hands clasped between us.

"It could be," I whisper.

"Nate," she whispers back, and I like that, my name whispered in that voice, a mix of hesitance, longing, and excitement there.

I step back, holding her hand until she's steady, watching the quick flash of disappointment in her eyes and fighting against everything not to smile.

"Come on," I say, stepping toward the back door but not letting go of her hand, not as I open the back door or as I walk along the walkway to the cottage, and definitely not as she uses her free hand to unlock the door, pushing it open.

"Goodnight, Nate," she says, stepping away from me but not letting go of me either, like she wants to hold on as long as she can.

I should let go.

I should let her move into her cottage and go back into the house to continue planning how I can remove her walls.

But I don't.

Instead, I let instinct win. I let my impulses win and tug her hand to me until she stumbles into my chest. I wrap one hand around her waist to steady her, the other finally letting go of her hand and cupping her chin.

"If this was a movie, I wouldn't leave without a goodnight kiss," I whisper against her lips.

Long, long moments pass while a million thoughts cross behind her eyes.

And then it happens.

Her mouth opens, lips brushing mine as she whispers, "Then kiss me, Nate." Her soft hand moves up my neck, warm against the cold air of December in New Jersey.

I don't give her a moment to second guess, instead leaning in the small millimeters to close the gap between us, pressing my lips to hers. It's soft and sweet, nearly chaste.

That is, until a small sigh leaves her lips, until the hand on the back of my neck presses in, pulling my face to hers, until her lips part, her soft tongue peeking out to touch my bottom lip.

That's when I press her back to the wall of the cottage, pinning her there and taking her mouth in mine. I let my tongue intertwine with hers, consuming her. I groan at the taste I thought I'd never have again.

Her nails dig into my neck now, and my hand on her waist moves down to her ass, gripping it tight and pulling her into me. She gasps again when she feels me through my jeans, her thin leggings doing nothing to hide my already hardening cock from the feel of her.

She grinds against it, a tiny mewl leaving her lips as she does. My mind races, trying to think of the best way to get her naked and writhing beneath me, how to get more and get it fast, and—

Flood lights turn on next door, nearly blinding me as I hear the jingle of dog tags, then the bark of my neighbor's Jack Russell terrier.

I groan quietly as I break the kiss, the groan much different than just moments before as I press my forehead to Jules's, our heavy breathing coming out in visible puffs in the cold air.

"Nathan, is that you?" Mrs. Tarte yells over the fence.

"Yes, Mrs. Tarte, it's just me," I say reluctantly.

"Oh, goodness, Buster thought it was an animal or something! I could have sworn I heard growls!"

I watch Jules's eyes light up, her lips rolling beneath her teeth as she fights back a laugh. At least she's not embarrassed or pulling away.

"Nope, just me," I say, waiting for her to go the fuck away.

"Oh, that's good. How are you, dear?"

"I'm great, you?"

"Oh, just peachy. Now, you remember to send that Sophie of yours over tomorrow, I made some special cookies for her!"

I send a silent prayer up to anyone who will listen that she'll leave.

"Sure will, have a great night, Mrs. Tarte," I say as I hear the jingle of tags move back toward her house, Buster deciding we aren't some great threat to the safety of the neighborhood.

"You too, Nathan." I think we're free, and then she says, "Next time, maybe do your canoodling inside, yeah?"

I look to the sky, bright stars overhead, and wonder why the fuck I stayed in this way too small of a town where everyone knows everyone's business and has absolutely zero sense of privacy.

"Got it," I grumble.

"Night, Nathan! Good night, Julianne!"

"Night, Mrs. Tarte!" Jules yells through a laugh.

The door finally closes right before Jules bursts out laughing, me following suit. When the laughter settles, I sigh, pushing her hair over her shoulder.

"You should get inside," I say when she shivers.

"Yeah." She bites her lips then looks up at me, a small, nervous smile on her lips. "It was a good date, Nathan."

Something in me explodes, and I fight the sudden urge to do a victory dance.

"Yeah, it was," I reply, feeling like I conquered Everest. "Goodnight, Jules." I press my lips to hers once more before stepping away, holding her hand until she finds her footing, her legs a bit shaky. I don't bother to hide the small, proud smile at that, and she rolls her eyes.

"Night, Nate."

"Night, Jules," I say, then stand there as she closes and locks the door.

A good date, indeed.

TWENTY-TWO

JULES

"So you kissed him?" Ava asks, brushing back the hair of one of the older girls for tonight's winter recital.

Harper is helping to make sure all costumes fit right and curtains open in less than thirty minutes, but the flutter of butterflies in my stomach isn't from the impending performance. I know the kids are going to absolutely kill it, no matter what.

No, it's the reminder that Nate and I kissed on Sunday.

Yesterday, I was out the door to the center early, hosting an adult workout class before spending the morning setting up the stage and making sure everything was ready for our Tuesday recital so I could get back to the house to get Sophie off the bus in time, not because her dad couldn't get there, but because I knew I'd miss her if I didn't.

When Nate came home, I was back here for the final rehearsal, and even though I didn't go to the main house after practice, there was a wrapped plate in the microwave and a sticky note on the top reading, *In case you didn't eat. -N.*

"To be fair, he kissed me."

"Oh, so you're telling me you didn't kiss him back?"

I guess I can't tell her that, can I?

"It was because Sophie was watching," I lie terribly.

"And the second time?" Ava asks, because I'm an idiot and told her about how he walked me to the cottage, pinned me to the wall, and almost made me come right then and there.

"I..." I start then groan, letting my head drop into my hands. "I don't know! I didn't know."

"It's okay, Miss Jules," Gina, one of the teenage dancers, says, coming over and patting my shoulder. "We all fall victim to hot guys scrambling our brains once in a while."

"And Nate Donovan will definitely scramble anyone's brains," another says.

I turn to her and glare. "What do you know about Nate Donovan, Chrissy? You're fifteen!"

"I know that when he came to renovate our kitchen last summer, my mom kept putting on her tiniest bikini, and she and my dad fought a lot at night once he left." Well, that would do it. "And I know he's hot. Like the surface of the sun hot. He was wearing this really tight T-shirt that was all sweaty and—"

"Again, you are fifteen, Chrissy," I shout.

"I mean, she's not wrong," Mrs. Johnson says with a laugh, and I glare at her, too. She's one of the moms who offered to help get everyone ready since Claire is gone, and I was grateful at the time. But now that she's hearing this...? "What? Everyone knows about Nate Donovan. He was a year or two under me in high school, but he's a Donovan, you know? When I was her age, I was drooling over his dad, but now that Nate's older?" She shrugs. "You're an idiot not to go for that. Plus, his family is the sweetest."

That part I couldn't deny, as I've had calls from all three of his sisters over the last few days, checking in and offering any help they could. Sutton is over in the other room helping Harper as we speak, just because Claire told her I might need an extra hand.

"Ten minutes," the stagehand says, popping his head into the dressing room, and I sigh with relief.

"All right, enough about that. Who needs last-minute help?" I say to the room at large. A hand pops up on the other side of the room, and I gratefully take the excuse to move out of the way and away from my friends while we finish the final touches.

Fifteen minutes later, I'm on the stage of the community center, lights nearly blinding me.

"Thank you all for coming," I say. Even now, when it's no longer my performance, I get butterflies up here, ready to show off all the hard work these kids did. I'm even more excited to see it's a totally packed house.

I give my normal thank you speech, thanking everyone who came to see the kids, the parents and guardians who took the kids to every rehearsal, the volunteers, and the center for hosting us before I remind the crowd of the courtesy standards.

And as the lights go down and I prepare to step back into the wings of the stage, pushing the kids out, I see him. Front and center, with Sophie right next to him, a brown paper bag at his feet and a wide, proud smile on his lips.

Nate came.

"You guys did amazing!" I shout for the millionth time, absolutely giddy as the kids start to pack up and head out with wide, exhausted smiles on their faces. "I can't believe how perfect you were. I'm so proud," I say, putting an arm around one of the older girls and pulling her in tight. This is my favorite part of a performance: congratulating my kids and seeing the tired pride all over them.

"Miss, Jules, there's some people here for you," one of the girls says as I help one of the stragglers pack up their bags. Most of the kids have gone off to their parents, flowers in hand and big smiles on their faces. I'll come back tomorrow and do the big cleanup, but at the very least, I like to make sure all of the kids' stuff is packed up after a performance.

"What?" I ask, looking over my shoulder at the door, but I don't have to ask another question.

There are six people standing in the doorway of the break room, four of whom I've met, and the other two I can guess. My heart skips a beat.

The Donovans are all here, except Claire.

Sophie runs to me with a big smile, and I'm barely able to stand up straight before she's barreling into me, knocking me back on one foot before I lift her, settling her on my hip as she starts to ramble, holding on tight.

"That was amazing!" she yells into my ear as if we're not inches apart. "I want to dance. Can you teach me? Please, please, pleaseeee!"

I laugh at her exuberance, pushing stray strands behind her ears as I smile.

"If your dad's cool with it, of course," I say, and her smile gets even wider before she wiggles for me to set her down. Then she turns to her dad, who has closed the gap between us, his sisters and his parents a few feet behind him.

"Can Jules teach me to dance?" she yells at her father, who uses his free hand to tug her in close. He only has one, because the other has a gigantic bouquet of peonies in it.

He smiles, then holds the flowers out to me. "You did great, Jules," he says, then leans in and presses a chaste kiss to my cheek.

The tiny contact sends shivers down my spine, and I hate my treacherous body for it.

I take the flowers he's handing me even though I'm not sure why he's giving them to me. "What are you doing here?" I ask, looking over his shoulder at Sutton and Sloane, who give me small waves.

Nate's brow furrows in clear confusion. "What do you mean?"

I look at the watch on my wrist. "Sophie has school tomorrow."

"It's your big night," Nate says simply.

"No, it's not, it's the kids' big night."

Nate tips his head in confusion mixed with a hint of frustration before shaking his head a bit like he can't believe me. "It's yours too, baby," he whispers before grabbing my hand, tugging me close, and turning to face his family.

"Mom, Dad, this is Jules. Jules, these are my parents. You already know my sisters," he says, tipping his chin to them.

I give them small smiles and fight the urge to step out of his grip and run away. "Hi, it's so great to meet you guys. I, uh, I'm sorry it's like this, at work." I glare at Nate, who just smiles.

"Are you kidding me? That was amazing! You did a phenomenal job with those kids," Mrs. Donovan says before stepping forward with a hand out. "Shauna," she says, introducing herself.

I grab her hand, which is soft and warm, and she puts her other hand on top, holding mine between hers. "I am so, so glad to finally meet you."

"Finally?" I wonder if she knew about me before the water break.

"Oh, yeah, my little love bug Sophie won't stop bragging about her new nanny," Mr. Donovan says. "Her real-life Ashlyn come to life. Can't say you're not a spitting image of her doll, though. It's kind of wild to see."

"I told you, Grandpa! She's my Christmas wish come true!" Sophie says, sticking her tongue out at her grandfather, who returns the gesture, making her giggle.

"I see that. Well, we couldn't resist the opportunity to support you and your students," Mr. Donovan says, then sticks his hand out, swatting his wife's away with a playful smile. "Tom."

"Hi, I'm Jules. It's, uh, great to meet you." Tom Donovan looks exactly like his son, but with graying dark blond hair and a red flannel shirt stuck into a pair of jeans that just fits the whole image of a wholesome grandpa.

"Do you have much more to do here?" Nate asks me, and I look around the room. I see the final kid waving as she steps out of the room with her parents, and I shake my head.

"No, I'll be back tomorrow to clean things up, but it's all good for tonight. We try to tidy as we go, so when everyone is done and exhausted, we can just leave."

Nate nods.

"Well, then it sounds like it's time for a celebration with ice cream and pie," Mrs. Donovan says with a clap of her hands.

"Please tell me you made pumpkin," Sutton says with a look to the ceiling like she's throwing up one last prayer.

"And chocolate cream," Mrs. Donovan says. "And an apple one."

"Three?" Sloane asks, and Mrs. Donovan blushes.

"I wasn't sure what Jules liked, and it's her big day." My heart warms at the most precious, sweet family, and I fight the urge to compare Shauna to my own mother, who has never once been to one of the performances my kids put on.

"Chocolate," Nate says before I can say anything. "For desserts, anything chocolate." I look at him with a face, but there's no time to argue before he turns to me.

"Anything you need me to grab? I can drive us to my parents, and we'll drop you off at your car on the way home."

"I—" I start.

"No room for arguing," he mutters under his breath. "You might hurt my mom's feelings." There's a small tilt to his lips telling me it's probably bullshit, but I go along with it all the same.

"Yeah, that works," I say.

"Pie time!" Sophie yells, grabbing her grandfather's hand and running for the door, leaving us all giggling as we follow her.

We leave the Donovan family home after eating way too much pie, but the fullness I feel isn't in my stomach but in my chest. Something about being around this sweet, supportive family that nudges and teases each other but in a way that's laced with love all the way through healed something in me I didn't know was frayed.

It turns out the Donovans are a romantic comedy family: incredibly tight-knit, incredibly kind, and incredibly funny, and I'm now adding another thing to my movie-worthy life list.

There are long goodbyes, more come back soons, and an invite to the family Christmas party before we get out the door, two hours past Sophie's bedtime.

"It's a special occasion, Jules," Nate said when I mentioned it. "Rules are off on special occasions."

She falls asleep in the car almost the second Nate starts it, despite it not being even a ten-minute drive from the Donovan house to the community center. We're parked in the lot next to my car, but I'm reluctant to leave this warm little bubble Nate has built for me.

"Thank you," I say into the quiet. "For tonight. For coming. For bringing your family. It means a lot to me."

"They insisted once Sutton told them she was helping and once Sophie told them all about you. This has been planned for a week."

"Why didn't you tell me? That you were coming?"

"Well, you see, ever since Sunday, you've been avoiding me, so..." His words trail off, and I feel a blush burn over my cheeks.

"Sorry," I whisper.

"All good, Jules," he says, reaching over to grab my hand. "You're steering this. We're going at your pace." I should say that we can't be going at any pace at all, but something stops me.

Silence fills the car again before, finally, Nate breaks it.

"Your mom wasn't there tonight."

I turn to him and see he's looking at the building in front of us as if he doesn't want to pressure me into talking but wants to know all the same.

I sigh, and maybe because I'm tired, or it's dark and quiet, or because I'm blown away by his gentle kindness, I respond. "Yeah, she's not really into the whole...thing."

"Dance?"

I shake my head and laugh. "No, no, she loves that. She was the one who got me into it. She's not into my owning a business."

That has his head jerking, turning to me. "What?"

"She wishes I'd focus on...other things."

"Why?"

I shrug but answer all the same with a deep sigh.

"When my grandmother passed, I got a small inheritance. Nothing crazy, but it was enough for the down payment on the building and a bit of money for renovations. She wanted me to use it to buy a house, preferably in a nice neighborhood with single bachelors who would wife me up and make me a stay-at-home wife."

He snorts out a laugh. "In Evergreen Park?"

I shook my head and bit back a laugh of my own.

"No, she lives in Dalton." Naming the expensive and exclusive town has Nate nodding with understanding.

"Ahh. So she doesn't approve of your self-renovations, I assume?"

I shake my head.

"She set me up with my ex, who offered over and over to just pay to have it all done, and she has no idea why I wouldn't just take him up on it instead of doing it myself. Now whenever anything doesn't go according to plan, she turns it into some big 'I told you so' lesson."

"That's why you didn't want to stay with her after the pipe burst."

I nod, not wanting to add much. It's been a long day, and I just spent the night laughing and talking with a family who doesn't know me but showed me more support than my mother ever has.

I'm too tired to unpack all of that tonight.

Nate must see that in my face, because he leans over in the car and puts a hand to my cheek. He then gently pulls me forward as he presses a soft, barely there kiss to my lips before pulling away and resting his forehead on mine.

"Well, you've got the Donovans now," he whispers like it's all I'll ever need in life.

I can't help it. A small, soft smile hits my lips. "Yeah, I've got the Donovans."

TWENTY-THREE

NATE

I send the text after contemplating what exactly to say for at least ten minutes, like I'm fifteen and texting a girl for the first time instead of thirty-five and texting a woman I've fucked multiple times, made out with last night, and lives in the cottage behind my house.

Julianne Everett makes me feel like I'm a teenager again, and I never thought I'd mean that in a good way. But when she texts me back in less than a minute, my stomach flips with excitement, and I fight the urge to dissect exactly what it means that she texted me back so quickly.

When she doesn't respond immediately, I inevitably worry I toed past a line I should have stayed behind. I contemplate sending another reply telling her I'm just kidding or that I meant to say that to someone else or something just as juvenile, typing and deleting at least a dozen replies before she texts me back.

> Sorry, I was walking, and I hate people who walk and text.

My chest eases, and I wonder if I'm too old for this, if the constant push and pull will be bad for my old man's heart.

> I just did my last class of the day and cleaned up the center this morning. Setting up at my favorite coffee shop

My favorite coffee shop is three blocks from the studio. They make this coffee with vanilla and almond syrup...it's amazing.

I remember her saying that the morning after we met, with a small smile on her lips and a dreamy look in her eyes. I also remember going out of my way multiple times that January and February, hoping I'd bump into her but never actually doing it until I decided it was a torture on its own and to let it go.

There are three coffee shops in Evergreen Park, something I always find interesting, considering it's a town that's barely two square miles. Two are relatively busy chain shops, not very Jules's style, and because I checked multiple times, I know neither has the flavor combination she told me was her favorite.

In that moment, I make a decision. It might be the wrong one, and it might push her more than she's ready, but considering I too am done with work for the day, I grab my jacket and keys and head downtown to her favorite coffee shop.

When I step into the doors of Evergreen Brew, I'm happy I made that impulsive decision, even if parking is a bit chaotic with the town lighting tonight, just like I'm happy I went into that bar that night instead of going home and moping once again about how I was single on New Year's Eve.

Jules is sitting at a table, her laptop in front of her, wearing a slouchy light pink sweater with her gorgeous dark hair pulled up with a clip, her face concentrating on her computer screen. But when she looks up and sees me walking in, a smile takes over her expression as she closes her laptop.

"Nate! What are you doing here?"

"I came to see you." I see it then—the brightness that comes to her face at that. God, nothing has changed since the very first night, and even she has to know it, even if she's too scared to jump. "Are you busy this afternoon?" She shakes her head. "Want to help me out? I need to do some Christmas shopping for Sophie and my sisters, and unfortunately, I hate shopping."

Without even asking how, she nods happily.

"I would love to. I feel like these scales are so unbalanced as they are." She starts to stand, putting things into her bag, and I shake my head.

"You can finish what you were doing, I don't mean to—"

She laughs and shakes her head.

"No, no, I was just wasting time, scrolling through social media. I'd much rather wander the towns and shop with you." She grabs her to-go cup and smiles. "Let's go shopping till we drop."

With a groan, I grab her bag and sling it over my shoulder.

"Why do I feel like I'm about to regret this?"

"Because you probably are. I love shopping." I roll my eyes, and she laughs, but she has no idea that even though I haven't wanted to step into a store for anything other than food or home improvement things for years, choosing to avoid my least favorite thing and shop online, I'd shop all day every day if it meant I could do it with her at my side.

"So, who's on your list?" Jules asks as we step out of the coffee shop once she finishes her drink. We move toward where my car is parked to put her duffel and laptop inside before we walk the three blocks to mainstream Evergreen Park, lined with stores and boutiques, perfect for shopping. There are workers and volunteers everywhere, putting the finishing touches on street lights, benches, trees, and shrubs to make sure everything is perfect for tonight.

"Uh," I say, putting a hand behind my neck and holding myself there. My free arm brushes against hers, and I curse the thick clothes between us, desperate to feel her against me. I kissed her last night, but I feel like I'm having withdrawals from her, which is insanity considering I didn't even see her for nearly a year. "My mom, Sophie, Sutton, Sloane, and Claire..."

She snorts out a laugh. "So, everyone?"

"I've gotten my dad," I say defensively, shoulder-checking her a bit, and she giggles. She stumbles a bit and I use it as an opportunity to put an arm around her shoulders, pulling her close to steady her and not letting go. "And gift cards for Sophie's teachers. I also got the guys who work for me. It's just..."

"The girls?"

"The girls," I say with a laugh. "It doesn't help that Sophie refuses to give Santa a list."

Jules sighs and leans into me a bit.

Another win. A subtle one, but a win all the same.

"Next time I watch her, I'll try and get her to put together a formal list," Jules says. "We'll make a whole thing of it. Stickers, markers, and glitter glue." She looks almost as excited as I know Sophie will be, and I laugh. "Don't worry, I'll make sure to clean it all up before you're home."

"No, no need. I was just thinking how much Sophie is going to love that. She loves her some glitter."

"So I've noticed. A girl after my own heart," she says with a laugh.

"She's off from school on Friday," I say. "Any chance you can watch her?"

"Lucky for you, I have no classes tomorrow, so I'd be more than happy to. We'll have a girls' day. Paint our nails, watch movies, eat junk food..." she starts, smiling as we move toward a boutique I know Claire has shopped at before.

"She'll really love that." I open the door, and Jules steps in, but instead she turns to look at me over her shoulder.

"So will I." She smiles and claps her hands excitedly before stepping in further, me right behind. "Ooh, we can bake cookies!" I chuckle as we move to the wall where a plethora of girly tchotchkes are lined up.

"You're the only person I've ever met who babysits and makes it into an entire itinerary."

"Are you joking with me? This is going to be a landmark day. The first Jules and Soph day. A special occasion to celebrate if I ever heard of one."

I think about how perfect it would be to give my daughter that all of the time, Jules and Soph days. To have a person by my side who loves my girl as much as I do.

"You do that a lot, make special occasions out of ordinary days. Snow day snowman pancakes, glitter glue for Christmas lists. You're throwing a party for the kids?"

She nods before explaining.

"I don't know. I like to celebrate the little things. Life has enough strife. If you romanticize the little things, every moment can feel special."

I love this about her—how she looks at the world like it's some fantasy she gets the honor of living, while the rest of us are over here just trying to survive each day. I wonder what the world would look like through Jules's rose-colored glasses. She makes it seem like after last year, she took them off, but I think she just hid them behind darker ones, hiding her softness that I love so much.

"Were you always that way? I think Sophie's a bit like that, too," I ask.

"Oh, for sure. I know a kindred spirit when I see one. And yeah. I'd do everything I could to make things special. First days of school, last days of school. God, you should see me on my birthday. It can be excessive. Oh! Claire would love this," she says, lifting a frame in the shape of a heart with a big bow on top. "Put a picture of her and Sophie in it, or a picture Sophie drew?"

"Genius," I say, leaning to grab a handbasket lined up along the wall and putting it in. Jules grabs a few other things, putting them in beside the frame.

"You can add these," she says, grabbing a pair of fluffy socks. "And a pack of those chocolate bars she likes, and you're all set." She gestures to a second matching frame and a coffee mug. "These are for my best friend, Ava. She loves this store, too. They're almost the same person, if I'm being honest."

"That's terrifying. But okay, one sister down. So, you make small moments special. Did you get that from your mom?" I ask, desperate to know more about Jules in any way I can. "My mom is like that, constantly celebrating everything. She threw Sophie a tooth-themed party when she lost her first tooth, and she sprayed a dollar with glitter spray for me to put under her pillow and everything."

Jules smiles. "God, I love your mom. She's the coolest." Then she sighs and shakes her head. "No, my mom...she didn't know how to do that. She didn't know how to romanticize the little things and just enjoy where she was at. She was always looking for what was next, something more, something better. Maybe before my dad, she did, but I barely remember that. I think after he left, she wanted the opportunity for...more. To prove him wrong, maybe? I don't know." She laughs, brushing it off and lifting a pink pen with a big puffy pom-pom on top, throwing it in the cart.

"Don't get me wrong, my mom was fine, she loved me and never made me feel like she didn't, but...maybe my expectations are too high for what a mother-daughter relationship should be. I always wanted sisters—someone to do all the girly things with. I have Ava and Harper now, but when I was younger, I wanted that."

I grumble, remembering the years when my sisters teamed up and tormented me, no matter that I was the oldest.

"You're lucky, you know. What's it like to have sisters?"

"A pain in the ass," I say with a smile, and she elbows me in the side. I use it as another opportunity, hooking my arm around her shoulders and pulling her in close. For a split second, her body is tight before it goes lax.

"I always wanted sisters." I don't speak, waiting to see if she'll elaborate, and I'm rewarded with my patience. "I guess, technically, I have a few half siblings, but they aren't...we weren't raised as siblings, so we're not close. Not the way you are with your sisters. It's great that Claire was so willing to nanny for you."

I smile, a pang of guilt filling me I refuse to give light to.

"Yeah, she's pretty great. When Sophie's mother decided she didn't want to do the whole mom thing, it was a shock. They all pitched in by making a schedule, and Claire moved in. It got a lot easier once Soph was in school full time."

The memory hangs heavy between us as Jules continues to pick up trinkets, inspecting them then placing them back before she turns to me.

"Okay, enough with the heavy. We're on a mission. Operation Knock Out Nate's Christmas List is in action." She makes a Charlie's Angel type pose, and I laugh.

"God, you're fucking cute," I say, then put an arm on her shoulders once more, tugging her close as we head to the register to check out.

An hour later, we're still wandering, a couple more shopping bags in hand, when Jules's steps slow, looking up at the Swift Building, the tallest building in Evergreen Park. When it was being built with broad promises of a mix of new work spaces and luxury hotel rooms, there were two very clear factions at the town hall meeting: half of the town loved the idea of bringing in more business and more room for people to stay in town, while the other half thought it would take away from the small-town charm.

My dad was on team "this is going to ruin Evergreen Park," and my mom was on team "it's good for the economy," making it an incredibly rough time in the Donovan household. Thankfully, once it was built (and his son got a good chunk of the contracting work), Dad agreed it didn't absolutely destroy the town as he kept worrying.

"What's your take on it?" I ask, watching her eyes go glazed as she looks.

"What?"

"What's your take on it? Everyone in Evergreen Park has an opinion on the Swift Building."

"I love it," she says simply, surprising me.

"You do?" I ask, since she seems much more on the side of small-town charm than big city hustling.

She shrugs. "I don't think it takes away from the town, just adds... something more. It's not like it's the goddamn Empire State Building, the way some of these people act. Plus, I hear you can see the entire town from up there, which is cool."

I look at her aghast and in shock. "You've never been up there?"

She shakes her head, and I make a split-second decision, grabbing her hand and moving toward the front door.

"Hey, Henry, how's it going?" I ask the doorman with a smile. A doorman isn't exactly necessary here, but when kids started sneaking up to the top of the building regularly, the town decided it was best to have someone keeping track of who was going where.

"Can't complain. Got a job in one of the suites?"

"No, I just found out Jules here has never been to the top," I say with a smile.

His eyes go wide. "Really?"

Jules shrugs and smiles. "Never had an opportunity."

"Well, you know sunset is the best time to go," he says with a wink to me before stepping to the side.

"Thanks, man. I owe you."

"Anytime," Henry says as the elevator doors close.

We ride the fifteen floors up, getting off on the top floor then moving to a flight of stairs that lead to the rooftop. A cold breeze knocks the air from my lungs, but the look on Jules's face is what keeps me from feeling it, total awe and excitement as she moves in a small circle, taking in the town below.

"Oh my god, you really can see the whole town," she whispers to herself. "Look, there's my building." Jules points to where her dance studio is excitedly before turning again. "And your house." She's like a little kid discovering something new.

"There's my parents' house," I say, pointing to the west where the sun is starting to dip below the treeline that surrounds the town of its namesake.

"Wow. This is so cool," she says, stepping closer then looking up at me. "Thanks for bringing me here, Nate."

"Thanks for coming shopping with me. You know, Henry was right. This is the best place to watch the sunset in town," I say as a breeze rolls through, making Jules shiver. I pull her to me, her back to my front, and I'm pleased when her body never goes tight, instead sinking into me almost instantly.

Progress.

"It is pretty," she says low, watching the sun sink beyond the boundaries of our little town.

When I was a kid, I hated Evergreen Park. I hated how small it was, how everyone knew everyone, hated that I couldn't go anywhere without getting stopped, without someone asking how my mom was or something about my sisters.

But as I got older, after I left for school in New York, I missed it. I realized a town like this doesn't exist much outside of fiction anymore, and I was lucky to have it. It's why, when I found out about Sophie, I immediately bought a house here, fully intending to raise my daughter in this small, idyllic town.

"This has to be in at least one of your movies, watching a sunset together."

"In *Sleepless in Seattle*, they meet on the Empire State Building at sunset," she says, briefly looking at me over her shoulder.

"What's that one about?" I ask, watching the colors of the sky change.

"A widower."

"Sounds depressing." She huffs out a laugh, trying to elbow me, but I hold her tighter. "What else?"

"Well, there's a meddling kid," she tells me.

"I'm familiar with that," I say, and she laughs again.

"His kid makes him call up this radio station to talk about how lonely he is and how much he misses his wife. Then the entire country falls in love with him, people send letters...it's chaos. But this one woman tells him to meet her at the top of the Empire State Building."

"Ah, I see."

"It's a classic I can't believe you've never seen it."

"Add it to our list," I whisper, leaning and pressing a kiss to the top of her hair.

"Our list?" she asks.

"What, you're not making it your mission to give me a full education of romance movies?"

"I, well, I..." she says, then tries to turn, but I hold her tight so she can't, instead staring at the setting sun. "We can watch something else, you know. If you don't—"

"I do," I say quickly, cutting her off. "I love learning what you like, what movies make you happy. It's like a small look into the world of Jules. I gotta take what glances I can get."

"Not much to know," she says. "I'm pretty boring. I'm just a girl who doesn't know to drip her water lines and watches too many movies and lives in delusion most of the time."

I don't like the tone of her voice, like she's embarrassed or thinks she's not everything. When I turn her to look at me, I see the same look over her face. I wrap my arms around her lower back until her chest is pressed to mine, her hands moving to my neck.

"I'm totally crazy for you, Jules. Whatever version, whatever bits of you you're willing to share," I whisper. A long moment passes where my heart pounds, thinking she's going to say something that will break this moment.

"I'm really fucking scared," she whispers, and despite the negative tone, this confession of hers feels like a win. She's no longer telling me she's done with the mere idea of love but that she's too afraid to try. "If I fall, I could get hurt. Really, really hurt, Nate."

I'll take it.

I shake my head. "I'll always catch you."

Her eyes warm, and I realize I said the right thing when she moves to her tiptoes and presses her lips softly to mine just as the sun sets.

That's when it happens: the town lights up. A short, stilted gasp leaves Jules's lips, and I take the opportunity to resume my lips to hers, a perfect fit as always.

It's a moment out of the movies, and in it, I realize I'll do whatever it takes to make her entire life like this: a series of movie-worthy events to take her breath away.

I convince Jules to let me drive her to her car. She's parked at the community center, a good half mile from where I parked outside the coffee shop, and even though it's a short walk, I'm desperate for more time with her.

"So how else do the women get wooed in your movies?" I ask, turning onto Maple Road. I'm taking the long way to where she's parked, trying to squeeze any extra moments I can with her. I know once she gets space between us, she's going to start overthinking again, putting what's left of her wall back up. I know it's starting to weaken, that I'm finding cracks in it to show her I want her, want this, and I'm safe, but she's still hesitant to give in completely.

"What?"

"During the courting process. What's on your list of what happens in the movies?"

"Are you asking for courting tips, Nate?"

"Absolutely. I'm man enough to admit I want to make sure I don't fuck this up with you. If this was a movie, what would be the next step?"

She bites her lip, thinking before shrugging. "I don't know. Sometimes they call."

"They call?

"Yeah. You know, they call and then they flirt all night. She twines the phone wire around her finger and lays on her back, staring at the ceiling while he whispers sweet nothings to her, wooing her."

"That's what I want to do, you know," I say, parking next to her car.

"Twine the phone cord around your finger?" she asks, confused, and I laugh. It might not be smart, but I lean in, pressing a soft, gentle kiss to her lips before pulling back, smiling at her dazed face.

I fucking love that, how the smaller kisses put that look in her eyes. "No, I want to do the whole nine of movie-worthy wooing. Sunset kisses and buying you flowers and phone calls that keep you up late at night. I want to win you."

"What if...what if I'm not ready to be won?" she asks, biting her lip. I know this is her thing, her being too scared to give into this, afraid it's going to fall away again, but I'll wait for as long as I have to.

"Then I'm going to be doing a shit ton of wooing," I say simply, then step out of the car, moving to her side. I fight a laugh as I watch her head follow me, mouth slightly open like she's in shock. When I open the door, she looks up to me, speaking.

"Nate, I—" she starts, but I cut her off, grabbing her hand and tugging her from the car before speaking.

"I'm taking your lead. I want more—so much more—but I'm not going there until you're sure. I get that you're scared, and that means I'll stand here every day until that fear goes away. I'll wait for you to be as sure as I am. I'm in this for the long run. I know what a year without you felt like after I found you the first time and I didn't like it. I'm not making the same mistake twice."

She stands there, stunned, mouth open, before she starts to make noise.

"I—I..." she stutters, a mix of panic and relief rolling over her face, telling me I'm making the right choice. "I don't—"

I shake my head.

"You don't have to say anything. I just want to be as clear as I can about what this is between us. It's more, Jules, and you know it. I'm not going to fuck it up by rushing it when I can just have you for a lifetime if I wait."

"Nate, we can't—"

"We can, and we have been, and we will. If we need to dance around it for a few weeks, months, fuck, years, I'll be here, waiting." Then I lean down, pressing my lips to hers gently before moving to press my lips to her forehead and step away.

"Now get in your car," I say, tipping my chin toward her car. Dazedly, she turns, digging in her bag and unlocking it before moving to sit inside. I grab the door before she can close it. "I'll call you tonight, Jules," I say before closing the door.

And as I walk back toward my truck, I can't help but smile to myself when I hear a girlish squeal from her car.

TWENTY-FOUR

JULES

I'm in my pajamas in bed when my phone rings. My entire body jolts when I see Nate's name on the screen. I got ready quicker than ever before, brushing my teeth and washing my face at record speed. Then, I impatiently waited for him to call me like I was fifteen and waiting for my first boyfriend to call.

"Hello?" I ask.

"Hey," he says, his voice low and sweet.

"Hey. You get Sophie to bed, okay?" I miss her, and I kind of regret not going to the main house after our little date, but I am also so nervous about pushing my luck.

"Yeah, she told me to say hi to you. She's super excited for tomorrow."

"I am, too," I say with a smile. I spent my time waiting for Nate to call me, looking up recipes, and thinking of what fun stuff I can do on our girls' day.

"So, are you watching a movie?" Nate asks, and I sigh into my bed, cuddling in.

"No."

"Why not? I thought you watched one every night? Do you need me to set it up?" He sounds concerned, and it's cute.

"No, no," I say with a giggle. "I just…" A blush burns over my cheeks as I spit it out. "I just knew you were calling, and I didn't want to get distracted."

"I like that, Jules," he says quietly. "I like this, actually. I never did this in high school, sitting on my phone for hours with a girl."

"No?"

"Hell no. I had three nosy little sisters, and the house wasn't big. They would have eavesdropped for sure, tattled on everything. So I'm not really sure what we are supposed to do," he says with a laugh, and I groan inside, fighting the all-consuming urge to just hang up, feeling nervous and a bit silly. But I don't, because I want this, chatting with Nate.

"We just…we talk," I say. "Nothing crazy. Get to know each other."

"Without the temptation. I get it. All right, I can do that," he says. "So, what's your favorite color?" he asks, and I laugh before answering, asking him for his.

"You make the cutest fucking noises," Nate says an hour later when I laugh at something stupid he said.

I'm cuddled up in my bed, listening to him talk and laugh, and it's been everything. Just like high school when you'd get that rush and want to stay up all night, except more, better, because Nate's using it as an opportunity to learn anything he can about me and vice versa.

From favorite foods to childhood vacations to first kisses, we've covered it all.

"Makes me wish I was there."

"What's that?" I ask, a smile in the words.

"Jules, when you make those noises, it makes me want to kiss you. I mean, I wanna kiss you all the fucking time, but especially then."

My smile grows, and I'm not sure if it's the endorphins or the late hour or what, but I don't think before the next words leave my lips.

"So you'd kiss me if you were here?"

"Hell yeah," he says immediately.

"What else would you do?" I ask, my voice husky even to my own ears. I should be embarrassed, but in the dark like this, I can't find it in me.

"What?"

"If you were here. What would you do to me?" I clench at the mere idea, my belly twisting and my panties going wet.

"I don't think this is what you meant when you said talking all night to court you, Jules." I smile despite myself. "Not exactly PG."

"You've seen me naked, Nate. I think we're okay to have phone sex. It won't push any boundaries beyond what we haven't already toppled over."

"Jesus fuck," he groans, and it sends a thrill through me. "This is a terrible idea."

Silence fills the line alongside my embarrassment, and I fight the urge to hang up and throw the phone across the room.

"Oh god. I'm the worst. I'm sorry, this is so embarrassing and inappropriate, I didn't mean to pressure you into something you aren't—" I start rambling, but he cuts me off.

"Stop right there," he says, and I find my entire body tightening. "Stop because there is nothing I'd love more than to hear you make yourself come over the phone, except maybe to run over there and fuck you until you realized how fucking perfect we were together. I am just terrified of moving things too fast with you and you pulling away."

"Oh," I say low. "So...you're not against it?"

Why am I the way I am?

"You moaning in my ear after a year of not having that? Fuck no, I'm not against it, Jules."

Silence fills the line, and all I can think about is how I'd also like to hear Nate moaning in my ear, jacking himself off. All common sense is gone, my singular focus being that possibility.

So I decide to be brave. I might not be able to be brave when it comes to our relationship, but I can attempt to be brave with this. My fingers slide up under my pajama top, moving to my breast and cupping it before rolling my nipple, my breath hitching as I do.

"What are you doing, Jules?" Nate asks hesitantly

"Playing with my nipples," I whisper, and the groan that comes through the line has me smiling. I like that—knowing something so simple brought that noise out of him. "It feels nice." Another groan, then a rustle of sheets before he speaks again.

"If we're doing this, we're doing it my way."

"Your way?" My fingers move to the other breast, the nipple already peaked as I pinch it.

"You do what I say when I say it."

I bite my lip, my heart pounding with excitement.

"But are you going to..." I don't know if I could handle this as being one-sided. I'm brave, but not that brave.

"Yeah, baby, I'm going to jack off while I listen to you make yourself come." I moan then, picturing it, and he moans in return like he really fucking liked the sound of that. "Jesus, Jules."

I'm already panting, my nipples hard, my phone cradled between my ear and my shoulder as I lay back in bed.

"What are you wearing?"

"That's what you're starting with?" I ask with a giggle.

"You're right; let's just cut to the chase. Take your pants off. And your panties."

"I—"

"Mine are coming off too, Jules." There's a rustle again, and slowly, I start to shimmy my pants down, speeding up when I hear a deep groan come through the line. "God, I'm already so fucking hard."

"Okay, they're off," I whisper breathlessly.

"Good, baby. Now, take your hand and slide it down your belly. Slowly. Once you reach your pussy, glide a finger down, but don't finger yourself, okay? I want you to tell me what it feels like."

I do as he asks, my fingers leaving a trail of fire along my skin as I do. Finally, I reach my slit, gliding over my clit, my middle finger running over me gently, then back up.

"I'm so wet," I whisper. He groans loudly, and it sends a bolt through me, my fingers moving to circle my clit.

"God, I want to be there. Wanna see that."

"You could be," I say, even though I don't know if that's something I'm ready for right now.

"No, no. This is good. This is really good, Jules." I let out a shaky breath with the heat in his words. "Circle your clit. Play with it, baby."

"Shit," I moan, my now wet middle finger sliding in a circle around my clit before zeroing in on it, rubbing fast, then slow, then repeating the motion.

I'm teasing myself, listening to Nate's heavy breathing on the other line. My eyes drift closed, thinking of what he would look like. Is he in pajamas? Did he leave his shirt on? Are his pants off, or just lowered just enough to let his cock out?

Another wave of pleasure rolls through me at the image I like best: Nate on his back, phone to his ear, shirt hiked up, those sweats he's always wearing pushed just low enough to jack himself off. The head swollen with arousal, a drop of pre-cum—

"God, you sound so pretty like this—whimpering and moaning."

"I'm thinking of you," I admit, my filter gone altogether.

"Fuck, that's hot." He groans loudly. "Stop playing with your clit and slide one finger inside you, baby," he demands.

"But I want—" I start to whine.

"I said stop playing with your clit and slide in one finger, Julianne." The words are firm, and something about the tone and the way he uses my full name has me whimpering. "Only one."

"Okay," I whisper, doing as he asked and sighing at the feel as I clamp down instantly, my body wanting to be filled.

"You like that, don't you?" he asks.

"Yeah." I sigh, sliding my middle finger out and then back in. "I want more, though."

He chuckles. "I meant me using your full name. You like it?"

"I mean." My breath hitches as I slide the finger out once more. "It's hot. Since you never use it. Except...last time you did." I'm reminded of the last time we fucked and he bossed me around, using my full name like it was a command.

"Mmm," he says, contemplative, before a sigh of his own comes over the line.

"What about you?"

"I'm not really into being called Nathan, sweetheart."

I laugh and shake my head even though he can't see it. It's strange, laughing when I'm fingering myself, my body wound tight, but it's also...us.

"I meant, what are you doing? I've got one finger in me—" He moans loudly, and I can almost picture it, the way his eyes would close, the way his Adam's apple would bob. I bite my lip before continuing, my voice breathier now. "What are you doing?"

"My hand is wrapped around my cock," he says, not beating around the bush.

"Oh."

"And I'm pumping it, wishing I was inside you. I remember, you know. How you fucking squeezed me, how you sounded. How you tasted. I've been thinking about it for a year. Every time I jacked off, I came to the sound of you moaning my name."

"Shit, Nate. I want you so fucking bad. I'm close. God, I'm close." My hips shift, trying to get more despite my following his directions of only one finger and no clit.

"Next time," he groans. "Next time I'm with you, where do you want it?" The pleasure builds, a mind-numbing orgasm coming despite the lack of friction, and I can't comprehend what he's even asking.

"What?"

"The next time I fuck you, when I'm inside of you, where am I coming, baby?"

"Oh." My mind stops altogether.

"Move back to your clit, but stop fucking yourself so you can listen." I moan at the way there's a demand twined in the words and the way I listen without a second thought. "Good girl," he says, a smile in the words. "Now, Julianne, the next time I get the honor of fucking that tight cunt, where am I coming?"

I clench, my fingers gently circling so as not to tip me over the edge, panting at the thought alone. "You liked when I came on your tits, if I recall." My eyes drift closed again, remembering when Nate made me come, told me to get on my knees, then painted my breasts with his cum. "And then, we were cleared for me to fill you, fuck you without a condom." I moan louder, hips bucking. "Ahh, that's it, isn't it? That's what my baby wants."

God, how is this man's mouth so fucking filthy?

"She wants me to fill her up, doesn't she?" I can hear his hand now, the slapping of skin on skin, the way there's a strain in his words. He's close, too. "Tell me, Julianne." The words are said through gritted teeth.

"Yes." I shiver. "God, yes, Nate. I want you to come inside me next time we're together. I'm on the pill."

"Good, baby. I'll do that soon, okay?" he coos. "You still being good, circling that clit?"

"Uh-huh."

"Good girl. Now slide in as many fingers as you can," he says, and I moan at the relief as I stretch around three fingers. "You're going to fuck yourself and do it hard. You remember how I like it, yeah?"

"Yeah, Nate." I start to pump, fucking myself and groaning at the slight relief.

"I'm going to come when I hear you, Jules, but you're going to put me on speaker. Put the phone between your legs, then finger fuck yourself and rub your clit until you moan my name as you come."

"Oh god!" I shout but fumble with the phone one-handed to follow his instructions, sitting up a bit to do it. I moan as my fingers hit my g-spot.

"That's it," his voice says through the phone, the sound filling the small room. If I close my eyes, I can almost picture him here across from me, jacking his cock and watching. "That's it. Come for me, baby. God, you sound so fucking wet. Come for your man, Julianne."

The plea in his voice is what has my body locking, what has the pleasure tipping over, exploding through me, and sending warmth washing over me. "Nate," I scream, my hips bucking, my fingers deep as I fuck myself with them. My body jolts, wave after wave crashing over me.

Through the haze, I hear Nate groan my name. It's the hottest sound I've ever heard and one I'll be using years and years from now to be the star of all of my fantasies.

Silence fills the line as we both come down, and I reach over for tissues to clean my fingers before grabbing my phone and taking it off the speaker. I cradle it in my shoulder, suddenly shy as I catch my breath.

"You were so right," Nate says, a laugh in his words, his breath still heavy.

"About what?"

"Phone calls are a great idea."

And with it, the nerves are gone, and I'm laughing, falling back into the comfort I always feel with Nate.

TWENTY-FIVE

JULES

The next morning, I wake up and already have a text from Nate.

Wanna come over and wake up Sophie with me?

I type back, smiling sleepily at my phone.

What's in it for me?

He sends back a photo of a cup of coffee, and I smile once more, a seemingly constant state of being at this point. I roll out of bed and get ready for the day before shuffling over to the main house.

I'm not surprised to find the back door unlocked, knowing he probably did so as soon as I texted him back, but I am surprised when Nate walks around the corner as soon as I quietly click it closed behind me. He pulls me into his arms and presses a small chaste kiss to my lips.

"Morning," he whispers against my mouth, and I smile.

"Morning. What was that for?"

"Decided I'm done wishing I gave you a good morning kiss every single morning. Just gonna take it until you tell me not to."

"Does it mean I'll get a goodnight kiss again, too?" I whisper against his lips, and I feel them spread into a grin against my own. "Or a call?"

"Don't tease me, dollface."

I open my mouth to say something I might regret, to poke the bear and see what happens, but then Sophie's little voice, singing in her room, makes its way to us.

"Girls' day! It's a girls' day!" She sings some made-up song, and her dad shakes his head and sighs.

"Save that idea for later, yeah? Let's go get our girl."

As we walk toward the room, his hand on my lower back and leaving only when he opens Sophie's door, I can't help but think about how much I like the way he said *our girl.*

An hour later, I'm putting Sophie's hair up into pigtails, sitting on the couch in the living room, when Nate steps out of his room dressed in another well-fitted sweater, this one navy blue with Donovan Contracting written in white on the back, and a pair of perfectly faded jeans, making my hands go still.

It should absolutely be illegal for any man to look this good simply going to work.

"All right, I'm on my way out. Have fun, girls," Nate says, leaning down to press a kiss to Sophie's head. "I'll see you later." He looks at me. "I should be done by seven at the latest."

I shake my head.

"No rush, we're going to have a girls' day." I wink at him, and he smiles wide.

"GIRLS' DAY!" Sophie sing-shouts.

"Yeah, no boys allowed. We'll do our nails, bake cookies, and watch girly Christmas movies."

"Blech, definitely a girls' day," Nate says, giving his daughter a fake grimace.

Sophie looks at her dad with all of the sass of someone three times her age. "Well, you weren't even invited, so there," she says, sticking her tongue out, and I fight the snort of a laugh.

"Shoot, before you go, would you mind if we stop by Ava's today? Their new place is almost ready, and I want to go see it. It's in Ashford, maybe a fifteen-minute drive, so if you're not—"

"The one marrying a bodyguard?" I nod, and he smiles. "Yeah. See if you can set up a double date soon. I think I'd like that guy." I know he would, though I don't know if Jaime would do much more than grunt at Nate when he attempts conversation. Still, the idea of a double date with one of my best friends sends warmth through me.

"Got it," I whisper with a small smile.

"Is Ava the princess?" Sophie asks as I tie off the last pigtail.

"A beauty queen, but yeah, kind of."

She turns to her dad. "Dad, Jules so is Ashlyn because she has a queen for a friend. And a dressmaker!"

I laugh thinking about how Harper might not exactly love being called my dressmaker.

"And Ava's got the cutest cat you'll just love," I say, thinking about Peach, the kitten Ava found in an alleyway on her pageant tour.

"A cat?" she shouts, standing up excited before looking at her father's big round eyes. "A kitty, Daddy!"

Nate groans and glares at me.

"Did I just touch on a sore subject?"

Sophie turns to me, hands on her hips. "I've been begging him for a kitty for *years*, and he keeps saying I'm not old enough." She might as well stomp her foot with all the irritation painted on her face.

"Years is a bit of an exaggeration considering you're barely five," Nate says, deadpan, as he shrugs a jacket on.

"My whole life, I've wanted a cat, Dad," she says, cutting the daddy from it like she's a snippy teen.

"Yeah, yeah, got it. And I told you when you're older and more responsible, you can have one."

"How am I supposed to learn if we don't have a pet?"

"She's got a point," I say, mostly because I'm finding the back-and-forth increasingly entertaining. Nate glares at me now, and I laugh before turning to Sophie. "Maybe one day we can babysit Peach for Ava and Jaime. Then you can learn just how much work it is to take care of an animal before you get one."

Sophie turns her glare at me as if I just betrayed her, and I fight the laugh bubbling in my chest. She takes me in as I raise an eyebrow in challenge before she sighs.

"Yeah, yeah. I guess that's a good idea."

Nate looks at me at her acquiescence and gives me an approving nod for dodging that bullet. I wink at him.

"All right, my girls," he says, grabbing his bag and looking at Sophie and me. A rush of warmth and butterflies fills my belly when he does. "I'm out of here." He walks over to Sophie, bending over her and pressing a kiss to the top of her head. "Bye, princess," he says.

"Bye, Daddy," she shouts, forgetting her previous irritation with him before he moves to me.

"Bye, dollface," he murmurs, voice lower, huskier now. Then he bends down, a rough hand moving to the bottom of my chin to gently tip it before pressing a chaste kiss to my lips, barely even a brush. He steps back, winking once more before turning toward the door. "Soph, lock this behind me, yeah?"

"Got it!" she shouts, bounding toward the front door, leaving me stunned.

A moment later, she's back, little feet pounding on the wood floor before she's standing before me, a wide, gappy smile on her face, hands on her hips.

"My dad so likes you," Sophie says with a smile.

TWENTY-SIX

JULES

A few hours later, we're at Ava's nearly finished place. We're watching her and Jaime bicker as they tend to do while Sophie pets Ava's orange cat, Peach.

"I want a kitty just like Peach," Sophie says with a wistful look, scratching the cat behind her ears the way Ava showed her Peach likes it.

"You can probably just go in an alleyway and find one. That's how Ava found hers," Jaime says under his breath, and Ava elbows him in the side.

"Are you insane? That's not safe, Jaime."

He raises a thick, dark eyebrow at her, tilting his head. "So you admit it was a bad idea."

Ava glares at her fiancé, jaw tight. "I will do no such thing."

Jaime lets out a bark of a laugh.

"You absolutely did, Princess. You just said it was unsafe for Sophie to do it. One would assume that it would also be unsafe for a famous pageant queen with a stalker to run off from her bodyguard into an alleyway to get a cat."

Ava sighs, throwing her hands into the air.

"Would you rather Peach just be motherless in some alleyway right now? You're cruel, Jaime Wilde," she says, crossing her arms over her chest and glaring at him.

"I'm pretty sure we covered this; Peach absolutely had a mother already, and you stole her from her."

She waves him off with a hand, and I smile, watching them go at it like a tennis match. I've never met two people more meant to be together who also bicker about anything and everything.

"Are they always like this?" Sophie asks, and I snort, nodding.

"Pretty much. It's all in good fun, though," I tell her. "They love each other; they just show it funny."

Sophie nods in that all-knowing, wise way of hers.

"Just like you and Dad?" I choke on my sip of coffee before she continues to answer. "You two pretend you don't like each other, but you secretly love each other." I open my mouth to say something, but she just keeps going. "Actually, it's really just you pretending. Daddy is obviously in love with you. Aunt Sloane says girls like to play hard to get sometimes. Is that what this is?"

I gape at the little girl, and Jaime lets out a deep belly laugh.

"I like you, kid," Jaime says, bending to grab Sophie and putting her on his hip, Peach cradled in his other arm.

"You're not bad," she says nonchalantly. "My dad says you should go on a double date with Jules," she tells him, looking up at the big man. "I think you and my dad will be friends."

"Yeah? Why's that?"

"You're both really, really big, and you give Ava the same gooey look my dad gives Jules."

"A gooey look, huh?" Jaime says, a small smile on his lips, that dimple Ava loves coming out. He sets her back down to the ground, ruffling her hair a bit.

"Oh yeah. Jules's my Christmas wish, you know. So they're going to fall in love and give me a little sister."

"A sister," Ava shouts with a laugh.

I shake my head, frozen in shock at how this cute little wish has truly evolved into utter chaos.

"Yeah, Dad has three sisters, and Aunt Claire said having a brother is kind of boring. You can't dress them up."

"You know what, girl? That's so true," Ava says, a smile all over her face as she turns to face me. "What do you think, Jules? Are you gonna give Soph here a little sister or a boring brother?"

I glare at her. "I think I should have known better than to put the two of you in a room together."

Jaime lets out a laugh at my response. He tries to disguise it as a cough when he sees my expression, but fails miserably. Ava snaps her head in his direction and gives him a glare that could kill.

"Excuse me?" Her hands go to her hips, and with her long blonde hair in curls, she looks shockingly like Nate's daughter, who is standing the same way.

"You and a tiny version of you are the kind of shit scientists should study. A cataclysmic event could happen, nuclear warfare level," Jaime grumbles.

Ava's face goes smug. "Yeah? And what happens when we have a little girl, huh?"

He laughs again, shaking his head. "Only boys for me, Princess. Don't ever have to worry about that."

Her mouth drops open as she stares at him, then smacks him in the chest. "But I want a little girl! A mini me to dress up."

He sighs, staring at her, then pulls her into his arms and presses a kiss to her hair. "Then you'll get it, Ava. When have I ever been able to tell you no?"

Ava smiles, turning into Jaime's chest and sighing.

I smile blissfully at my best friend and her happily ever after, and for the first time since they got together, I don't feel that guilt-laden jealousy eating at me.

And even if that should scare me, it doesn't. Instead, I send a text to Nate with a photo of Sophie holding Peach.

"Hey, Jules?" Sophie asks hours later, lying on the couch, her head in my lap.

My fingers move, brushing her hair back, gently untangling the knots that, even though I brushed her hair an hour ago, still seem to be there.

We went to lunch before coming back home and getting right into jammies to bake cookies, do facials and our nails, then eat a girl dinner, which consisted of a menagerie of snacks and probably too many cookies before we got ready for bed and put a movie on.

"Yeah, sweetie?"

"Do you like my dad?"

"What?" I ask, my fingers stilling for a moment before continuing their movement as I try to play it cool despite my pounding heart.

"Do you like my dad?"

"Well, of course, honey. He's a good friend."

She turns to look up at me.

"I mean, like like. Do you want to marry him?"

I sigh, trying to figure out how to answer this.

"I...I think your dad is really great, Sophie, but I don't know him that well. You don't just marry anyone, you know? That would be silly. You have to get to know them, make them your best friend, then decide if you want to spend every day with them." There's a long pause that has me holding my breath before she seems to accept what I'm saying, nodding against my legs.

"That makes sense." I let out the breath I didn't realize I was holding. "But I think I'd really like it if you were my mom, Jules," she says, and a part of me breaks at that, at a little girl lost in the world.

I get it; after all, I was that girl once. I think I am still, in more ways than I care to recognize.

"You're the coolest kid I know, Sophie. Whoever ends up marrying your dad is going to be the luckiest girl on earth," I say.

That seems to appease her as she turns back to the movie.

It doesn't take long before her breathing evens out and she falls asleep in my lap. But her words never stop swirling around my head. And the scariest part isn't that she said it out loud; it's that I think I'd like to be a part of this family too much.

TWENTY-SEVEN

JULES

Sophie is still asleep in my lap when Nate walks in an hour later, looking exhausted. He smiles at me with tired eyes as I put a finger to my lips and then look at her.

"She looks like she had a lot of fun," he says quietly with a smile.

"She did. She's shot, but she had fun. Gotta warn you, though, she may want a cat sooner than later. She was really good with Peach."

He shakes his head, a small smile on his lips as he moves closer to sit on the couch next to me. His hand reaches out, brushing Sophie's hair back, and in her sleep, her lips tip up like she knows her dad is near, making my heart nearly explode.

"Yeah, I think I can handle her."

I snort out a quiet laugh because I listened to her spend an hour with Ava, planning on how to convince Nate to let her get a kitten. Ava gave her advice based on her own experience of forcing Jaime to fall for Princess Peach.

"Sure, bud," I say before we fall into a comfortable silence, watching a grown-ass man throw snowballs at children on television.

"What are you guys watching?" he asks.

"*Elf.*"

"God, she conned you into that? That one's the worst." He says it with a wide smile, and I feel around gently for a pillow to smack him with. He laughs quietly, and I reach for another to launch at him, hitting him square in the face this time. "Okay, okay!" he says, hands raised. "I surrender."

"*Elf* is a classic, and I will not hear you dishonor its name like that."

"It's not a rom-com, though," he says.

"Are you kidding me? It's totally a rom-com."

"So *Top Gun* isn't a romance, but *Elf* is? Isn't it about a guy who finds his dad?"

"For one, no one tragically dies in *Elf*. Yes, he goes to New York to meet his dad, but then he also meets Jovie, who doesn't like Christmas and convinces her it's the best thing with the ultimate Christmas date," I inform him, feeling self-righteous. "It's definitely in the top five Christmas romantic comedies."

"That high, huh?"

"Oh, for sure. It goes *Love Actually*, *Serendipity*, *Elf*, then *The Holiday*. *Four Christmases* comes in there, too, depending on my mood, but a relationship in distress isn't my favorite, so I have to be in the mood."

"Noted. I've only seen two of those."

"Let me guess, I'm the one who made you watch them?" He smiles, and I roll my eyes. "I'm so sorry I subjected you to my girly trash."

He reaches over, grabbing my hand, and suddenly, his face is less joking.

"It's not trash, Jules. You like it, so I like it. That's how this works. If it means I get to spend a few hours on the couch with you, I'll choose it every time." I still do not know how to reply when Nate looks at me like he means every word he's saying, but I don't have to respond as Sophie shifts in my lap.

"Hey, Soph," Nate says.

"Tired," she replies, rubbing her face further into my lap.

"All right, honey, let's get you to bed," he says, standing and scooping his daughter up from my lap and starting to move away.

"No, no," she mumbles into her dad's neck. "Jules."

"Sophie, we—"

"I want Jules to put me to bed," she says, her eyes opening and a tired panic creeping over her face as she reaches for me. "Both of you."

"Okay, girlfriend," I whisper, grabbing the small hand she extends my way. "I'll come." Her lips tip up, and if I hadn't watched her fall asleep and enter zombie mode, I would have thought it was her little matchmaker side faking it.

We easily get Sophie to bed, me tucking her in and watching Nate press a soft kiss to her forehead before she rolls over, cuddling Ashlyn to her chest.

"Thank you," he says as he steps out, clicking the door shut. "Really. I'm not usually this late, but when I am, it's nice not to have to pick her up at my mom's and then drive her home."

"It's all good. I think I had more fun than she did, if we're being honest. I wouldn't be surprised if she got enough of me to last a while."

He shakes his head with a small smile.

"Doubt it. Us Donovans could never get enough of you." I bite my lip, not sure what to say. "But really, thank you. I can tell she had a great day. I can't wait to hear all about it tomorrow."

"Anytime," I reply, meaning it, then stepping toward the back door, but his hand grabbing my wrist and pulling me close stops me.

"You can stay, you know. Finish your movie," he says, making my heart flutter.

I'd be lying if I said I hadn't been hoping he'd offer, considering how much I really like our movie nights. But also, he's been working all day, bound to be exhausted...

"You've been working all day. I'm sure you want some alone time."

He shakes his head, taking a step closer, then grabbing my hand.

"I missed you. I had alone time all day, away from you. I want my Jules time."

Something in me melts, something I refuse to look at too closely, but before I can overthink anything, Nate moves, tugging me by my hand over to the couch. Eventually, he lets go, and I awkwardly sit and start my movie. I'm confused when he walks away without a word, but I understand when he walks back five minutes later wearing a T-shirt and sweats, clearly having gotten out of his work clothes.

He moves, sitting close to me.

"We can watch something else, you know," I say, leaning forward to grab the remote and pause the show.

"Just hit play, Jules."

"You said it was stupid," I remind him.

"It is. It's about a grown-ass man who somehow didn't realize he was, like, three times bigger than every other person around him until he was thirty-something."

I glare at him. "Then why do you want to watch it?"

He looks at me, a small shake of my head before he shifts, putting an arm around my waist and tugging me until my legs are draped over his lap. My shoulder is tucked under his arm, and his chin is resting on the top of my head before he hits play on the remote I didn't realize he had grabbed from me.

"Because you like it, and I've found I can learn a lot about you just through these movies." I sigh, snuggling deeper into his strong chest, more comfortable than I should be. "Now, hush and watch your movie."

An hour later, we've barely moved, and a new movie is starting on the streaming service, something I'm grateful for because I do not want to move.

Like at all.

If I move, I might break this moment with Nate—this blissful sweet moment where I don't have to second guess or overthink every single interaction. Where I don't have to worry about if I should or if I shouldn't or worry about my past or some future we just can't have together.

His thumb has been brushing the bare skin between where my sweatshirt stops and my leggings start, and that's all I've been able to focus on since it started. The constant contact of his thumb on my sensitive skin sends my mind reeling, my body slowly shifting with each gentle movement.

But when it slides again, his calloused finger scraping and, this time, just barely dipping beneath the waistband of my leggings, my breath catches, hitching and stopping altogether.

I shift then, my body just barely turning toward his, but it's all Nate needs to put his hand to my jaw, tip my chin up, and press his lips to mine. His hand slides up so it's resting on the skin of my ribs right beneath my thin sleep bra.

When I gasp, the kiss instantly moves deeper, and suddenly, we're devouring each other. My body moves, trying to get closer to him as if some fragile thread of decency and common sense has snapped. My hand moves to his neck, pulling us even closer. He groans, and my leg shifts, trying to straddle him, but before I can, he's moving both of us until my side is to the couch, and he's lying right beside me.

With this new position, my leg can move to hook over his hip, and when I do, I feel his hard cock pressing against me, his thin sweatpants letting me feel the heat of him where I want him most of all.

He groans at the feel, his hand moving to my ass to pull me in close so I can grind on him. A low moan builds in my throat, silenced by his lips as they continue to move with mine, testing me, pleasure building in my belly.

"God," I whisper, hips bucking into him, his cock pressing right into my throbbing clit where I want him to touch me. All I can do is think about how badly I want Nate Donovan to make me come, how it's been nearly a year since I've had his hands on my skin, and how no one has touched me since.

"You're so fucking hot," he groans, his lips drifting to my neck and sucking there. His hand on my ass pulls me into him rhythmically.

"Nate," I whisper, all common sense and reality falling away as the throbbing heightens, as his hardness grinds into me.

My leg curls around him, pulling me closer to him before he shifts again until I'm on my back, his strong thigh between my legs, one hand holding himself up on the couch. His hand moves, sliding up, and he groans loudly before dipping a hand under my bra, cupping my small breast.

I've always been a bit self-conscious of my boobs, of how small they are—barely a handful—but I remember how much Nate liked them when we were together. The deep groan he lets out tells me he still does.

His fingers move, rolling along my nipple, and I moan, hips bucking to grind against the hard of his thigh. If I had any kind of shame right now, I'd be nervous about leaving a mark, but all I can think about right now is the pleasure folding in on itself, building and building.

"I've missed you so much, Jules," Nate pants into my ear. His body moves in time with mine, helping me grind on his leg, mimicking fucking me in a way that shouldn't be attractive but is somehow one of the hottest experiences of my life. "The way you feel, the way you sound. Fuck, the way you taste. It's consumed me for a year."

I groan, unable to keep up this kiss, instead panting as his lips move along my jawline, and the pleasure builds and—

Then, without my permission, I should note, his hips slow, his hand stopping pressing on my ass to drive me forward.

"We should probably stop," he whispers against my lips, his forehead pressed to mine. I pout, and he laughs. "You have an early morning and should probably get to bed."

He's right: I have an early class, and he's been working all day, but even so, I can't convince myself to move. I have no desire to do anything other than lay on this couch and kiss Nate, feel him...and maybe some more. *All common sense has left my head.*

"Yeah," I whisper, but don't move. "Or we could..."

He chuckles, the feeling vibrating through me and making my body melt further into his, pulling a groan from him.

"Jules, as much as I would love to fuck you right here on this couch, we're not doing that. Not now, and surely not here."

I pout, shifting my body to see if I could maybe convince him to change his mind. I'm past common sense, past reality.

He presses a kiss to my lips, a hard, quick one, before shifting my leg from his hip and standing before me on the couch, giving me a hand. In his gray sweats, I can see his hard cock jutting out, causing my belly to flip again.

"Come on, gorgeous. Let's get you tucked in."

"Will you do the tucking?" I ask with a smile.

He shakes his head, then reaches down, grabbing me and lifting me until I'm standing. He presses his lips to mine briefly before grabbing my hand and walking me to slip on shoes.

"No, I'll be leaving you at your door because I can't trust myself near a bed with you. And Jules? The next time I fuck you, I'm doing it when you can moan my name loud because no one else is home." I bite my lip at his words, and he leans down once again, giving me a gentle kiss. "But if you agree to keep it PG tonight after I jack off in the shower, I'll call you. We can talk all night if you want. I feel I've already fucked up pushing you too far, too fast."

A rush of warmth runs through me, and I smile.

"Deal."

Then he walks me to the cottage on shaky knees, giving me another chaste kiss before pushing me inside and waiting for me to close and lock the door behind me.

And when I do, letting out a small squeal of excitement, I hear his deep laugh as he walks back to his house.

Thirty minutes later, he calls me, and although we don't stay on the phone all night, it's well past midnight when I do finally fall asleep with a smile on my lips.

TWENTY-EIGHT

NATE

"We gotta talk, Dad," Sophie says the next day as I make her lunch.

I look over my shoulder at her, raising an eyebrow at her stern tone, and see she's glaring at me.

"Oh yeah?" I ask, and she nods emphatically.

"Yeah. We're cutting things close, you know."

I turn back to the sandwich in front of me, spreading peanut butter on the bread and fighting a laugh. "Things?" I never know what crazy shit is going to come out of Sophie's mouth, but I always love to hear it.

"Jules isn't in love with you yet," she declares. "And that's because you're doing it all wrong!"

I fail, letting out a small laugh, and I move on to the jelly. She's not completely wrong: there hasn't been a major breakthrough between us, no confession of love or outward acceptance of something between us, but I'm okay with it. My sisters and Sophie might think I need to go full speed ahead, but I'm playing it cautious, afraid to scare off Jules before she lets her walls down. Instead, I'm basking in the small wins, like her calling me at night and talking all night about absolutely nothing or watching movies in my lap.

"And how am I doing it wrong, exactly?"

"You haven't even taken her on a date," my daughter, who is much too wise for her age, nearly shouts. "You gotta take her out. Give her a grand gesture. That's how you make a girl fall in love with you."

I slide the sandwich into a zip-top bag, put it into her lunchbox, and close it before turning to face my daughter, arms crossed on my chest as I lean on the counter.

I sent Jules a text this morning asking if she wanted to get coffee, but considering we were up late as can be talking on the phone, I think she's probably sleeping in. Last night she told me she didn't have much going on today except for the holiday party for her kids tonight at the center, which is why I planned on taking her to get coffee and try my hand at a bit more wooing before she has to go.

"What do you know about grand gestures?" I ask.

"Jules taught me all about them. In all of the movies, that's how the guy wins the girl. You're never going to convince Jules to stay forever if you don't give her a grand gesture!"

I sigh, knowing my daughter is not going to like what I have to say next. Neither do I, if I'm being honest.

"Soph, I need to make sure you know that after Christmas, Jules is going to move into her house again." Her eyes go wide, and I see the dramatics start to win. "Eventually, if things go the way I'm hoping, she'll move in with us for real, but she's got a place of her own, baby. And the dance studio. The deal was she'd live in the cottage until things were all done."

She glares at me now, moving from sad to annoyed.

"But," I say, cutting off whatever rampage I know is impending. "But if we play our cards right, she'll be back." *I've got a plan, kid. Just give it some time.*

The plan is a bit hazy, if I'm being honest, and changes day-to-day to fit what I think Jules is ready for, but it's there. She takes in my words before finally, thankfully, nodding as if she now agrees we're on the same page.

"Well, then, what's your plan?" she asks, arms crossing her chest to mimic mine.

"My plan?"

She sighs as if I'm the most exhausting person on this planet.

"Your plan, Dad. To make her fall in love with you. You've gotta take her out."

I could brush her off, but considering Sophie has spent a good chunk of time with Jules, too, lately, I decided to pick her brain. Maybe I can get some good ideas from her.

"What are you thinking?" I ask. "I'm planning to take her to coffee and on a date today. What should I add?"

She smiles deviously.

"I've got an idea," she says like she's been waiting for this question, and I can't help but laugh.

Fifteen minutes later, I'm just getting off the phone, and Sophie is sliding on her jacket when Jules shuffles in the backdoor in sweats and a pair of slippers. As if she rolled right out of bed into the main house without much of a hesitation. I love that—how she's eager to get here and how she's getting more comfortable in my place.

"Jules!" Sophie yells, dropping her jacket altogether and running to hug her legs. "I thought I was going to miss you before school."

Jules's hand moves, gently brushing back Sophie's hair I had to do myself this morning, much to her dismay, and smiling down at her.

"I'm sorry, sweetie. I was more tired than I thought, I guess. I usually wake up without an alarm, but I was out like a light. I was up really late last night." Over my daughter's head, I give Jules a knowing smile, and she blushes.

She's so fucking cute.

"Well, today, you need to go with my dad," Sophie says, fists on her hips and glaring up.

"Do I now?"

"Soph," I warn. "I've got it." The girl can be a great wingwoman, but with Jules, we gotta play it smart, not overwhelm her. She shifts her glare to me, and I glare back, a battle I win for once when she rolls her eyes and sighs.

"Fine."

"Now, come on. Get your jacket on, and grab your backpack. You don't want to miss the bus." I look to Jules, holding up the discarded jacket as Sophie slides her arms in. "Want to get coffee and check your place out today? I'll explain all of this"—my hand moves in the direction of my daughter—"then."

"Yeah, I'd love that. I have the cast party at six, but until then, I'm all yours," she says with a smile.

"All right, perfect. Go get dressed, and we'll meet back here in ten." She nods, sleep still in her eyes. "And Jules? Dress warm."

Once I get Sophie on the bus, I step back into the house to see Jules waiting for me in a pair of thick leggings, an oversized cream-colored sweater with a thick jacket over the top, her hair loose and long. It's casual and so very Jules, and she's never looked more gorgeous.

When I get close to her, I smile and grab her hand, tugging her to me before pressing her back to the door as I close it and covering her body with mine. When I press my lips to hers, she tastes like the mint of her toothpaste and the strawberry lip balm she likes so much, and I get lost in it.

We stay like that for long minutes, with a good morning kiss and then some before I pull back, pressing my forehead to hers and smiling. This is what I want for us: this easy, free feeling, kissing her without her hesitation, without her second-guessing. I want this every fucking day, and I'm doing whatever it takes to get this. Yesterday, I had to fight with myself not to let things go further, not to make her come on my thigh, because I'm not sure how she'll react to it, or if that would be too much, too fast. I feel like I'm walking a careful tightrope with Jules sometimes, but my eyes are on the prize at the end.

Her.

"Hey," I say eventually.

"Hey," she whispers, then clears her throat. "So, what is going on? I feel like I walked into a trap."

I smile wide at her, grabbing her hand and leading her out of the front door and to my car.

"I mean, you kind of did. Sophie yelled at me this morning, told me I'm fucking up making her Christmas miracle come true because I haven't taken you out on a proper date."

"A cardinal sin," she says with a small smile.

"Yeah, nothing like the movies, as you know. Apparently, all of the movies have a grand gesture, and that's where I'm slacking."

"Oh, is that right?" she asks, her smile widening, the words playful as her arms stay looped behind my neck, and hope ignites in my gut again.

I just need to maintain this lighthearted, easy way with her. Jules only shuts down when she starts to think we're moving too fast or when she gets nervous. If I can keep her comfortable and prevent her from overthinking, I think we can work to get past her fears. I help her into my truck, closing the door behind her and walking to the driver's side.

"So I figured I could appease her, I suppose, take you to coffee," I say jokingly, and she giggles. "Then we can go check on your place before you head out to your party. My mom is picking up Sophie today, so I don't have to be back until later," I say as I pull out of the drive and make my way to downtown Evergreen Park.

With a wide smile, she reaches over and grabs my hand, holding it gently.

"I can be on board with that," she says.

TWENTY-NINE

JULES

When we pull into a parking garage in downtown Evergreen Park, the butterflies start, which is silly because we're just getting coffee. Plus, this is Nate we're talking about, the man I've had coffee with almost every morning this month. The one I've spent more time with in the past month than I have with any of the people who matter most in my life.

Still, he smiles at me, and my stomach flips as if he's some stranger I have a crush on.

It's a reminder of just how fucked I am.

When we step out of the car, Nate gives me a goofy grin, and I can't help but return it as he grabs a plaid and fur trapper hat. He slides it on his head before he grabs my hand and starts leading me toward the exit.

"What's with the hat?"

"I'm getting into character."

"Into character?" I ask, confused.

"We don't have time to go on a full-out movie date, but this will do." I feel it then, my heart skipping a beat, yet another part of me falling for him despite the risks.

This was a bad idea, the cautious voice inside my head that sounds a lot like my mother says.

"How much time did you guys have to plan this?"

He smiles wide.

"Fifteen minutes, maybe. She approached me about my slacking while eating breakfast. I think she'd been planning to ambush me about my lack of effort when you weren't around."

"Hmm," I say. "Sounds very Sophie." So what's this grand plan you got together?"

"Buddy took Jovie on a date through New York based on what he thought was the best date ever."

Another skipped beat of my heart as I stare at him, my books clicking on the concrete as we walk out of the garage and into downtown. Everyone is preparing for the town lighting and every surface is wrapped in garland and lights, making it look like a winter wonderland. The only thing missing is a dusting of snow.

"We're not in New York," he continues, "but I have to say I think most people would agree Evergreen Park at Christmas time is even better than the city."

I don't disagree: While I made the trek to Rockefeller Center in December, the bustling crowds and utter chaos of New York weren't for me.

I prefer our cozy small town.

"So we're..." I start.

"First, we're going to get the best cup of coffee," he says as we turn a block and see my favorite coffee shop glowing brightly.

In the front is a chalkboard bistro sign that reads *Best coffee in the world, as proclaimed by Jules Everett! Come in and get the Jules Latte, one pump vanilla, one pump almond!*

My heart stops beating, I think.

"When did you do this?" I ask, but he ignores me, continuing to explain our upcoming date.

"Then we're going to go look at the windows on Main Street and come to a consensus on who decorated theirs best. We'll go through the revolving doors at Evergreen Department Store, but only once, twice max." He smiles at me, and I give him a shaky one back because I feel the wave of uncontrollable emotion coming. "It would be a bummer for our date to be cut short because I got arrested."

"Yeah, probably. I don't think your sisters would like me anymore if I got you arrested," I say breathlessly.

"Not true, they'd definitely blame me. But then we're going to lunch at the diner. I thought about taking you to a steakhouse or something fancy, but it didn't feel very *Elf*. So we're getting pasta, though the maple syrup on top is optional."

"Thank god for that," I say with a smile as we stop outside the coffee shop. "So you're taking me on the *Elf* date?"

"I know you like *Love Actually*, but I think *Elf* is much more of a romantic comedy."

"You said it was stupid."

"And then I watched it with you, and it wasn't," he says, his voice low, his eyes sincere. I bite the inside of my cheek to fight another wave of emotion but clearly fail. "Hey, hey, I'm sorry. Fuck. I'm fucking this up." He pulls me in close. "I think *Love Actually* is great! Really! If you want, we can skip all of this and go back home and watch it. Three times if you want! This was silly, I—"

I push on his chest and glare up at him.

"Absolutely not, Nathan Donovan. I'm not upset, I'm...overwhelmed."

He raises an eyebrow at me.

"Overwhelmed?"

"Yeah, I mean, this..." I wave my hand at the coffee shop. "You didn't have to do this. It's too much."

He looks at me, confused, before shaking his head.

"It's a sign at a coffee shop, Jules. It's not too much."

"Nate, it—"

"It's not too much. Nothing is too much for you, Jules. You deserve the world. You deserve your life to be the most romantic, cinematic masterpiece that was ever created, and I'm making it my mission to help you see that."

"Nate," I start, but he shakes his head.

"You deserve magic," he says low.

"Magic?"

"You said you'll make Christmas magic for Sophie, but not for you. So I'm making it for you because that's what you deserve, Jules. The fantasy of your favorite movies but in your real life. Every day. The second you give me the go-ahead, dollface, I'll make every day a movie for you. Until then, I'm taking you on this date. "Then he presses his lips to mine, silencing me before he grabs my hand and tugs me into the coffee shop.

As always, the coffee is spectacular, but we get it to go with a not-so-hidden wink from my favorite barista before we wander mainstream to check out the storefronts.

I've passed them a dozen times since Thanksgiving, but I haven't had a chance to meander and check out all of the cute, intricate details the shops always make sure to include. After perusing all the shops, we decide that the flower shop, Evergreen Grows, has the best display.

"They're so pretty!" I say, gawking over the blooms and leaves, both real and artificial, mixed with fake snow and painted cardboard to make the most magical storefront. "Look! Those peonies are gorgeous, even if they're fake. They're my favorite," I say with a smile.

When he's quiet, I look over to see he's taking his phone out and opening a screen, looking like he has a mission.

"What are you doing?" I ask with a smile, watching him diligently tap on his phone with determination. "Is everything okay?" Maybe he got a text about Sophie or—

"Just making a note," he says.

"What?"

"A note. I don't want to forget what kind of flowers you like."

"You don't..." I start, confused. He turns his phone to face me, and I see my name on the top of a notes app. My hand reaches out to grab it. "What is that?" He tries to pull it away, but I've already got it, pulling it from his reach and looking at the list.

Jules Likes is the title of the note, and below are various items.

Coffee: milk, one pump vanilla, one pump almond.
Snack: snowcaps with popcorn
Movie: romantic comedies
Christmas movie: Love Actually or Serendipity
Color: Pink or purple

It continues, a dozen or so minute things I've probably mentioned in passing, ending in Flowers: peonies.

"When did you start this?" I ask, but I'm already tapping at the top to see the creation date when my hand stills, my breath caught in my lungs.

January 1 of this year.

The morning after we met.

That's why coffee is the first one: I mentioned it first thing that morning. His hand gently reaches out, grabbing his phone from my still hands. My eyes move to him, a sheepish smile on his lips.

"I wanted to make sure I didn't forget anything important."

"How I take my coffee isn't important, Nate," I tell him, but my voice doesn't sound like it belongs to me. Instead, it's breathier and shocked.

"It is to me. Everything about you is important to me, Jules." He keeps staring at me, and I wonder if he knows how much he's impacting me, how he's changing me and making me shift how I view things and how I believe I should be treated and valued.

"Come on. Let's go get lunch."

We go to the diner, where he clearly has connections there as well, since the table in the back corner had a white tablecloth instead of the normal laminate, and we were served pasta, complete with

M&Ms and maple syrup on the side. He gave me the cutest, goofiest smile.

The next stop is ice skating, where I quickly learn that I don't know how to skate, but I get to have Nate's hands on my hips the entire time, which is a win all around. I giggle as he effortlessly glides me around, telling me how he played hockey in high school just to try and get girls, an effort that backfired when he realized between his job at the grocery store, practice, and homework, he had no time for girls, so it only lasted a year. But, it taught him how to skate, "which, right about now, is serving me really well."

When I shiver one too many times, we step off the ice, and he insists on unlacing my boots for me before finally and slightly begrudgingly, we make our way to my place so I can check things out before I have to head over to the community center for the cast party.

THIRTY

NATE

"It's actually... not terrible," she says with a smile, stepping around her place.

I don't tell her I cleaned up immensely the last time I was here, throwing out anything that might reveal the level of damage. The pipe that broke must have been leaking for some time, making it more susceptible to bursting because there was a good amount of dried water damage in the area. I don't tell her, of course, that the town came here a few days ago and approved the updates. Even though it still needs a good cleanup and some paint, it's mostly done.

"What did you think I've been doing this whole time?" I ask with a laugh, and she shrugs.

"I hadn't really thought of it. I've been a bit...distracted."

"I like you distracted. But go, check things out. Just watch out for tools and whatnot," I say, tipping my chin toward where she's walking. "There's shit everywhere."

She looks over my shoulder at me.

"Don't worry, I'm a dancer—" Jules doesn't finish her sentence as she falls forward, tripping on a box and catching herself with her hands on a sheet of plywood. Running over, I grab her and her help up.

"Are you okay?" I say as she looks at me with wide eyes. She nods.

"Yeah, I think I just wasn't paying attention." My lips tip up as I grab her hands, but my face moves from humor to concern when she flinches. Turning her hands over, I see one has a splinter. I move toward the kitchen, sitting her down on the kitchen counter to get a better look.

"I'm fine, really."

"Humor me, okay?" I ask, turning to grab a first aid kit and fumbling inside to find a pair of tweezers, an alcohol wipe, and a Band-Aid.

"It's just a splinter, Nate."

"I told you. When you're with me, if you get hurt, I take care of you," I say, quoting what I said to her that first night we were together.

I take her hand again and stretch the skin of her palm so the splinter is clear. It's barely in, mostly just sticking out, but still, I gently grasp it with tweezers and pull. Then I grab the wipe, clean it, and put a Band-Aid on the spot. When I'm all done, I lift her hand to my lips.

"My hero," she says sarcastically. "You know, you seem to like this, fixing injuries and helping damsels in distress."

I smile at the reminder of the first time we were together.

"Yeah, I guess. But only with you." I move to get closer to her, standing between her legs. The counter brings her to the perfect height, and I fight the urge to think about possibilities as her hands move up, hooking around my neck.

"Is that so?" she asks with a teasing smile.

"Oh, definitely," I murmur, then drop my head, pressing my lips to hers.

It's not a gentle kiss, but an intense all-consuming one. My mind loses track of time and space and common sense as an arm moves to her back, pulling her closer to me.

My tongue intertwines with her, tasting coffee, chocolate, and her strawberry lip balm. She sighs into my mouth as my other hand moves to her hair holding her where I want her, need her, so I can take what I want.

She arches her back, pressing into me, and I groan, getting already hard at the small mewl that comes from her. I continue to kiss her, our tongues battling against each other like we can't get enough, my teeth nipping at her lip, her breathing getting heavier.

My lips move to kiss down her jaw, up to her ear, her fingers gripping my hair.

"God, I can't get enough of you," I groan into her neck, my hand slipping up her sweatshirt and under her tee, only to find she isn't wearing a real bra, just a thin bralette. My hand moves up, thumbing over the peaked nipple and dragging a moan from her.

"I need—" she starts, and I know I would give her anything, absolutely anything she asks. There's something about her sitting before me on a counter just like that first time that has something in me snapping.

"I know what you need, Jules." My hand moves to her knee, her leggings a thin barrier as I tentatively slide up, my thumb grazing over the seam. She moans, hips moving to get more and I smile, pressing my lips to the pounding pulse in her neck.

"You need me to play with you? Don't you?"

"Yes," she whispers. "Yes, Nate." My head dips, planting kisses along her neck, her head tipping to the side to give me better access. My thumb presses down on the seam right over her clit, her hips shifting to get more contact. "Oh god."

"Fuck, you're already so wet for me, aren't you? I can feel it on my thumb, through your leggings." I press on her center, pushing her underwear into her cunt and feeling her pulse through the fabric. My hand moves up, hesitating at the top of her leggings. "Is this..."

"Please, Nate. Please, please touch me. I need it."

"You sound so pretty, begging for me to finger fuck you. Who am I to deny you?" My fingers slide under the waistband, right into her panties, until the front of my fingers rubs over her swollen clit. "Jesus, baby. Kissing me got you this wet, didn't it?"

"Yes," she whispers. "Take them off," she says, lifting her hips, and I oblige, my hand moving to the waistband of her leggings and tugging them and her panties down until they're around her calves.

I step back just a bit to take her in and look at my handy work, but a small growl comes from her lips as she reaches out, grabbing the front of my sweatshirt and tugging me toward her until my lips crash into hers. I let out a laugh as her mouth moves along mine, but she's clearly past the point of joking and niceties. Her hand moves to grab mine, moving it down her belly and toward her wet pussy.

She lets go when the tip of one finger hits the top of her close-cut curls, and I take over, sliding along her slit slowly, up and down, then circling her entrance, not touching her clit. I tease her for a moment before finally sliding two fingers inside.

"So fucking perfect," I nearly whisper as I slide the fingers out, then back in slowly, her head lolling back. I move slightly back to watch as I continue my slow ministrations, looking down to watch my fingers move in and out, feeling her pussy tighten around me. I continue my slow and torturous pace before her hips buck, trying to get more, get my fingers deeper into her.

I chuckle, reveling in this. "My baby wants more, doesn't she?"

"Yes," she moans, moving a hand down her belly to try and touch her clit while I finger fuck her.

"No, no. Not until I say so. Hands on the counter." She groans but doesn't fight me, making me smile as I watch her hand move to the countertop, the back of her head resting on the cabinet behind her.

"So good, aren't you?" I reward her with three fingers, sliding them in once slowly before starting to fuck her with them, curling the fingers and swiping over her swollen g-spot.

"Fuck!" she shouts, making me smile.

"That's it, baby. You feel so fucking good. I can't wait to have you on my cock again soon." The thought alone has me throbbing. I've been trying to take things as slow as Jules needed, but feeling her wrapped around my fingers, moaning my name, has me feeling suddenly impatient.

"Yeah. Yes. Nate, please, fuck me."

I groan loudly, wanting that but knowing that's not what this is.

This is making Jules feel good, reminding her how fucking good we are together, and, admittedly, a bit of torture for myself. This is me telling her I can behave as long as she needs me to, even if that just means making her feel good until she's comfortable enough for more.

"No, no. Not today. Not now. This is just for you." She starts to argue, but then my thumb moves, swiping across her swollen clit. Her hips buck, a squeal leaving her lips, and I smile.

"Lean back," I finally say, groaning when she plants one of her hands further back behind her on the counter, widening her legs to give me more room. She moans when I slide back in, hooking my fingers and hitting a new spot with the new angle.

"Nate," she pants, and I can't do anything but look at the beautiful fucking sight of her spread for me, my fingers deep inside her pussy. Her hips start to move, fucking herself on them.

"That's it, baby. Ride them," I say low.

"Clit," she whispers. "My clit. Please." Because she asks so nicely, I give in.

"You can rub it, baby," I tell her, then watch her eyes drift shut as her hand slides down from where it's been pinching her nipple beneath her sweatshirt to her clit.

She moans loudly.

"Oh god, baby, you should see how pretty you look. Your fingers rubbing yourself, me three fingers deep, your cunt stretch around them."

"Nate," she whines, clearly close to the edge, and I can't take it anymore.

"Make yourself come, Julianne," I demand, watch her fingers speed up on her clit. "But do it looking at me." Those eyes snap open, her pretty browns locking on mine, her lips parted, and then I feel it when her eyes stop on mine. Her pussy tightens, her entire body going still except for her hand that rubs harder and faster as she cries out, my fingers sliding in deep and pressing on her g-spot as she comes.

"Nate," she screams.

I've never heard anything prettier than my name on Juliann Everett's lips when she comes.

And as she pants my name with each small aftershock, all I can think is how I cannot wait to do it again.

And again.

And again.

THIRTY-ONE

JULES

I'm panting as Nate slides his fingers out of me, my body still gently pulsing with pleasure, but my breath catches when I watch him lift those fingers, slide them into his mouth, and lick them clean.

His eyes are locked on mine to gauge my reaction, and his lips tip up when he gets the one he was clearly hoping for.

My eyes move down to his jeans, a thick outline there that I really want to see. And touch. And taste.

"Now..." I start, eyes drifting from his eyes down, implying it's now his turn.

But then, because my phone is a cockblocking bitch, the alarm goes off, reminding me Ava and Harper will be at the community center in an hour to help set up for the cast and crew holiday party.

He smiles and shakes his head.

"As much as I'd like that—and trust me, Jules, I would really fucking like that—the first time I come with you since last having you is going to be in your pussy, in my bed."

My breath hitches, my mouth dropping with his words.

He smiles wider.

"Now. Do you need anything while we're here?" I shake my

head, still a bit speechless, and he smiles. "Perfect. Go clean up in the bathroom, and then I'll take you to the center."

I nod and do as he asks, moving to the small bathroom off the side of the kitchen while I hear him wash his hands in the kitchen, moving things around.

"You know, I bet this place would rent well," he says as I wash my hands.

"What?"

"Or you could turn it into a few more studios. Or a lounge for the dancers or your teachers."

I'm drying my hands as I step out, brows furrowed in confusion, giving him a small smile.

"That's great and all, but where would I live?" I ask with a laugh.

"Well, you'd move in with us," he says like it's the obvious answer, and my entire body stills, whatever happy endorphins are left from my orgasm flying out the window instantly.

"Move in?"

"Not right now, of course," he says casually, but my panic is so all-consuming I barely register his words. "But someday, this place will be empty. You could easily rent it out to cover your mortgage. Or expand, add another studio, or make this your office." He looks around like he can already envision it.

I stay silent, my pulse pounding at the reality of where we are, of where he thinks we are. Eventually, he looks at me, his eyes going wide, stepping closer, clearly seeing my nerves.

"Oh, Jules, I don't mean now. I just mean eventually. When you're ready. When we're ready." He steps closer, but I step back, trying to move away from him. My heart is pounding as I realize what he's suggesting.

"Eventually," I say, my voice low, cold panic creeping in my veins. Eventually isn't a maybe; it's a certainty. He thinks that, at the end of the day, that's where this is heading. He's talking about a future between him and me. One where I'm moving in with him and his daughter.

"That's...that's where this is heading, Jules. Right?" he asks, stepping forward, and I step back once more.

The panic continues to build.

How did we get here?

One minute I was safe, building First Position and cheering my friends on and avoiding even the faintest whisper of dating, keeping myself safe in my little fantasy world, and then Nate is here and talking about *eventually*.

How did this happen? How did we go from safe and strictly platonic to him fingering me on my kitchen counter and talking about moving in together?

This is too much.

This is too fast.

"This is moving too fast," I say, feeling like I'm floating, checking out.

"What is this, Jules?" he asks quietly, a hint of defeat in the words that make me want to say, *just kidding*!

But I can't. As much as I want to, I can't. I need to let common sense win. I've been letting my emotions win too often these past weeks, and that's exactly how I got hurt last time.

Building this with Nate, or even thinking about building anything with Nate, is far too dangerous for me. The last time I let myself fall into romantic daydreams, I couldn't get out of bed for a month except to go to work.

The last time I lost Nate, I built a wall around myself and swore off romance. What happens if I lose him again?

"This is you helping me out with my place and giving me a place to stay. It's me watching Sophie in return and helping with her Christmas wish because she deserves that little bit of magic." I explain our original agreement.

"Jules, come here," he says, an arm out to me. I shake my head. "Jules, baby. Please. Come here."

"No! No. No touching," I say, stepping back, and Nate fights a small smile.

"No touching?"

"No! Because every time you touch me, my brain goes scrambled, and I lose all common sense."

"Your brain goes scrambled when I touch you?" he asks, the smile winning and humor in his words. He thinks I'm joking, that I'm being silly and flirty, but I mean it. When Nate isn't holding me, when I'm not under his spell, I can think straight. I can see a future where if I let myself fall completely, I could get hurt. When he holds me, all of that goes out the window, leaving me lost in just how good being his feels.

"Yes! Every time you touch me, my snaps fail, and I make dumb decisions. Dumb, unsafe decisions. And if you touch me right now, you're going to convince me it's all okay and everything will be just fine, but we can't do this."

The humor in the atmosphere around him fades quickly, and he looks at me differently now.

"I thought you just said it was moving too fast. Now we can't do this at all?" I cross my arms on my chest and avoid looking at him, but he steps closer, bending a bit to force me to look at him. "Why are you so dead set on keeping your wall up, Jules? You're safe. You're safe with me."

He says it with so much conviction, so much softness and kindness, and I know he thinks that, but I also know the truth. Real life isn't like the movies. It's scarier, and a safe happily ever after isn't promised. It's safer to keep my heart protected at all costs.

His hand reaches out, the now familiar calloused hand tipping my chin up to look at him, and then, finally, I break.

"Because I could barely leave my bed for weeks last time, and we barely spent a weekend together, Nate. What happens next time if this falls apart?" The words come out louder than I intended, and I pause, breathing heavily and taking in his shocked face before continuing. "I saw what losing my dad did to my mom, how it changed her as a person, and I don't want that to happen to me. I'm not the same as I was a year ago. I'm not an idiot, believing in signs and messages when there's nothing there. I stay rooted in reality, where I can't get hurt that way again.

"This? This is great, Nate. You're great, and one day, you're going to make someone *so* fucking happy. You deserve someone who can trust in everything you can give her and not be looking over her shoulder, waiting for the other shoe to drop. Because with me? It always fucking drops. And I'm tired of picking up the pieces when it does."

"Okay," he says, low and easy before he stares at me, his hand still on my chin, reading every flash of emotion and thought and shift of my eyes.

I worry I went too far, exposed too much, and for a split second, I regret my words, even if I believe it to be all true and for the best.

"Okay?" I ask, my stomach dropping, and he nods.

"Okay."

"What? Okay, what?"

"Okay. I see it. You're terrified, and this is moving too fast."

My mouth drops open, and I gape at him.

"I don't—" I start, but he shakes his head and smiles.

The man is smiling. Why is he like this??

"We'll slow this down. We'll do this your way." With that, he moves, walking closer to me before his hand moves to my jaw, barely a graze, but I feel it all the same. "But know, I know it's a lie," he whispers, empathy and guilt clear as day in his eyes.

"What?"

"That's a lie. It's all a lie you're telling yourself to try and protect yourself. You know this is right, the same way I do. You know that if you just trust that what we have is special and real, you won't get hurt. But the trusting part? That's what you can't get past. Your fear is stopping you from just *jumping in*."

I can't handle that, the small bit of proof that he sees so much more than I want him to, so I look away from him. He doesn't let me for long, though, instead once more moving to my chin, grabbing it firmer this time and forcing me to look at him.

"But I'll be here, Jules, when you're ready. Waiting for you. And when you're ready to jump, I'll catch you." After a long moment, he steps back from me. "Now, are you ready to go?"

My brow furrows. "What?"

"You have your party. I'm driving you to the center." I shake my head, the idea of being stuck in the car with him after all of this horrifying.

"You don't have to drive me, Nate. I can walk; it's only a few blocks."

He smiles at me softly, grabbing his work bag off the floor.

"I know. But I want to."

"Nate—"

"Just humor me, Jules."

He stares at me until I sigh and nod, grabbing my bag and sliding my jacket back on before we head out the door in near silence.

When we get to the community center, I fiddle with my keys as he parks, then walks around to the passenger side to pull me out. Once I'm out, he leans into me, pressing his lips to mine gently, and I revel in it. I'm already craving more when he breaks the chaste kiss, and that's when I know I'm so fucking screwed.

"I'll call you tonight. We can talk," he says, and I shake my head.

"I can't, I won't be home until late." It's not a lie per se, but saying it aloud after whatever just happened in my place feels like one.

But I need space. I need time. I need to think.

He must know that because he nods before speaking. "Then we'll talk in the morning when you come over for coffee."

I smile weakly and nod. He presses his lips to mine once more before walking me to the front entrance of the community center.

"Later, Jules," he whispers.

"Later, Nate. Thanks for...today."

"Anytime, dollface."

He pulls me into his arms, and I take a deep inhale of Nate's woodsy scent as he presses a kiss to the top of my head before stepping back. And then I watch him walk off, start the car, and wave as he drives away.

THIRTY-TWO

JULES

The party goes fine, both Harper and Ava coming to help out, and I'm relieved when I don't have to spend too much time with them, constantly getting pulled one way or the other.

I know the second they get me alone, one or both of them are going to try and pick my brain, and I'm scared of that.

I'm scared for Ava to tell me to jump in without fear or confirm I'm just a big baby, letting my old wound be an excuse for why I'm not going all in with Nate.

But I'm also scared for the more cynical Harper to give me her opinion, to tell me I'm right to be cautious considering everything that's happened, the way I got hurt last time.

And as I wave off the last kid, wishing him and his family a great holiday, I walk back into the center knowing my time is up.

"Okay, what's going on?" Ava asks as we start cleaning up the community center together.

"What?" I ask, tossing a greasy paper plate from the pizza I bought the kids into the trash.

"What's going on? You're moping around like you've just been dumped, but you aren't even dating anyone. Unless…"

The statement hangs in the air, waiting for me to fill it with the truth we all know, but I don't answer, and Ava continues.

"Unless you started something with Mister Hot Dad, and you're so stuck in your head you don't even want to talk to us about it."

I keep moving, grabbing cups and dumping them into the sink in the corner before tossing them.

"I think that's pretty obvious, Ava," Harper says. "They started something the day she agreed to their little deal."

Ava nods, tossing a chip from the bowl into her mouth and chewing thoughtfully.

"Here's my theory: you got in there, and it all felt the same as it did in January. It was like there wasn't a whole year between the two of you. And that was all fine until it started to feel a little too real. And then you, our sweet, soft-hearted, scaredy-cat girl, keep thinking about the what-ifs."

I glare at her but don't respond.

"Let me guess: he gave you an ultimatum? Make a decision or get out?" Harper guesses.

"Oh, if he did, you have to get rid of him, that's not—" Ava starts, but I can't take it anymore.

"No!" I say finally, the urge to stick up for Nate is all-consuming. "No, he didn't do that. He'd never do that, you guys. Everything is... everything is great." Ava tips her head at me, brows furrowed, clearly not believing me. "They are! We even went on a date today," I say, trying to act normal, even though the reminder of our conversation from a few hours ago makes my stomach hurt.

Nate wants more.

Nate wants more and wants me to admit I want more, but I don't know if I can. If I'll ever be emotionally ready to take that leap, to take the risk. I've been acting this entire month like it's just some silly fantasy world, but the reminder that I would be moving back to my place eventually and that we were already in the deep end was a dose of reality I wasn't prepared for.

"Then what is it, Jules? I can't figure it out. Why are you moping around like someone killed your dog if everything is so great?"

"He said we'd be moving in together."

"Okay? That feels obvious, Jules. He has a daughter, and your place isn't that big. Did he say it had to be soon? Or that you had to get rid of First Position?"

"No. He was mentioning I could rent out my place or build a lounge or more studios."

"Okay...? That seems like the ideal situation, Jules. What's wrong?"

"I just...I didn't expect it. I hadn't really thought of this moving beyond Christmas. I told him from the start I didn't want this to be anything because I want to focus on my friends and my—"

"Oh my god, can we stop with this lie?" Harper snaps, exasperated.

"What?"

"It's a lie, Jules. You aren't focusing on us or your business. You're focusing on finding any excuse you can to keep your heart safe."

The brutal honesty hits hard, and I still as my friends walk over to me. Ava reaches over and grabs my hand, and I feel it then: the wobble of my chin.

"I know in January, when you thought you found something special and then thought it was all a lie, you were hurt. And it changed you, Jules. We all saw it." Harper nods. "We saw you shut down and build a wall up. But I also saw you with them last week, and I saw that wall was down, babe. So what's going on? It seemed like everything was going well."

I take a deep breath before confessing. "I'm scared."

"Well, duh. You feel everything deep, Jules. It's your superpower," Harper says.

"My superpower?"

"I've never met anyone with more empathy than you. I've never met anyone who sees fairy tales in everyday moments and who believes in the best of things. Ava, she's our go-getter. I don't even think she thinks the sky is the limit. She sees something, she wants it, she gets it. She saw Jaime and made that man hers.

"I am the realist: I overanalyze and pick everything apart, and it's worked out well for me. I have Jeremy, and I have the fashion line, and I'm happy."

I don't touch on how she doesn't even seem to be convincing herself on that.

"But you, Jules, you're the dreamer, the optimist. You see the best in everyone, and in the past year, you've seen that as a weakness. You've hidden it so far, and we were worried it would be gone forever. But it's back, and you seem...like you again. Your romanticism isn't a weakness, Jules. It helps you see the real potential of things and turn them into reality. Just look at this place," she says, waving her hand at the mess left from the party. "First Position was just a daydream, what, three? Four years ago? And now it's booming. You're proving everyone wrong, and that's because you liked this run-down building and knew the potential."

"And look what happened," I say with a scoff. "I didn't know what I was doing, and it flooded."

"There's mishaps in even the most angst-free movies, Jules. If this was a movie, that would be the beginning of your own fairy tale. You just have to be brave enough to take the leap."

I wait long moments before finally, *finally*, I confess what's been eating at me for a year.

I felt the way I changed when I thought Nate broke my heart, and I didn't like the road I felt I could fall down.

"What if it turns me into her?" I whisper.

"What?"

"My mom. What if I get my heart broken and I turn into her? Turning marriages into opportunities and using people. I remember that she used to believe in love. And now she's some Stepford robot."

Ava rolls her eyes like that's a ridiculous question.

"You could never turn into her. Have you met you, Jules? You're a hopeless romantic. You believe in true love at every turn, except when it's looking you dead in the eyes." Harper glares at me like even *she* knows that what Ava is saying is true.

"You think Nate's my true love, too?" I ask.

She sighs, looking out the window and not at me when she answers.

"I think I'm too much of a realist to believe in something as grand as that, but if I did, I'd think you found it. I think Ava found it. I don't think whatever higher being that exists would put Nate in your path twice if there wasn't a reason. I know that when you lost him, your mood had never been worse."

I glare at her and smile.

"I think tomorrow you have to put on your big girl panties and talk to him. Tell him what you just told us and that you're scared, but you want to try." That makes my stomach flip. "You tell him you're crazy in love with him and it's scary, but that being scared is a part of life."

"I'm sorry, *what?*" I ask, that stomach pit turning into full-blown nausea. Ava rolls her eyes.

"Harp, she's clearly not ready to address *that* truth right now," she says. "Even if we all know it is true. And Jules, he loves you too, which I think you know."

Do I know that? Do I know that Nate loves me? Or that I love him? That's crazy, right? A month ago, I was swearing off even the *idea* of love, and now...

"But...but it's been a month," I argue, and Ava gives me a small, pitying smile.

"And when does time ever come into play with matters of the heart? And it's been a *year*, Jules." She sighs, then links her arm through mine. "But enough moping around for now. I think we're mostly done cleaning up. We can go to my place and watch movies and dissociate until I have to take you home. You can talk to Nate in the morning." I smile at her weakly.

"You know what this calls for?" Harper asks, grabbing a package off the counter.

"Cookies?" Ava asks, and Harper smiles wide.

"Cookies. Cookies cure everything," she says, looking at me before putting the leftover snacks into a bag to bring to Ava's where we eat way too much junk, laugh way too hard, and drink a bit too much wine, so Jaime ends up being the one who has to drive me home.

When I eventually make my way into the cottage, throwing my bag on the floor, I see a vase on the tiny counter, filled with peonies. My stomach flips and simultaneously plummets when I read the note.

See you tomorrow for coffee. Miss you. -N

It's then, I know that no matter what, I have to talk to Nate tomorrow, and I have to be brave.

THIRTY-THREE

JULES

I stare at the text on my phone and then out the front doors of the community center, trying to organize my thoughts as I watch silent, fat flakes of snowfall.

I left the cottage before the sun even rose to go to the community center and dance, needing to clear my head before I went to Nate's for our talk. I'd been up most of the night, restless dreams plaguing me anytime I tried to fall asleep, but mostly thinking about the chaos of the last few weeks.

The disaster that was my place was flooding.

Finding Nate again, the instant pull we have snapping back into place.

Settling into life with Sophie and Nate and the way it felt normal.

Kissing him at the top of the Swift Building, and it feeling like a movie.

Nate and his whole family coming to my recital to support me, even though they barely knew me.

His mission to woo me, no matter how much I dodged his efforts.

It's been just a few weeks, and they both have dug themselves so deep under my skin, so far into my daily life, I can't escape them. More importantly, I don't *want* to escape them. While, logically, it tells me I need to just give in and give Nate the chance he's asking for, all my anxiety-prone mind can do is focus on the aftermath.

What if this ends horribly? If I can't survive a weekend without wanting to be by their sides, what will it feel like if we go a month, four months, a year, and things go sour?

It would destroy me. That much I know for sure.

For hours on end, I've practiced and moved, working through old routines and perfected routines I'll be teaching in classes in January, trying to numb and block out the never-ending thoughts.

But each time they came through, knocking down the wall, I kept trying to erect them back up. I used to be able to hide away in dancing, the secret place I'd go to escape, but today, it isn't working.

With each turn and leap, I think about my mom and how we'll never, ever see eye to eye.

About my father and the way he helped create this reality where I guard my heart.

I think about all of the superficial relationships I've had in the past, keeping every potential suitor at arm's length and then cutting them off when they inevitably didn't live up to the ideal I'd built up in my mind.

I think about Ava, who found love when she least expected it, and Harper, who has been trying to convince herself for far too long that Jeremy is the one for her.

But mostly, I think about Nate. How, for the first time in my life, I feel like I have someone. Someone outside of Harper and Ava who truly believes in me and wants whatever it is I want for myself. Someone worth taking that terrifying leap for.

I know Nate wants me to come to him and tell him I'm ready to take the leap, but if I'm being honest, I don't know if I'm brave enough. I don't know if I'm brave enough to tell him I'm ready to take a chance on him, on us.

But I'm also not brave enough to tell him no.

Which is why I sigh when I type out my answer, knowing he is absolutely going to know I went to the community center with every intention of avoiding him for as long as humanly possible.

> At the community center.

I set my phone down and begin to walk away from it to the stage, but I'm turning back around when it bings again almost instantly.

> A blizzard is coming.

His response is confusing and makes no sense, considering I expected him to start hounding me, telling me it's time to make my decision.

> What?

> We're supposed to get two feet of snow, Jules. Today.

I take a deep breath, looking out the window on the front door and seeing there's already a thick layer of white on the sidewalks and street.

Once again, Julianne Everett made a stupid, impulsive decision. I can almost hear my mother now. I quickly pull up the weather app on my phone, seeing every hour for the next ten says heavy snow is expected. Sighing, I come to the realization I'll be stuck here for a while, then shoot a text to Nate. Thankfully, there are water bottles and snacks here, so I should be just fine.

> It's fine; I'll stay here for a bit.

Actually, this might even be the best-case scenario. Maybe I'll be stuck here for days, no one able to reach me, and I'll be here alone with my thoughts. I can put off this conversation for as long as I need, give myself time to continue to break apart the pros and cons, and convince myself the best option is to walk away before everyone gets hurt.

Because, in the end, everyone always gets hurt. Right?

> Jules, a BLIZZARD is coming.

I roll my eyes, knowing he's probably pacing the house, running a hand through his hair, an irritated grimace on his face, looking all cute, and—no, Jules. Stop thinking about how cute Nathan Donovan is. We need to be thinking about this with some kind of rationality.

> Got it. I'll stay here until it stops and the streets are clear.

Again, he responds almost immediately.

> You're joking, right?

> I'm not stupid enough to drive in this weather.

I type this as I watch the snow come down harder, large flakes building quickly. With my last reply, Nate stops texting back, and instantly, I feel the loss of him and wonder if this is it, the moment he decides I'm too much of a headache, that I'm not worth the chase.

It would be for the best, of course, and would solve all of my problems. And in reality, patient, sweet, kind Nate, with the most precious daughter and the best family, deserves the world. He deserves someone trusting, with no baggage, who can jump in without looking.

Someone who, when a miscommunication happens, acts like an adult and confronts them instead of blocking their number and disappearing for a year. It should be an easy answer. I should protect everyone: Nate, Sophie, and myself, and bow out while I still can.

I spend the next fifteen minutes not dancing to distract myself but lying on the stage and staring at the ceiling, wondering how I got in this position. When the front door to the community center swings open, a burst of cold and fluffy snowflakes coming in, I sit up quickly, spotting a dark figure in the doorway, my heart pounding with panic.

"Come on," Nate's voice says, the panic turning into a different kind almost instantly. I continue to stare at him in the doorway, covered in a fine dusting of snow.

"What are you doing here?" I ask, beyond confused.

"Lock up, shut everything down. We have to go."

I blink at him, still unmoving, trying to put the pieces together.

"What are you doing here?" I repeat.

He steps in, the door slamming behind him and his face becoming clearer—a mask of frustration there. "Jules, there's a fucking blizzard. Please, get whatever you need and get in the fucking truck."

"I don't—" I start, then watch him grab my jacket, turning off lights as he moves around the room.

"Do you have boots?" he asks, looking at my socked feet.

"What?" I ask, feeling like that might be the only thought I can actually finish right now.

"Boots, babe. Do you have any?" His voice is softer now, sweeter, somehow making me more confused.

"I don't—"

"We don't have time for this. Snow's piling up quick. Where's your bag?"

"My bag?" I ask in confusion, but he's already moving to where my slouchy bag sits on a chair, grabbing the items nearby and shoving them in without hesitation.

"Anything else?" Finally, I get it together enough to actually answer, shaking my head. "Great." Then he slings the bag over his shoulder before making his way to me.

"Wha—" I start, but then shriek as he bends, lifting me gently and cradling my body before making his way toward the exit. "Nate, put me down!"

"When we're in the car," he says, pushing open the door. The snow is coming down hard now, an inch or three on the sidewalks. Nate's boots crunch, compacting the snow with each step as he moves toward the truck idling outside the community center.

"Nate!" I shout, though not moving as thick snowfalls cling to the arms of my sweater, arms that are wrapped around Nate's neck. I don't have shoes on, after all. Thankfully, I guess, he continues to ignore me, using one hand to open the truck door, a wave of heat enveloping me as he slides me into the seat, tossing my bag on the floor of the truck.

"Keys," he says, putting a hand out.

"Keys?" I repeat.

"For the community center so I can lock up."

I don't argue; instead, I dig into my bag to grab the key ring, separating the one he needs. He grabs it wordlessly, slamming my door shut as I bend once to grab my comfy but not waterproof boots from the bag. Finally, I tug them on before sitting back in the chair, arms on my chest, watching Nate as he locks the front door.

A moment or two later, he's jogging around the front of the truck to the driver's side, opening the door, and sliding in. Slowly, he begins to drive in silence.

"Where's Sophie?" I ask quietly, noting she's not in the back seat and assuming school was canceled for the day.

"Staying at my parents for the storm," he says simply.

I try not to look over at him, but when my curiosity wins, his jaw is tight, and he glares down the road, driving slowly. The roads are empty, and I'm relieved to note a few of the busier roads have been plowed, even if they're quickly filling back up with heavy snow.

"Where are we going?" I ask as he turns left on Acorn Street, going a different way than I'm used to, probably to stay on the main roads that are more likely to have been cleared.

"Home," he says, voice low and almost threatening. I should argue and tell him it's his home and mine is under construction, but for some reason, I don't. "Back roads are all a mess; it's better to take main roads when I can. It might take a bit longer, but at least we'll get there safe."

I bite my lip, suddenly feeling ridiculous that he had to come all this way just because I wasn't smart enough to check the fucking weather before I left this morning. I was so caught up in my nerves and, admittedly, my lack of sleep that all I could think of was getting out of there before Nate came to try and talk to me.

"You didn't have to come get me," I say as we drive at a snail's pace the mile to Nate's place, clearing the road before us as he does.

"I wasn't going to leave you alone during a blizzard, Jules."

"I would have been fine."

"I'm sure you would have been," he says. "That's what you want, right? To prove to everyone you're independent and fine being alone?" I stare at him, but his eyes are on the road, not looking at me. "That way, you can hide in your safe little box where no one and nothing can hurt you."

I know he's not talking about being safe during a blizzard anymore, so instead of responding, I bite my lip and look out the window.

"Stay here. I'm going to shovel a path to the house, then we'll go in," he says a few minutes later when we pull into the driveway.

"Nate, I'm going to the cottage," I say low, my stomach in knots.

"No, you're not."

"Excuse me?" I ask, feeling my own irritation building because he can't tell me—

"Power's out, Jules. The cottage is going to get really fucking cold really quick. There's a fireplace in the house, we can stay warm, and I have a generator to keep things going as needed."

"Oh," I say quietly, slightly embarrassed.

"But don't worry, I won't bother you."

My head snaps back with his irritation. "What?"

"You ran off in a goddamn blizzard to avoid me, Jules. I told you to come over, and we'd talk in the morning, and instead, you drove a mile into town and planned to stay there with a blizzard coming. Clearly, I've been pushing too much, and I'm pushing you away. So I'm just going to...stop." With that, he opens the door, stepping out and slamming it.

I should be relieved.

I should be relieved that I don't have to have some big talk with Nate to push myself to do something that's going to scare me.

Instead, I feel an all-consuming sadness take over me.

I fucked up. I took too long. I pushed him away too much.

Tears start to fall against my will as I come to terms with how big I've fucked this up. I just wanted to clear my head, not push him away. And now I think it's too late.

I watch as he moves to the side of the house, grabbing a shovel and carving a clear walkway between the passenger side door and the front door before unlocking it. Then he comes back to my side, opens the door, and puts a hand out to me.

"Come on. Be careful; it might still be slippery."

I stare at his hand, then the path he just made for me, then finally, up at Nate. When our eyes meet, his brow furrows with concern.

"What's wrong?" he asks, opening the door further, but the softness isn't there. My Nate isn't here, the one who teases me and pushes me out of my comfort zone because he knows I need him to, or else I'll stay in the safety of the familiar, lonely but safe for the rest of my life.

Now there's a wall in front of him, and I wonder if this is how he's felt the whole time.

"You're mad at me." I shiver, staring at my hands, snowflakes floating into the open door, landing on my leggings and melting, but I barely pay them any mind.

"What?"

"You're mad at me."

He sighs deeply before saying, "I'm...I'm frustrated."

"With me?"

He groans, then looks at the gray sky. When he looks back at me, a dusting of snowflakes is on his eyelashes, and I want to wipe them away, but I don't think that's my right anymore.

Maybe it never was. I never really earned it, after all.

"Yes. No? I don't know. I'm mad at myself for pushing you so much to the point you felt you needed to flee in a snowstorm to get space. And with you because you refuse to give us an honest chance." I open my mouth to argue, but he continues speaking. "January hurt you. But you weren't the only one wrecked by that, Jules. There's been no one here for me."

I hesitate before asking for clarification. "I don't understand."

"I've been praying every day that I'd get to see that girl again, that I'd find out what happened. That you would show up right when I needed you most. And then you did. You can't tell me that's not a sign."

I shake my head because I can't fathom what he's saying, can't process it, but he interprets it as me disagreeing.

"I forgot. This new, closed-off version doesn't believe in signs anymore, right?"

I shake my head, tears welling again, desperate to explain, to tell him I wanted to come here and talk to him, but I needed to clear my head first, beat back my fears, and simply lost track of time.

"No! I wasn't running. I'm just...scared, Nate. I'm terrified."

"So what?"

"So what? I'm scared, and you say 'so what?'" I say loudly, the sound buffered by the snow around us, and Nate throws his hands into the air.

"Yes! News flash, Jules, life is fucking scary if you're living it. You don't like to be scared, you don't like risks? Too bad. That's what life is about."

My breathing comes heavier, his words fracturing something in me, some barrier I've built up, the truth of them shaking me.

Have I been living? Or have I just been hiding, doing the bare minimum to get through each day without the danger of getting hurt?

"I don't know if you've ever let yourself live, baby. But I'm trying to get past your wall so I can make sure you do. I'm trying to make sure from here on out, you live. I want you to chase your dreams and get your happy ending. And do it scared because you know I'll be there, ready to catch you if you slip. But I can't do that if you keep hiding, if you keep denying you're mine."

Finally, those tiny cracks split open, letting out everything I've been holding in, and I put my hands on his chest.

"Of course I am!" I shout, pushing and watching him stumble with shock. I don't even have time to register the embarrassment I should feel at finally snapping at him because my heart has taken over, my mind and self-preservation taking a backseat. "Of course, I'm yours, Nate! I'm in *love* with you and I have been for a whole year! It makes no sense at all. None! Do you know how crazy it feels to have your heartbroken after just two nights with someone? Do you know how insane I felt, mourning the mere *promise* of you for an entire year?" His eyes are wide, but I'm past common sense, I'm past watching my words. "That's what is so terrifying. I spent a weekend with you, knew you for a week before you broke my heart by accident, and then I spent an entire year mourning the loss of you. What happens if it's longer? How will I survive that kind of hurt?"

I feel it then, a single warm tear on my cold cheek dropping, but I'm too far gone.

"Jules, baby," he says low, stepping toward me like I'm a scared animal who might bolt.

"No! You don't get it, Nate. If this happens, if we happen, I need it to last. I need us to last, or I'll end up like my mom. I just know it. I'll become her, cynical and not believing in love or romance or dreams coming true, and what kind of fucking life is that? I told myself I'd rather live in my world where I believe in all of that magic but watch it from the sidelines because it was better than getting hurt again and becoming her. So yeah, Nate, I'm fucking scared." Nate steps closer. "But I was going to come to you and tell you I was going to try."

Finally, he pulls me into him, and I don't fight it. The wall I built has tumbled down, taking all of my mental strength to do it; I'm running on emotions only. My body rejoices at him being this close. His warm breath flutters against my lips.

"You're in love with me, and it terrifies you," he says. "I love you, Jules. I love you, and I'm going to fight back your fears every day until all you know is feeling safe."

"I—" I start to argue or maybe confirm his words, then stop because he shakes his head, little snowflakes stuck to his eyelashes.

"Shut up," he mumbles, and then he moves, one hand moving to my jaw, tipping it up as his head lowers.

I should be mad.

I should be scared.

Instead, I feel like I'm home.

Instead, my fingers move up, tunneling into his hair as I tug his face down to meet mine. As I press my lips to his, moving to my tiptoes to make the contact easier.

THIRTY-FOUR

JULES

The kiss morphs quickly into something all-consuming, my hand moving behind Nate's neck to pull him in as close as possible to meld his body with mine. My final layer of restraint is gone, torn off, and thrown aside.

His hands grab my ass, and he lifts me, my legs wrapping around his hips. Slamming the truck door closed, he moves toward the front door of the house, never breaking our kiss as my fingers bury into his hair.

I can't get enough of him—the way his lips feel on mine, the way he tastes, the way his groan vibrates through me—despite the multiple layers between us. His feet move up the steps before opening the front door and moving inside.

My tongue slides against his, and his teeth nip my lips as he closes the front door behind us, then pins me to it, my arms around his neck as he unzips my sweatshirt and struggles to get it off my arms before throwing it to the ground, never breaking the kiss.

I laugh into our kiss when he tries to take off his jacket without dropping me. He gets it eventually as I kick off my boots, his hands going back to my ass as he grinds against me. I moan at the feeling, knowing this time it's going to end in pleasure for both of us.

"God, you're so fucking beautiful," he groans as he slides a hand up my side, under my shirt, and up to my breast. He cups it, a thumb sliding over my hard nipple.

The shirt needs to come off *right now*, I decide. I need less between us as soon as possible. My arms cross, tugging up my sweatshirt and thin sports bra at the same time before throwing it to the ground.

The groan he lets out tells me I made the right choice as he pins my back to the door and shifts his body in order to watch his hand pinch my nipple. The rush of pleasure shoots directly to my clit, need blooming there.

"Nate," I moan out in a whisper.

"I know," he says, then moves his hands, one up my back, fingers burying in my hair, the other holding my ass before stepping toward his bedroom. His lips trail over my neck, the hand in my hair forcing me to give him the room he wants while my hands gather his sweatshirt to try and take it off even though he doesn't move to help me at all.

This moment encompasses all of the built-up tension and panic and hope finally coming out in chaos and need and impatience, and it's absolutely perfect.

Finally, we make it to his room, and he sets me down, moving to a knee before me to tug my leggings and panties down my legs. He leans his head in as he does to pull a nipple into his mouth, like he can't resist himself. I moan, my knees going weak until I'm forced to use his shoulders to steady myself.

When he stands, his hands go to my jaw, pulling me up to him and pressing a hard kiss to my lips before they move to my waist, lifting me and tossing me to the bed, where I bounce with a giggle.

I expect him to crawl up the bed after me or to at least start undressing himself, but instead, he stands there, arms crossed on his broad chest, watching me as I lay on his bed, propped up on my elbows, completely naked.

"Nate," I murmur, a small, nervous smile playing on my lips, suddenly a bit self-conscious.

He shakes his head at me, knowing what I'm feeling in the way only Nate is able to do.

"No, no, baby. Don't. I've been waiting a long fucking time to see this again. Just let me soak it in. You, naked on my bed, your hair everywhere, smiling at me. Fucking beautiful, Jules."

"Can you at least even the playing field?" I ask with a laugh. "It's a little...unfair."

He looks at me, then himself, still dressed in his boots, jeans, and sweatshirt, and smiles.

"Fine. Lie there and look pretty while I do, though," he says, walking up to the bed. He slides a hand up my thigh slowly, eyes locked on me, and I revel in the feel of his rough, work-worn fingers on my soft skin.

Even more when his thumb grazes gently from my center to my clit, stopping there and pressing, rolling my clit in a lazy circle, pulling a moan from me. Then he steps back, moving to the storage chest against the wall facing the bed, sitting there and beginning to undo the laces of his boots.

His eyes are locked on me the entire time, my chest moving up and down with each bated breath. My body hums, dying for more. He's a tease of the worst variety, and when he smirks at me, I know he knows exactly what he did and what he's *doing*.

Deciding two can play this game; I move to just one hand on the bed, the other brushing my hair back over my shoulder, exposing my breast, my nipples tight with arousal. Trying to be as seductive as possible and, admittedly, feeling a bit silly, I slide a hand down my middle, spreading my legs wider. "I guess I could give you a show if you're not going to take care of me yourself."

"Absolutely the fuck not," he says, and I smile wider, my hand sliding down further, stopping right above my clit, which is already thrumming with need.

"You're still fully dressed, Nate," I say with a tip of my head to his hands stopped on his first boot. He quickly undoes the laces and then slides the boot off, tossing it with a loud thump. I let my hand slide down another inch, my finger landing on my clit, and let out a low sigh.

"Jules, I said no."

I ignore him altogether, eyes locked on him as I circle my clit and moan. I'm wet already, my body dying for us to finally end this wait we've been enduring for weeks.

Another boot clunks to the ground, and I smile, my fingers moving down to my entrance.

"Julianne," he says in warning, and I smile, watching him stand and tug his sweatshirt over his head. When his broad chest is bared to me, I slide one finger in, whimpering at the feel.

It's not enough, not stretching me the way I know Nate will, not satisfying my need to be filled, but still, I groan all the same. Nate's hands move to the button of his jeans, and I slide the finger out and move it back to my clit, rubbing the slickness there.

My hips buck, and my eyes close with the feel of it. Pure fucking bliss.

Then the bed dips, a now naked Nate moving quickly to grab my wrist and pin it to the bed above my head before covering me with his body, his lips just an inch from mine.

"That's mine," he whispers, and I can't help but smile at the way he says it.

"You liked it last time," I say with a smile, reminding him of the first time we fucked when he asked me to show him how I touched himself for research.

"And I've been replaying that moment for fucking months, so it's well burned into my brain. I don't need you to show me what you like again."

"What if something changed?" I ask, my head moving up to kiss him. He deepens it, his hard cock bobbing between my spread legs, sliding through my wetness. My hips move to try and get more of him despite my baseless arguments.

"Then you can tell me another time. This time, I'm just fucking you, Jules. It's all I've been able to think about, sliding into your tight, wet pussy." He groans as my hips move again, as the head of his cock slides over my entrance, a tease.

"Then do it," I whimper, then moan as his free hand moves between us so he can feel just how wet I am.

He moans as he slides a thick finger into me, filling me better than I did, the pleasure skyrocketing as his thumb hits my clit too. It's still not enough, though. Not when I have the promise of *everything* right before me.

"Please, fuck me, Nate."

His fingers keep working me as he speaks. "Before we do this, I need to know you understand that if we do this, you're mine."

I roll my eyes, hips bucking to get his fingers deeper, to get more of whatever he's willing to give me.

"Didn't we just cover this?" I whine.

"Yeah, but this cements that, Jules. If we do this, there's no going back. There's no letting your fear get in the way, just trusting I'll keep you safe." I open my mouth, but he keeps talking. "I'm not saying you can't be scared, just that you won't let it stop you. Stop us." His fingers stop moving as if he wants me to concentrate, and I stare at him for long, long moments.

I don't want to be scared anymore. I don't want to live in fear, waiting for the other shoe to drop. I want to trust in this, trust in Nate and this thing between us that has been there since the beginning.

I want to be Nate's and more, I want him to *know* I'm his. I don't want him to keep harboring that concern that I'm going to run scared at any minute. Nothing is promised—not tomorrow, and surely not forever. But I know in my soul that if I trust in it, if I give this a shot, I'll live happily ever after.

My free hand moves to his cheek, feeling the scruff beneath my hand. He must not have had the chance to shave this morning, not with his panic about my being stuck in a blizzard alone. His face dips closer to mine, pushing into my hand, and our noses brush.

"I'm yours, Nate. I'm yours. I've been yours since January, even if I was too stubborn to admit it." His smile goes wide then, something that, with the closeness of our faces, I feel on my hand more than see.

"You are pretty fucking stubborn," he says, the hand between us moving to his cock to line himself up with me.

I moan as the head notches, and he slides in just enough to settle in me, but then he holds it there unmoving. My hips try to move, to buck up and get more, to get *all of him*, but he shakes his head, the hand on himself shifting to hold my hip down in place.

"Uh-uh. My way," he whispers, then slides in an inch. The stretch is phenomenal, better than I remembered, and my head tips back, my hand still on his jaw, and I moan.

"Fuck, who's stubborn now?" I whine before he slides in another inch, and I moan again. "Nate."

"I lied," he grunts out, sliding in another inch.

"What?"

"I lied. There is something better than hearing you moan my name as you come." I tighten around him, and we both groan this time.

"What?"

He slides out, then slides back in, going slightly deeper this time but not all the way. It's the worst tease in the entire world because I know just how perfectly he's going to fill me once he does.

"Nate," I whine.

"That." He slides out and in again, the glide seamless with how soaked I am, before he answers finally. "You moaning my name with my cock inside you. That's the best sound I've ever heard."

Finally, I hook a leg around his leg, my hips widening to give him more room as I do, then attempt to pull him in deeper. The new angle makes his slow, shallow thrust scrape along my g-spot before, *finally*, he plants himself deep inside of me, his hips flushed to mine.

"Fuck, Jules," he groans.

Not Julianne, not dollface, not baby.

Jules.

"Nate," I whisper, his lips against mine, wanting to tell him just how good it feels, how magical it feels, like a part of me I was missing has returned.

"I know," he says. Because he does. He knows how perfect this is and how perfect we fit. "I know."

Still, I want to tell him.

"I'm yours, Nate." His head drops to my neck, another sound coming from him, filled with soul-deep pleasure he can't control. "I'm yours."

"Jules," he groans.

"I know," I whisper now because I do. I know how wonderful and all-consuming it feels to be connected to him like this again and to know there's nothing standing in our way anymore. "I need more, though."

There's a bit of a plea in my words as my hand glides down his back until I reach his ass, my hips lifting slightly and pushing him toward me to get more, and thankfully, despite the sweet moment we just shared, he gets the hint, sliding out, then back in.

I sigh with relief, and he laughs against my neck before moving until he's hovering over me. He looks down at me, with broad shoulders and strong arms supporting him.

"My baby wants me to fuck her." I nod. "Then that's what she's going to get."

And then it starts. The pleasure swirling in my belly with each slam of his cock into me, the way his pelvis grazes my clit. Not enough to take me there, but just enough to grow the powerful orgasm building.

It builds and builds until I know I'm going to shatter soon, detonate and destroy any part of me that ever even considered we weren't made to be together.

"God, you feel so fucking good. So fucking mine," he groans into my neck, slamming in deep. It feels perfect in every way: being Nate's, him filling me, the fierceness of it.

It's all-consuming and overwhelming, and so, so right.

"Yes, Nate," I moan, my hips moving to meet his with each thrust.

He starts grinding each time he fills me, pressing against my clit now to take me closer, warmth tightening all the muscles in my lower back as I feel it coming.

"I want you to come with me," I groan as he slams in hard before pulling back out and repeating the cycle.

"Fuck," he moans through gritted teeth, his forehead coated with a thin sheen of sweat.

"I want you to fill me, Nate," I shout as he fucks me hard, eyes locked on my face like he's afraid if he blinks, he'll miss something life-changing before finally, he slams into me, hitting deep and staying there, grinding against me and tipping me over the edge.

I come hard, stars shooting behind my eyelids as they slam shut. The room goes quiet; the only thing I can hear is the pounding of my heart. Pleasure crashes over me, my back arching as he plants himself deep.

His hips dig into mine, grinding against my clit as I come and come and come, his name a prayer on my lips. My hips tip up to try and get him in deeper, and it's then I hear his own groan of release, his teeth biting into the place where my neck meets my shoulder and causing another mini-orgasm to roll through me as I feel him pulse inside of me, filling me.

We lie like that, coming down from the all-consuming high of now being together, and even when I search for it, I can't find that fear I'd be holding on to. And when Nate looks down at me, his eyes go soft like he, too, knows it's gone.

It's just him and me and the promise of cinematic happily ever after.

THIRTY-FIVE

JULES

I sit bundled in the living room, staring at the fireplace as Nate continues to poke it, shifting the wood or adding more. The power is back, but I think Nate just wants a distraction, something to keep himself busy.

"Are you still mad at me?" I finally blurt out. It's been bugging me since we cleaned up post-mind-blowing sex.

Nate, normally so chatty and outgoing, has been quiet and contemplative. Though I let him be, I know if I continue with this elephant in the room, I'll start to overthink everything, and that's not good for anyone. If I want to move forward without this cloud of dread and panic hanging over me, I need to actually talk to Nate and tell him what I'm thinking.

He looks at the fire, closing his eyes and sighing before standing, crossing his arms on his chest. He's in just a pair of sweats while I'm in one of his way-too-big-for-me tees, and he looks absolutely delicious. A flat stomach that's just a bit soft that has a light, happy trail disappearing beneath his dark gray sweatpants, and arms and shoulders that I now know from personal experience are strong enough to hold me against a wall while he fucks me breathless.

My pussy clenches, like now that we've crossed that barrier, she has a lot of making up she would like us to do.

"Are you still going to pretend there's nothing between us?" he asks, an eyebrow raised and a small smile on his lips. I shake my head with a similar smile because there's no point in that anymore. "Then no. I'm not mad at you."

"So you were mad at me?" I ask, my stomach turning in on itself.

He sighs, sitting on the edge of the couch. The fire lets out a loud pop that catches both of our attentions before he looks back at me.

"A little? I don't know." He looks at his hands before continuing to speak. "Frustrated is probably the right word. I was frustrated you were standing in the way of something we both really wanted. I was frustrated that you couldn't look past your fear and take the leap. But you also have really great points: there is more than just you and me to worry about if things go sideways. There's Sophie and Claire. My entire family is already obsessed with you."

"Most have barely even met me yet!" I say with a laugh.

"Claire has been talking about you for the last six months, Sophie screams about you every chance she gets, and, of course, there's me."

"You?" I ask with a smile. "Are you talking about me to your family?"

"Every chance I can get, dollface. They're very excited to spend more time with you at the Christmas party next week if you'd like to be my date." My stomach roils thinking about it, but he just smiles. "All that to say, I'm not mad *at* you. I was just frustrated that you wouldn't give us a chance. We can be great, baby. I just want you to allow us to be."

"I'm going to do my best," I say low. "But I can't guarantee I'm always going to be...brave."

"All I ask is that you talk to me, Jules. You're allowed to feel the way you do, there's nothing wrong with that. But when you're scared, I want you to talk to me. If you're confused, you talk to me. We can do almost anything, so long as we talk it through."

I smile, loving this. This new relationship is based on open, honest communication, and him already knowing all of my faults, shortcomings, and fears. Even more, I love that he doesn't see them as shortcomings, but more as something we have to work through together.

That's beautiful, if you ask me. Something even better than the movies because there's no obnoxious miscommunication or anything.

"All right, enough about this. I'm crazy about you, you're crazy about me," he says, a wide smile on his face as he moves toward me.

I squeal as he throws back the blanket covering me, slides under, and cozies up to me, pressing his lips to my neck.

"Say it again," he whispers there, his hand moving under my shirt to soothingly rub up and down my back. I close my eyes at the feel and sigh.

"Say what?"

"Tell me you love me, Jules. I want to hear it when it's not in the heat of the moment and we're arguing." I take in a deep breath, my heartbeat picking up with nerves. "But only if you feel it. Only if you're ready. If you're not, I'll wait," he adds hesitantly, picking up on those nerves.

But they aren't because I don't love Nate. They aren't because I'm not ready for that. It's just because I know as soon as I say it, there's no turning back. There's no putting space between us because I'm scared or hesitant. There's no more protecting myself from potential future harm, there's just trust that this is going to work, that we will work together to get our forever. If I tell Nate I love him, I'm putting my heart in his hands, and that's a scary thing.

My hand lifts, resting on his cheek and forcing him to look at me while I take a deep breath before I give him everything. "I love you, Nate," I whisper, looking him in the eye, letting him see everything: how much I love him, how deep that goes, that all of my walls are completely crumbled. He waits a moment before sighing deep, relief in the noise and resting his forehead on mine, then pressing his lips to mine, a gentle, easy press of lips that means more than it lets on.

"Nothing more beautiful," he whispers against my lips. "Nothing more beautiful than you giving me that. I love you, Julianne. Thank you for giving me this. For giving me you."

It confirms I made the right choice, that he understands what it means that I'm giving him myself, and that he's going to make keeping my heart safe the utmost priority.

His head moves to my neck then, holding me tight and pressing a kiss there. I sigh contentedly, my hand running through his hair. We lay like that for long moments before finally, I break the comfortable silence.

"Snow days seem to be our thing," I say.

A laugh moves through Nate as his head moves back and his fingers run through my hair. My eyes drift shut, not because I'm tired but because being in his arms feels so damn good. I've always loved having my hair played with, but add laying on a couch with Nate, a cozy blanket pulled up tight, and a fire in the fireplace...it doesn't get better than that.

"Yeah, I guess they do." There's a long pause—not an uncomfortable one, but one all the same. Eventually, I feel his eyes on me, despite mine being close. "Every time it snowed, I thought of you," he whispers.

"Really?" I ask, eyes opening.

"Last year was the snowiest winter in ten years; it felt like the schools were closed more than they were open," he says, not exactly explaining.

I remember that, the way the schools were forced to stay in session almost until July in order to make up for all of the extra snow days they had to take.

"It was the winter I met you, and the winter I lost you. Every time I saw snow in the forecast, I hated it, knowing I'd remember laying in my bed, your head on my chest just like this, the world quiet." A small, humorless laugh comes from his lips. "It felt like the world reminded me of you, like it didn't want me to forget."

"I'm sorry I didn't talk to you, Nate," I whisper, the guilt of it heavy. I should have been an adult, reached out, and confronted him. This all could have been so much different if I had.

"No, no. You did what you thought was best for you. I'd want my sisters or Sophie to do the same if that's how they felt. It just sucks it happened to us. I missed a whole year of this."

"Fucking?" I ask.

His laugh has much more humor in it, and he shifts, rolling me so I'm on my back, Nate hovering over me.

"Definitely lost a year of that," he says with a broad smile before doing a push-up, pressing his lips to mine. "But I meant this. You and me. Lying together, kissing you. Spending time together, learning you. You meeting Sophie, getting to know my family. I wish I could get it back."

I let the small whisper of a smile stay on my lips, battling the heartache of it all as I reach up, pushing his hair away from his face.

"I'm not going anywhere, Nate," I whisper. "Unless, of course, you come out of the woodwork with some hidden family I don't know of." I smile wide at him with that. "Then I might have to ghost you again."

"Mmm," he says. "No, no, I think you're good on that one. Plus, if you disappeared, my family would now come find you. Even they know I'm meant to be yours."

"Claire texts me at least once a day, making sure we're still together and you haven't fucked it up," I confess with a laugh.

"Gotta love her confidence in me," he says with an eye roll, then pressed his lips to mine once more. His hand moves down to grab mine, twining the fingers and bringing them to his lips, where he presses a kiss.

"I'm still really scared," I whisper my truth to him and watch the way his face drops just a tiny bit. It's so subtle that if I hadn't dissected his every move, I would have missed it. "I'm scared, but I'm going to try and be brave." That shadow of doubt vanishes, replaced by a wider, joy-filled smile. "I'm going to be brave because I know this —us? It's worth it."

A long moment passes, Nate staring and smiling at me before his hand moves, brushing my hair back.

"Thank you," he whispers. "Thank you for being brave for us."

I don't tell him how much I appreciate him not telling me I don't have to be scared or that there's nothing to worry about, invalidating my fears even if he means well. But I must show it on my face because his smile goes soft and knowing.

He presses his lips to mine again like he can't resist doing otherwise before whispering, "Pancakes, right? Snowman pancakes for a snow day?"

My smile is soft when I give it to him.

"Yeah, Nate. Snowman pancakes."

THIRTY-SIX

JULES

"Oh, look at you three!" Mrs. Donovan shouts at us as we stand in the doorway of the Donovan house, my heart pounding, holding a plate of cookies I baked with Sophie this morning.

It's the Saturday before Christmas, and we're attending the annual Donovan family ugly sweater party. Sloane came over yesterday, dropping off three matching sweaters with Christmas cats on them, telling me if we didn't show up in them, we'd stick out like a sore thumb. Nate told his sister to stop freaking me out, joking that he just convinced me to give him the time of day. He was mostly joking, but I felt the undercurrent of honesty there, like he is still afraid of scaring me off.

Since the snowstorm, things have been...easy.

I'm still scared shitless of the unknown, but I'm moving past it, forcing myself to look past my fears and jump in. Ever since the snowstorm, I've spent most of my day at the main house, shuffling over first thing in the morning to steal a few kisses and drink coffee with Nate, then get Sophie up and out the door.

I still sleep in my own bed at the cottage, nervous about what it might mean if we stop pretending I don't have my own place and how that might impact Sophie, but that's just about all I do there.

Being a part of his family has been...easy. Surprisingly easy.

But I like it a lot, this new little normal of ours.

And now, I'm being hugged and tugged from Donovan to Donovan as if I belong here, too.

"Our girl," Sloane says with a smile.

"I'm so happy he hasn't scared you off yet," Sutton says, pulling me away from Nate. "Though, the mere fact that you convinced him to wear this sweater is proof enough you're strong enough to endure our brother," she says, tugging at the sleeve of mine. When she brought them, Sloane told me there was a good chance I wouldn't be able to convince her brother to wear it, and I agreed.

But as always, he was a team sport, and he smiled as he shrugged it off. It was obvious why, when Sophie came out, she had the biggest smile on her face when she saw her dad.

"Come on, we have to talk," Sloane says, tugging my arm and looping hers through it.

"We do?"

"We need an update on how bad our brother is fucking this up," Sutton says, looping hers through the other. "Before everyone gets here."

"I, uh," I start, looking over my shoulder at Nate to save me, but he just smiles.

"Be gentle with her. Don't scare her off. I like this one," he says with a laugh. And then he winks at me, his sisters carting me off to another room.

Even though it's strange and different since I've never really confided in anyone but Ava and Harper, I filled them in on the last week or so, keeping out the gory details. It feels like what I always thought having sisters would be like, and I'm reminded of just another thing I would have missed out on if I let my fear win.

Being brave is turning out to be so fucking worth it.

Two hours later, I'm standing in the sunroom of the Donovans' house, watching Nate, Sophie, and a bunch of the kids who came to the party have a snowball fight. I grimace as I watch Sophie and an older boy tackle Nate to the ground, his hands going up in surrender as he laughs.

He's good with the kids, deciding when a little boy almost knocked over a vase after all of the kids were experiencing a bit of a sugar high that they needed to expend some energy, telling them to get on their jackets and head outside for a snowman-making competition.

It quickly devolved into chaos and, obviously, a snowball fight, and it's been entertaining to watch. He leans down, propping Sophie on one hip and his cousin's two-year-old toddler on the other. My heart flips at the sight, thinking of Nate holding Sophie and a kid we made together. *Slow down, Jules. We just got past admitting you love the guy.*

"You're Julianne Everett, right? You own First Position?" a man with a plate piled high with cookies asks, ripping me from my daydream.

"Uh, yes! I am."

"Hank," he says, putting a hand out. "Approvals for the town." Ah, so he's the one holding my place hostage.

"Nice to meet you," I say, taking the hand and shaking it.

"How's the place?

"Oh, you know, still waiting for the final improvements, but I'm excited to get back in."

His brow fires up, and his neck goes back. "Improvements? Is Donovan doing more to it? I don't think that came across my desk."

"I...I'm not actually sure what's next. He was fixing a water leak and redoing insulation."

"I approved that to residency this week," he says, confusion clear on his face.

"I'm sorry. What?"

"That was approved last week. All of it. Insulated installment, drywall, structural. He did a great job and did it quickly, too. Your building is completely ready to live in again."

"Oh, I..." My mind drifts off to when we were there the other day. Now that I think about it, most of the work seemed to have been done, just needing a bit of paint and for the tools and materials to be cleaned out.

Has Nate been done all this time?

I wait for the irritation to hit at that potential truth, but it doesn't come. Instead, I fight the urge to laugh at the hoops I'm realizing he was jumping through to convince me to stay longer.

"Excuse me, I think I just spotted Shauna's thumbprint cookies on that platter, and I've been listening to Tom brag about them for years." He walks off to a cookie platter, and I look around the room for Nate.

He spots me, a bit of nerves on his face, and I give him a look that makes him smile. I make my way to him, but Sutton grabs my arms, tugging me in the opposite direction.

"Oh my god, please do not leave my side right now. My ex from high school is here, and I want to die," she says, eyes wide.

"Where?" I ask, looking around.

"My god, you're terrible at this. Not a sneaky bone in your body, is there? Come on, I'm taking you into the other room to show something."

"What are you showing me?" I ask, increasingly confused.

"Literally anything that isn't in this room," she grumbles. "And you're not allowed to leave my side." Her head is tipped down like she's some starlet trying to avoid the paparazzi.

"Sutton, I—" I start, but she's already tugging me out of the dining room into the family room, Nate watching with a slightly amused shake of his head. As we leave, a man with bright green eyes and dark brown hair watches us leave, not even glancing at me, eyes locked on the middle Donovan sister.

"Can I help?" I ask, stepping into the kitchen where Mrs. Donovan is washing dishes in red-and-green striped gloves. She gives me a warm smile and shakes her head.

"Oh no, sweetheart, go on and enjoy the party!"

I step in further and give her a shaky smile. I came into the kitchen hoping for some vague semblance of peace, on account that I had spent the last hour and a half having Sutton drag me to meet every single Donovan family member in order to avoid her ex. I met aunts, uncles, and long lost cousins, all of them telling me how many wonderful things they have heard about me from one of Nate's sisters, Sophie, Mr. and Mrs. Donovan, or Nate himself.

To say I'm overwhelmed would be an understatement.

I bit my lip before confessing, "I'm not going to lie; it's so fun out there, but it's overwhelming. I'd love some quiet if you don't mind the company."

She looks at me with an understanding smile.

"Why do you think I'm in here? Tom loves this, all the people in our house, and don't get me wrong, I do too, but dang, it gets loud." I laugh and nod before she tips her head to the drying rack. "Grab a towel, you can dry."

I give a relieved smile before I move over to her, grab a holly-covered dishrag, and start to wipe off the dishes, stacking up the clean plates. We move in silence, Mrs. Donovan washing and me drying, my occasionally asking a few questions to know where to put some of them away before she finally speaks.

"You know, we're so grateful Nathan found you, and you've been spending so much time together. Sophie also just adores you, you know." I give her a genuine smile.

"I'm just incredibly grateful he was willing to help out with my place," I say, grabbing a platter that held the mini meatballs I absolutely need the recipe for. "And that he needed help with Sophie."

"Oh yes, the girls told me all about her little wish to Santa. My goodness, she really does have quite the imagination. I'm sure Nate was so relieved to have a way to make her wish come true. He's so terrible at telling her no. But you know, you really do look like her doll."

I smile and shake my head.

"No, I meant with the babysitting since Claire left."

Mrs. Donovan pauses, staring at me. "What?"

"Well, that's why I'm staying in the cottage. You know, to help get Sophie off the bus and..." My words trail off when Mrs. Donovan rolls her lips between her teeth, trying to stave off a laugh. "I feel like I missed something."

She turns the tap off, drying her hands on a free towel, and turning to me, arms on her chest.

"We're a big family, sweetheart. Up until recently, I was the one getting Sophie off the bus most days, and any night Nathan had to work late, we'd all take turns on who got to hang with our favorite girl." She looks at me, a twinkle in her eye, giving me a small wink that looks so much like her son's. "Except for recently, of course."

"So Sophie..." I pause, trying to process what he's telling me. "Nate didn't need a babysitter, did he?"

She shakes her head, a small smile on her lips. "That boy, always working to get whatever he wanted. He never lied as a kid, knew that would get him into the most trouble, but he would play around with the truth."

"Hmm," I say, lost in my thoughts and finding myself once again conflicted by what she's telling me. Nate lied about needing a sitter. Or, I suppose, *all* of the Donovan kids did, all to give Nate the chance to try and win me. A surge of guilt rises as I think about all of the trouble everyone went through just because I was stubborn.

"Just like his dad," she says, then gives me a small smile. "You know, when I first met Tom, I ran away from him."

I choke out a laugh. "I'm sorry, you ran away?"

Mrs. Donovan shrugs. "I was at some party in high school, just had my heart broken, and this cute boy comes over, talks to me all night, and buys me a soda. He was sweet, and I really liked him, but at the end of the night, I ran off and didn't give him my number." She smiles and shakes her head, grabbing a platter and putting it into a cabinet. "I was just scared because I just had my first real breakup, and I didn't want it to happen again. So I never talked to him again, and that was that."

"Except..." I started because, obviously, that was not that at all.

She smiles. "Except a year later I was moving into my dorm for college and he was helping the freshman. We bumped into each other, and he made me drop the box I was carrying. We both scrambled to pick things up, and lo and behold, he found the bottle cap."

"The bottle cap?"

"From the soda he bought me. I'd kept it for some silly reason. Tom had planned on letting me be, but he says he saw that bottle cap and knew I felt something that night, too. So he spent the next month wearing me down, asking me out, and flirting with me until I gave him a chance." She tips her head toward the living room with a smile. "The bottle cap is in a frame there."

My mind moves to a similar story, one where *I* ran away from Nate and kept my own memento.

"I like to think the Donovans hold some kind of magic. Like when we find our person, there's a bit of chaos, but in the end..."

"It's magic," I say with a smile.

"See, you get it," she says, the same smile on her lips.

"Were you still scared? When you met him again?"

"Ah, yes. I'd had my heart broken again in between and swore off men altogether." My heart stops beating at the familiar refrain. "But Tom never stopped prodding."

"Like father, like son." I smile, and she smiles back, some quiet secret passing between us that I like a lot.

The door to the kitchen opens, a wave of sound flooding the space as Mr. Donovan walks in.

"Ah, so this is where the pretty girls are hiding out," Mr. Donovan says with a smile, stepping into the kitchen and leaving the door open.

"Sometimes you just need some peace and quiet from this family," Mrs. Donovan says.

"You got any more of those thumbprint cookies? I think Hank ate 'em all before I could get any."

"That's a bald-faced lie, Thomas, because I saw you eat at least five before anyone even came here."

"I get them once a year!" Mr. Donovan tsks but moves, reaching for a box over the fridge. "I knew you loved me," he says, seeing an entire box of the cookies he loves there. But just as he reaches the box, the front door opens, slamming against the wall as it's flung open. All eyes move in the direction of the noise to see Claire standing there, eyes watering, a suitcase and a large duffel at her feet.

And then she starts to cry.

"Oh my god, Claire!" her mother says, shoving the cookies at her husband and moving. She moves at lightning speed, seemingly reaching her daughter before I can blink and wrapping her in her arms. "What happened?"

"He dumped me!" Claire cries into her mother's arms.

THIRTY-SEVEN

JULES

We drive home and put Sophie in bed in near silence, both of us lost in our heads.

After Claire got settled, I watched the Donovans do what I'm learning they do best: handle a crisis. Tom grabbed her bags and brought them into the house while Sutton, Sloane, and Nate gently and kindly ushered out the remaining guests at the party.

I stood with Sophie, trying to keep her both entertained and distracted while staying out of the way. When everyone was gone, Claire and the rest of the Donovans sat in the living room to hear her story. I tried to sneak out and clean up while they handled family business, but Shauna gave me a very stern motherly look and told me, *"You're a Donovan now, Jules, like it or not. Sit down."*

Then, Claire began her tale of arriving in California and it being a mess from the start. Her boyfriend, Paul, wasn't there to get her from the airport, spent nights out late, never telling her where to go, and even when she told him she was lonely and she knew no one there, he simply shrugged off her concerns. With each word, I watched Nate's jaw get tighter and tighter, hearing about how his baby sister was mistreated.

Finally, Claire gave Paul an ultimatum: either she gets treated better or she leaves. Unfortunately, it seems he chose door number two, leading her to come back home to Evergreen Park where she promptly broke down about seemingly losing everything.

Now we're on the couch, a movie playing, but I'm barely paying attention. I've made my decision, and even though I know Nate is going to argue with me, I need him on board.

"Claire will need the cottage," I finally say.

"What?" Nate asks, confused as he looks over at me.

"Claire needs the cottage. I'm going to move back home tomorrow."

"No, you're not," he says. "The city won't let you."

I give him a look.

"Hank from approvals talked to me at the party. According to him, my place was approved last week. I can move back into First Position at any time."

Nate's jaw goes tight, and even though he has both arms wrapped around me, he tightens them as he groans to the ceiling.

"Fucking Hank and his big fucking mouth," he grumbles, and I laugh.

"When were you going to tell me?" I ask.

"Never." I glare at him, and he rolls his eyes. "After Christmas," he says begrudgingly.

"Why didn't you tell me it was done?" I ask, my fingers moving to push his hair back.

"Technically, it wasn't. It still needed paint." I remember him coming home two days ago with paint dried on his hands and instinctively knowing he finished my place then but didn't tell me to keep me close for as long as he could manage.

"You know what I mean. It was safe to live in a week ago. Or longer."

He sighs deeply before taking a long moment to answer. "Because I knew the second you knew, you'd be moving out."

"Well, yeah..." I say, because he's stating the obvious.

"And at that point, you were still in your denial zone. So moving out of the cottage would mean moving out of our lives."

I bite my lip, knowing he's not wrong, feeling a bit guilty over it. "But I'm not there anymore," I say softly. "And I can't live behind your house forever, Nate."

He groans, looking at the ceiling. "Is it a crime to like having you close?"

I give him a soft, sweet smile, putting a hand on his cheek.

"No, Nate. It's not a crime. I get it. I love being close to you guys." He reaches over, grabbing my hand and squeezing before I speak again. "But it's time for me to move back home."

"No, it's not," Nate says, but he sounds more like a grumpy kid. It reminds me that once I get through to Nate, I'm going to have to get through to Sophie, who is going to be even more of a force to reckon with. I decided it might be better to play a little dirty, shifting until I'm straddling him. His hands instantly go to my ass, and I smile.

He has to know I can't live in the tiny cottage forever. I have all of my things at my place, it's close to my work, and I love the little home I built for myself.

"Nate, your sister needs a place to stay—" I say, trying to bring logic into the conversation.

"She can stay with our parents!"

"Nate," I say, giving him a chiding look. "She's going through a lot. She needs something familiar. And I need to go to my place. Lessons start up soon, and I'll have to be there for those."

He glares. "But I want you here."

"And I will be here, Nate. Just not...all the time."

He looks at me, weighing his options and clearly understanding that they are slim. Then his face shifts, like he's made a decision, something I'm suddenly nervous about.

"Sleepovers."

"What?"

"We get sleepovers. Four nights a week."

I scoff out a laugh. "Nate, four nights a week is over half the week!"

"And?"

I let out a sigh and roll my eyes. "How about we start at two?" It sounds reasonable to me, but I should know Nate is *anything* but reasonable.

"Three. And when you're here, you sleep in my bed."

"Nate—"

"I wasn't going to push it, you sleeping in my bed because you're close, which means you can stay late and come over early. But if you insist on spending four nights a week across town—"

"Five," I say with a laugh.

He ignores me, continuing. "If you insist on staying four nights a week away from me, I get you in my bed. I get to hold you."

The idea of that is utter bliss—Nate holding me all night or waking up wrapped around him. But there's other things to keep in mind.

"But Sophie—" I start.

"Sophie isn't going to notice, Jules. Right now, you're here before she wakes up, and you're here until she goes to bed. Where will it be different?"

I scrunch my nose because he's not wrong. That's been my argument with staying at the cottage and insisting I go back to my bed each night. But he's right: If I'm here when she wakes and I'm here when she goes to sleep, where is the difference?"

"Two nights," I whisper, placing my forehead on his and smiling.

"Three, and we work up to four."

As much as I love this new and improved version of *us*, common sense tells me we should move slow. I should give Nate and Sophie time to be themselves without my hovering everywhere. I should give Nate room to really think about when and how he wants to incorporate me in this little family. Right now we're in the honeymoon phase, and even though I'm secure in this relationship of ours, I'm worried about moving too fast and Nate having some kind of regret.

"Two," I whisper, my lips now grazing his. "And you have to break the news to Sophie." I'm testing my luck, I know, but it's worth a shot. I shift my hips a bit, hoping I can use anything at my disposal to sway him.

"Oh, hell no," he says with a laugh, pushing me back so there's a gap between us now. "I know what you're doing with your womanly wiles. You're not going to trick me."

I give him a very fake gasp, putting a hand to my chest. "I have no idea what you're talking about!"

"Don't play cute with me," he says, then grabs my chin, resting his lips on mine before pulling back. "Three nights a week." Then he flips us until I'm on my back on the couch, Nate hovering over me. He looks so fucking handsome like this, happy and smiling, broad shoulders holding him up. "That's my final offer."

My hand reaches up, grazing over his cheek, and I can't believe we're here, a year later, joking about making deals on how many nights he can convince me to stay here.

It's real, true Christmas magic.

"Deal," I whisper, and then lean up to press my lips to his, taking my prize.

THIRTY-EIGHT

NATE

The next day, I called Claire and told her she could have the cottage again if she's interested. Although she argued for a moment, worried she'd be taking the place from Jules, as soon as I explained to her that it was Jules's idea and we were good—solid, even—she sighed with relief.

"I can't stay here for another day," she said quietly as if our parents were near and might hear. "Mom is hovering over me like I'm about to break, and Dad keeps telling me my shirt shows too much skin. It's a cropped sweatshirt, Nate! They're driving me crazy."

I laughed even though I know it's all painfully true. This was, after all, why Claire moved out in the first place, considering she was twenty-four and they hadn't stopped treating her like a baby.

"But I don't want to move in if it's going to mess things up with you and Jules. You guys are so cute together, but Sloane told me she's being a bit stubborn."

I sighed, battling the urge to tell my sisters to stop fucking gossiping about me.

"She was just a little...nervous, is all. But if I have my way, she'll be moved in with me and Soph by summertime. So don't worry, Claire.

Just pack your things up. Jules is going to break the news to Sophie in a bit and start packing up. Have Sutton drive you over whenever you're ready."

Claire sold off her car before leaving for California, so I know she doesn't have a way to get around. I add that to my mental list of things to ask around about, to see if anyone has a decent car they're looking to sell.

"Good luck with that," Claire grumbled, and she wasn't wrong.

The next hurdle was telling Sophie, a feat that began a large rash of dramatics, even when we told her her beloved aunt would be moving back into the cottage and Jules would be here multiple days a week. The only thing that seemed to cut through the chaos, of course, is Jules's promise to come on Christmas morning with presents.

"I don't want Jules to leave!" Sophie shouts, her eyes glimmering as we give her the news.

"Sophie, sweetie, I promise I'll be here all the time. We'll still have girls' days. You know I was only staying here to help watch you while my place was getting fixed. Now your Aunt Claire is back to watch you, and your daddy fixed my place up!" Jules says.

"But what about my Christmas wish?" she asks, her voice cracking and her eyes watering. "Why isn't the magic working?" Her lower lip trembles as Jules's brows furrow.

"What do you mean?"

"The Christmas magic! It's supposed to make you guys fall in love so you can stay here forever with us." She's getting angry now, stomping her foot, and her face is going red with emotion.

My heart breaks for my sweet little girl.

"I know, honey, but—" Jules starts with a sigh.

"It needs to work!"

"Sophie, sweetie," Jules says, kneeling before her and getting to her eye level and holding her hands. "It worked, Soph. The magic worked. It helped me find your dad, and I care for him so much, really, I do."

"Then why aren't you in love and getting married? If this was a movie, you'd be getting married."

"Because real life isn't like the movies, sweetie," she says. Sophie's face falls, but Jules's smile gets wide. "It's better, Soph. It's better because it's real, and we get to live it. It's a movie come true, but it just takes a little longer." She shrugs and laughs. "A movie is only two hours long."

"But I have a Christmas present to give you," she says with a sniffle, no longer angry, which is a win.

"And I'll be here first thing on Christmas morning. I have to give you the presents I got you."

"Presents?" Sophie asks, all sadness melting from her face. "Like, two?"

I smile because my girl is so damn funny. She's sad and mopey, but she hears *multiple presents*, and her entire demeanor changes.

"Five," Jules whispers conspiratorially, and Sophie's eyes go wide. "You gonna help me pack up?" she asks, changing the subject, to which my daughter nods.

Hours later, when I'm back home after we helped Jules pack up, Claire *un*pack, dropped Jules off at her place, and then helped *her* unpack, I start to make a pile of things Jules left behind.

A sock here, a hair tie there, a shirt in the laundry intertwined with my and Sophie's things, the way she's supposed to be. Her perfume on my sheets, her shampoo in my bathroom from a fun shower after the storm.

She's on every single inch of this house. I can't escape her.

I don't *want* to escape her.

"Hey, Nate, I—" Claire says, walking in the back door with a small cardboard box balanced on her hip. "What's wrong?"

"What? Nothing," I say, using the pile to the side.

"He's *depressed*," Sophie says, a new word she probably learned from one of her aunts making me roll my eyes.

"Is that right?" my sister asks with a laugh.

"I'm not depressed, god."

"Where's Jules?" Claire says, looking around. Sophie glares at me, and I close my eyes, taking in a deep breath.

"At her place."

"Yeah, let's talk about that," Claire says, putting the box on the counter. I see it, too; she has a shit ton of Jules's stuff she left behind. "Why is she there?"

"Because she wanted to unpack, get settled, and said you should have time without her hovering." My sister rolls her eyes like she doesn't believe me and thinks I fucked up somehow. I wave a hand. "Trust me, we're good. We agreed she would sleep over three times a week." I don't tell her I am absolutely pushing for more than that as soon as I can manage.

"And you just let her *go?!*" my sister asks. "God, Nate, if I knew you were going to kick Jules out, I would have just stayed with Mom and Dad."

"I didn't kick her out! It was her idea!" Claire glares at me. "I'm serious, Claire. It was *her* idea."

"And you didn't even fight it?"

"I didn't want to push her too much!" I say, throwing my hands up. "I just barely convinced her to agree we were together!"

My sister shakes her head, moving to my fridge and pulling out a beer, cracking it, and taking a sip. She cringes like it's disgusting since Claire doesn't *drink* beer, then hands it to me.

"God, you are such a man, Nate," she says finally, arms crossed on her chest.

"What is that supposed to mean?"

"It means she loves romance movies. She loves the guy chasing his girl down at the airport, telling her not to leave."

"That's not even feasible anymore. You can't get past security without a boarding pass. She's also not getting on a plane. She's a mile down the road."

She sighs like I'm exhausting her.

"I just mean, Jules loves the moment where the guy says, '*No! Don't go! Stay with me forever and marry me and make babies!*'"

"I *know* that proposing marriage and kids would absolutely send her into a spiral," I deadpan, and Claire rolls her eyes.

"You're so fucking thick-skulled. You know what I mean, Nate. You told me you've been watching all of those movies, right?" I nod. "And in any of them, do they end with her going back home and them shaking hands?"

"We didn't shake hands," I say because I pulled her into her bedroom and made out with her against the door while Sophie watched TV for as long as she'd let me get away with.

"You know what I mean, you fucking moron." Then she slaps me upside my head. I should be offended, but instead...it makes sense.

Fuck.

I sigh, running a hand over my face and through my hair before turning to look at Sophie, who looks shockingly like her aunt right now, arms crossed on her chest, hip cocked out. "We messed up, didn't we, kid?" I ask her, and both women glare at me.

"We?" Sophie asks, with more attitude in the single word than I've ever heard. Claire snorts out a laugh, and I glare back at my daughter. "I wanted you and Jules to fall in love and for her to stay forever. *You* messed it all up!"

"She really did give you Jules on a silver platter," Claire says, and I glare.

"So what's your plan?" Sophie asks.

I look to Claire. "My plan?"

"God, Dad, did you learn anything?" she says, all sassy. In the time that she's spent with Jules, it's clear my girl's sassy, independent streak has rubbed off on my daughter, and made hers even wider, and fuck if I don't like it. "You need a grand gesture to win her back."

"Oh, definitely. He needs a grand gesture," Claire says with a nod.

"You lose the girl, you gotta win her back," Sophie says, and I roll my eyes.

"I don't think I lost her, Soph," I tell her gently.

"She's not here, is she?"

Fair point.

"So you think I need a grand gesture?" I ask, crossing my arms on my chest and leaning against the kitchen island.

"Oh, absolutely."

I start brewing on it, thinking about the past month, about all of the movies Jules made me watch, the ones that made her laugh and cry and blush while sitting at my side and realize my daughter isn't wrong. All of them have a grand gesture, some big moment where the hero does something to win her back.

My mind starts scrolling through all of the movies we've watched before finally, an idea blooms. I must show it on my face because Claire smiles, nudging Sophie excitedly.

"Oh, Soph, I think that means your daddy has an idea!"

THIRTY-NINE

JULES

When I bought this place, I thought it was magical. I was so proud to have a place of my own, something to work on and put myself into every inch of, that every moment here felt like a dream come true.

But after just four weeks of living behind the Donovans, of waking up and shuffling into the big house to have coffee with Nate, then getting Sophie ready for her day. Of putting her to bed and then watching a movie on the couch while Nate pretends to work just so I feel comfortable enough to sit with him.

I miss it.

I miss the way Sophie slams into my legs every time she sees me and the way she uses me to team up on her dad.

I miss walking into the main house and having Nate pull me into a corner to press a kiss on my lips when Sophie isn't looking.

I just miss *them*.

Part of me wishes I had just taken him up on his offer, moved in, and let this place be just my business, but that's too fast, isn't it? There's no rationality behind saying yes, no common sense. It's bound to end in disaster if we rush things.

But then again, is it really rushing things if I've been pining after him, missing him for an entire year? If he's been doing the same?

When I finally opened up to him and let him in, it was like we were always meant to do this, like we hadn't stopped. And now there's an aching hole in my chest where my two favorite people belong.

I've tried watching a dozen movies, but all of them feel pointless without Nate by my side, asking questions and giving his thoughts. I turn in my bed more than once to try and explain a trope or a scene to Nate, but I'm just...alone. The first tear falls down my cheek when I realize I may've totally and completely fucked up by going back home.

That's when something hits my window. A quiet *tink* that has my entire body going tight and turning toward the sound.

It would be my luck for something bad to happen just as I move back in. What if it's my windows freezing, cracking, and shattering, letting in all the frigid cold? I'll be like Tiny Tim, shivering in the corner while all of my expensive ass heat flies right out the window.

But this time, when it happens again, I'm staring at the glass so I can see it: a tiny pebble hitting my window. My brow furrows in confusion as I take a step closer and step back when a new noise fills the room. It's my phone in my hand with a new text lighting up the screen.

> Are you up?

> Yes...?

> Go to your bedroom window.

I move closer to the window, tentatively, before looking down at the sidewalk below, my Nate standing on the sidewalk. His truck is double-parked in front of some other car like he couldn't waste the time to move around back and park in my little lot. Sophie is beside him waving both arms. Both have identical wide smiles on their faces.

Lifting the window, I stick my head out and shout," What are you doing here?"

"Come down!" Nate yells.

"Yeah! Come down!" Sophie concurs.

"Why—"

"Just do it, Jules. Please." There's something white on the ground, stacked next to his feet among the piles of snow from the storm, and Sophie is jumping up and down, clearly overexcited. No matter what, I need to go downstairs to hug my girl and kiss my man, and maybe tell him I made a mistake and want to go home with him.

Three nights a week, my ass.

Nate is mine, and I'm his. We've already covered that, but the reality is Sophie is mine too. The way she snuck into my heart and stole it is obvious. I want to be in their family, I want to be Nate's, and I want to be whatever version of a mother figure Sophie is comfortable with me being. I always knew I wanted kids one day, and Sophie is everything and more that I've dreamed of.

I don't even bother to close the door to my place as I slip on a pair of slippers, running down the flights of stairs to get to my front door. I'm panting when I finally get there, swinging the door open to see Nate on my doorstep, with what I think is a boom box in hand.

"Where did you get that?" I ask as he lifts what looks like an ancient artifact, and he smiles somehow wider, beginning to look like it might crack his face in half.

"My mom has everything. You should see my old room, it's just piles of junk," he says. "But shush."

"Shush?" I ask, my head moving back.

He puts a finger to his lips, then hits play on the machine before setting it down, the sound of Christmas caroling coming through the shitty speakers. My confusion goes up a notch, but while I'm looking at the boom box, trying to decode what's happening, Sophie grabs what I now see are large white cards and hands them to her dad.

Nate holds them high and proud.

You cry at that movie even though it's creepy

The first card reads in bold black, familiar writing that isn't neat. Instead, it's sprawled there like he was eager to get it done, like he was in a rush to get...here?

That card drops, and I read the next one.

This is how it's done, Jules, if you really want to win the girl over.

My mind is still racing, trying to put together pieces that are somehow familiar, but in the chaos and overwhelm, I can't seem to identify what's happening.

But then I read the next one.

You are perfect.

Love Actually, the scene with Kiera Knightly that Nate said was a little creepy and weird.

What's more romantic, this or meeting your dream girl in a bar on New Year's?

The card drops, and I read the next.

Not just to me, but to everyone you meet.

It drops a few moments later.

You're funny and kind and independent in a way I hope Sophie can learn from you.

My lower lip starts to tremble as I read it, my eyes shifting to the little girl who is jumping up and down still, her excitement palpable.

I knew from the beginning you were meant to be mine. My first mistake was not chasing you.

The first tear drops, and I move to look at Nate, who shakes his head and nods, the card dropping and showing the next, like he knew what would happen.

You're such a crybaby.

"You're the worst." I sniffle as he drops that card, revealing the next. Absent-mindedly, I hope none of them drop into the snow and get damaged because I already know I want to keep them forever.

My second was letting you ever think I was in this for anything other than to make sure you fall for me and realize we were meant to be.

That you were never allowed to leave our side again.

The card drops, and I eagerly read the next one.

That first time you mentioned going back home, I should have told you your home is with us.

The tremble wins, and a small sob leaves my lips. Sophie's smile widens, and Nate's look softens, like he can't bear to see me *really* crying, but he needs to finish what he started.

This isn't a movie, this is real life.

Something in my mind niggles—an old memory of being wrapped up together on his bed—but I can't quite reach it. It comes back to me with the next card.

I love you madly, Jules. Let me love you madly.

That's when I make my way down the steps, launching myself at Nate. He drops the card, and I realize then that was the last one, not that I care.

"You're crazy," I whisper against his lips.

"Crazy about you," he replies. "I fucked up. I shouldn't have agreed to let you go home. Fuck needing space. You can get space in my house, under my roof."

"No, no. It's my fault. I shouldn't need space or time. Not when I have you."

He shakes his head, smiling at me.

"What a pair we are," he mumbles, kissing me finally, my soul complete as his lips move along mine, sealing this moment perfectly.

"Look!" Sophie shouts, and we both look at her, her face turned to the sky. "It's snowing." I see it then, light flakes falling from the sky and sticking to her hat, the cherry on top of this perfect scene. "It's a Christmas miracle. It's just like the movies," she shouts, and Nate looks at me, a goofy smile on his lips.

"Except better."

EPILOGUE

One Year Later
Nate

Her breaths are shallow as I press soft kisses down her neck, my fingers sliding through her wet pussy. "Please," she whimpers, hips bucking.

It's the night before Christmas Eve, and Jules is naked on her back in my bed, begging for me.

The perfect present, in my opinion.

We're supposed to be wrapping gifts for Sophie so we don't have to stay up until midnight like last year when we assembled a dollhouse at the last minute, but we got a bit...distracted.

That happens a lot with us.

"I'm gonna eat you, but you gotta be quiet, Julianne," I say low, pressing a kiss to her neck. When she looks at me, her hands in my hair tugging my head back, I'm reminded why I fucking love this woman.

"Make me," she says, taunting me, and I smile wickedly.

"Okay." Then I flip us so I'm on my back and shift her until she understands what I'm trying to tell her, moving until her pussy is over my face, my cock in front of hers. "Put your mouth on that; it'll keep you nice and quiet," I say, then put a hand on her hip to pull her down and run my tongue from her clit to her entrance.

She starts to moan, and my hand moves down, pressing on her back. And then she takes me in her mouth, muffling the cry. Instead, it reverberates down my cock to my balls, a torture of its own.

I groan in approval into her cunt, and her hips buck toward me, my tongue sliding into her. Then I start to devour her, alternating between sucking on her clit and sliding a finger into her pussy with fucking her with my tongue. Her mouth slides down my cock as she moans again, one of her soft hands moving to cup my balls the way she knows I like, and I groan once again into her.

We continue this cycle for what feels like a blissful and torturous eternity before she starts to move faster, riding my face, muffling her cries as she sucks me off. She's close, and when my hand moves back to slap her ass, her entire body shakes above mine. My cock slips into her throat as she moans, coming on my tongue. She continues to ride it out, my cock in her mouth, before her body slackens just a bit, her mouth moving faster to even the score.

But that's not what I want.

My hand slaps her ass. "Go, baby. You did good; now ride me."

She removes her mouth from my cock, her long, dark hair moving over her shoulder and grazing my thigh as she looks behind at me with a wicked smile on her lips.

"Glad I got your approval." I have a witty response on my tongue, ready to continue to banter with her, but then her hand wraps my cock as she shifts, tugging once, twice, three times, and I groan aloud. "Now, who is supposed to be quiet?" she asks.

"Still you. Now go," I say, and she laughs before moving down my body as she sits up and positions her wet cunt over me. She rubs the tip of me along her wetness until she notches the head inside.

A sigh leaves her pouty pink lips, ones I know are swollen from sucking me off, before she slowly, torturously slowly, sinks down on me, moaning as she does. My hands go to her hips, fingertips digging into lush skin to stop me from slamming her down, letting her take whatever time she wants or needs. It's a tight fit like this, the way she's leaning forward just a bit, and her knees are spread on either side of me.

Next time, we're doing this with a mirror in front of us.

Or a camera, making a movie of our own.

"Oh god, fuck," she moans, once she's seated and full of me.

"Quiet, Jules," I say through gritted teeth as she clamps down on me, slides up, and then slowly glides back down. "You have to stay quiet."

"I'm trying," she whispers now, a plea in her words. "It's so fucking good, though." She leans back a bit, a hand moving up to pull at her nipple. Her other hand rubs at her clit leisurely as she slowly fucks me, occasionally moving down, fingers spreading over where we meet, grazing the underside of my cock as she fucks me.

My balls tighten, wanting to spill inside her, and god-fucking-dammit, I need her to get there quicker. I shift us, moving so I'm sitting up a bit, changing the angle, and making her moan before moving her hand away and taking over playing with her clit.

"Nate!" she moans, her body stilling with the loud noise. My hand moves up, covering her mouth as she starts to move over me, fucking herself on my cock, my fingers rolling over her swollen clit.

"Bad girl," I groan. "Couldn't stay quiet, so now I have to keep you quiet." She moans again, her head tipping back to my shoulder, the wetness of her pussy loud in the quiet room. We need to get a fucking noise machine in here for nights like this. "You're so goddamn wet for me, aren't you? Can you hear it?"

She nods under my hand, her pussy tightening as I continue to murmur in her ear. "You feel so goddamn good, Jules. I want to be buried in you forever, fucking you always. Next time it's just us, I'm going to make sure you're so fucking loud the neighbors hear. I'm going to pound into you, make you scream my name. But right now, you need to be quiet, and you need to fucking come." Her hips buck, and I know she's close as a rush of wet slicken my cock.

"That's it, Julianne. Fuck my cock," I groan through gritted teeth. "Take yourself there and take me with you." Another deep moan is muffled by my hand, followed by the tightening of her pussy around me.

I've learned Jules loves this; this, *stay quiet, or I'll make you* game of ours. She loves being under my control, loves when I find creative ways to keep her quiet, be it with my cock or a pillow. Last month, I balled up her panties and shoved them in her mouth while I fucked her from behind.

She came especially hard then, but tonight, I think she's going to beat that one.

I tighten my hold on her mouth as she shrieks beneath my hand, as her hips buck, and my finger moves frantically on her clit before she tightens around me, her entire body going still.

That's when I let go, groaning into her neck to dull the sound as I lift my hips into hers to get deeper, filling her with pump after pump of my cum. I move my hand, letting her catch her breath as we both come down before flopping back on the bed, panting.

A moment later, she slides off me, both of us moaning with the loss, and she rolls beside me.

"Good enough?" I ask, and she mumbles something, probably a curse or two, before slapping me on the chest. I laugh, standing and moving toward the bathroom for a wet washcloth before coming back out and cleaning her up. She mewls with pleasure as I graze over her swollen clit, and I smile.

"If we wrap presents quickly, we can go for round two." She glares at me, and I laugh before rolling off the bed and throwing the washcloth in the laundry basket before moving back to her. "Come on," I say, slapping her ass. "We have some wrapping to do."

She looks over her shoulder at me, then groans, flopping on the bed with a sigh, and I can't help but laugh. "You were the one who bought Sophie eighteen thousand gifts and who says they all need to be wrapped."

"They do," she grumbles. "Even the stockings." Thankfully, all of the gifts I bought Jules were already wrapped in the spare closet, something I took care of while she was at the end-of-the-year party for First Position. "I just don't like leaving your bed."

"*Our* bed," I remind her. It's been a year since my grand gesture to convince Jules of where she belonged and her moving in for good.

"Yeah, yeah, yeah," she grumbles, standing up and reaching for her pajamas. "Our bed. Come on, Donovan. You're not getting out of wrapping just because you gave me an orgasm."

"Two," I correct her, and she rolls her eyes.

"Come on. I'll get the wrapping paper, and you will get the gifts."

And then, as always, we move as a well-oiled machine, wrapping gifts for Sophie, my sisters, Ava and Harper, and my family.

And we only take one more fuck break.

A success, if you ask me.

There is a pile of paper covering the living room floor, various patterns and colors, ribbons, and bows mixed in as Sophie opens her last gift—some new set for her Ashlyn dollhouse Jules decided she had to have.

"That's it, Soph," Jules says as she smiles at our girl, who is looking around like something isn't right. "What's wrong?" Jules asks, unsure.

Sophie takes a moment before pouting. "It didn't work," she says grumpily.

"What didn't work?" I ask, sitting back and fighting a laugh at her dramatics.

"The Christmas magic, it didn't work."

"What do you mean, sweetie?" Jules asks. She's absolutely the worst at keeping secrets, as evidenced by her widening smile she can't fight. It's why I didn't even tell her my plan until a couple days ago, instead having Jaime help me secure and hold on to Sophie's gift for a bit. As Jules assumed, Jaime and I have become fast friends, both constantly dealing with the chaos that is our women and the schemes they brew up. He's a quiet guy, but when he does talk, it always makes me laugh.

"Last year, I told Santa I wanted Daddy to marry the real-life Ashlyn. And you guys aren't married, but we're working on it, you know?" She gives me wide, knowing eyes that Jules misses, thankfully.

Jules snorts out a laugh before nodding. "Okay?"

"And this year, I told him I wanted a cat because Dad said I wasn't ready, but if you ask Santa and you're good, *you get what you want.*"

"Well, that's not exactly how that works, Sophie," I say, sitting next to Jules.

"But it is how it works," she says, flailing her arms. "And I was good! What was the point?!"

Jules rolls her lips into her mouth to fight a laugh before finally putting our girl out of her misery. "You know, I think there's one last gift," she says, tipping her chin toward the tree, where deep in the branches is a pink wrapped gift.

"What? No, there—" she starts, then spots it, bolting up. She's gotten so fucking tall in the last year, my little girl is not so little anymore. I can't help but wonder how long Jules will want to be married before she'll want to try and give Soph a brother or sister.

I hope it's not too long. I don't know if Jules knows yet, but since they got married last summer, Jaime told me he and Ava are starting to try for a kid of their own. I know Jules would love nothing more than to have kids around the same age as her best friend.

Sophie grabs the small box and starts tearing the paper without any hesitation. Jules looks at me with a soft, serene smile as she stands, quietly walking toward our room to get the gift Jaime dropped off last night after Sophie went to bed. Soph opens the box to find a small pink collar, her eyes going wide as she looks at me.

"Daddy?" she asks, but her eyes move quickly to the hall where

Jules, in the matching pajamas she bought all of us, is stepping out of our bedroom, a small white cat in her arms. "OH MY GOD!"

"Merry Christmas, Sophie," Jules says with a smile. "It's not from Santa because he can't bring real animals on his sleigh, but he told us you wanted a cat, and your dad and I decided you've been so responsible, watching Peach and all, that you earned one of your own."

Sophie's eyes start to water, and I watch Jules's follow suit.

I shake my head. My two girls, total crybabies.

"Can I hold her?" she asks, her voice soft.

"Sit down," Jules says, and Sophie runs to the couch before Jules hands Sophie the incredibly gentle and chill kitten. Instantly, it curls up into our daughter's lap, settling down to go back to sleep. "Oh. My. Gosh," she whispers, eyes wide. "Daddy, do you see it?"

I nod, and I look up to see Jules taking photos and videos of Sophie. "She's cute, Sophie. But you've gotta take care of her. That means cleaning the litter box, making sure she's fed, and playing with her every day."

"I will! I promise!" she shouts, and even though she's only six and I know she probably won't remember most of the time, I smile and nod.

"I know." Jules and Sophie talk about the cat, Jules probably sending a million pictures to everyone we know, and I move, grabbing one last gift I hid in the corner before setting up my phone, knowing that's what Jules would want.

"Hey, dollface, I've got one more," I say, and her brow furrows. We'd talked about making sure all gifts were done before we gave Sophie Ashlyn, the kitten, but I also knew then I was lying. "Humor me."

She rolls her eyes, sitting next to Sophie right where I expected, and I hand her the box, sitting on the edge of the coffee table to watch her unwrap the box, then taking the lid off. When she gasps, I can't help but smile. She lifts out a frame—the matchbook from that very first night—between two panes of glass.

Her hand goes to her face as she looks from the frame to me to the frame again, her eyes watering as she does.

God, she's so fucking cute.

"Just like your parents," she whispers, and I nod.

"There's more," I whisper, watching her brow furrow, but she sets the frame aside, Sophie now watching along smugly as she reaches down into the box, pulling out a small matchbox.

Strike up a happily ever after, it reads on the outside.

"Nate," she whispers, and I move, grabbing the small box from her.

"I ran through every movie we've watched where he proposes and tried to think of one to recreate, but nothing fit. In *Love Actually,* he proposes at her work, but that isn't your style, even if I could have used the kids and gone full *Meet the Parents.* In *Sweet Home Alabama,* he closes down Tiffany's for her, but that engagement ends, and I'm not letting in any bad vibes. In *The Wedding Singer,* Adam Sandler sings on a plane, but I think you'd rather die than have that happen."

She laughs and sniffs, her lower lip wobbling before nodding her agreement.

"So I went with the one that feels the most...us."

"A matchbox," she whispers, a single tear falling.

I swipe at it, then slide open the box, grabbing the ring before moving to one knee. Jules gasps even though I know she's already put together what's happening. Sophie squeals with excitement, stomping her little feet and probably terrifying her new cat, but my eyes are on Jules.

Like they always are.

"You want to be loved madly, and I am absolutely crazy about you, baby. I want to make every single day movie-worthy for you. I want you to make Sophie's Christmas wish come true: become my wife, become her mom. I want to convince you to give her a brother or sister or maybe two."

She's crying full out now, and I swipe at her tears once more. "Such a crybaby," I whisper, and she slaps my shoulder.

"But I love you. I love you so damn much, Jules, it's insane. I know to my soul that you were meant to be mine and that there was always some string tying us together. Even when we tried to ignore it, it pulled me to you, and I'm so fucking grateful it did. I'm so grateful you were in that bar on New Year's. That your pipe broke and that Claire was moving out. That Sophie made that wish, and all the pieces fell into place until we found each other again."

I sigh. "Let me love you madly. Let me make your life a fantasy. Let me give you the fairy tale ending you deserve. So, Jules, will you marry me?"

I hold my breath as I wait for her answer, but I don't have to wait long as she nods rapidly, holding her hand out so I can slide on the ring. Once it's there, a classic princess-cut Ava and Claire helped me pick out; she stares at it in awe, like she can't even imagine this just happened.

"If this was a movie, I think this is where you guys would kiss," Sophie says, breaking Jules from her reverie as she laughs out loud through the tears, swatting playfully at her.

But I take our daughter's advice, putting a hand on each side of Jules's face and pulling her toward me, pressing my lips to hers as we start our own happily ever after.

ABOUT THE AUTHOR

Morgan is a born and raised Jersey girl, living there with her two sons and daughter, and mechanic husband. She's addicted to iced espresso, barbeque chips, and Starburst jellybeans. She usually has headphones on, listening to some spicy audiobook or Taylor Swift. There is rarely an in between.

Writing has been her calling for as long as she can remember. There's a framed 'page one' of a book she wrote at seven hanging in her childhood home to prove the point. Her entire life she's crafted stories in her mind, begging to be released but it wasn't until recently she finally gave them the reigns.

I'm so grateful you've agreed to take this journey with me.

Stay up to date via TikTok and Instagram

Stay up to date with future stories, get sneak peeks and bonus chapters by joining the Reader Group on Facebook!

ALSO BY MORGAN ELIZABETH

The Springbrook Hills Series

The Distraction

The Protector

The Substitution

The Connection

The Playlist

Season of Revenge Series:

Tis the Season for Revenge

Cruel Summer

The Fall of Bradley Reed

Ick Factor

Big Nick Energy

Evergreen Park Series

Passenger Princess

If This Was a Movie

The Ocean View Series

The Ex Files

Walking Red Flag

Bittersweet

The Mastermind Duet

Ivory Tower

Diamond Fortress

All My Love